PETER C
NEVER A DULL MOMENT

REGINALD Evelyn Peter Southouse Cheyney (1896-1951) was
born in Whitechapel in the East End of London. After serving
as a lieutenant during the First World War, he worked as
a police reporter and freelance investigator until he found
success with his first Lemmy Caution novel. In his lifetime
Cheyney was a prolific and wildly successful author, selling, in
1946 alone, over 1.5 million copies of his books. His work was
also enormously popular in France, and inspired Jean-Luc
Godard's character of the same name in his dystopian sci-fi
film *Alphaville*. The master of British noir, in Lemmy Caution
Peter Cheyney created the blueprint for the tough-talking,
hard-drinking pulp fiction detective.

PETER CHEYNEY

NEVER A DULL MOMENT

DEAN STREET PRESS

Published by Dean Street Press 2022

All Rights Reserved

First published in 1942

Cover by DSP

ISBN 978 1 914150 99 9

www.deanstreetpress.co.uk

CHAPTER ONE
AM I THE ONION!

NEVER a dull moment!

You're tellin' me! Maybe you're one of those guys who leads a routine existence an' knows just what he's goin' to do every day. Well, I wish I was like that, because so far as I am concerned life is so goddam funny that sometimes I do not even know what I did yesterday.

Am I the onion or am I?

Maybe some of you bozos have heard of me. My name is Lemuel H. Caution—Lemmy Caution to you—an' I carry a Federal Bureau of Investigation ticket an' a whole goddam load of trouble. I have spent most of my life chasin' thugs, crooks, rollers, finger-guys, counterfeiters, Inter-State skulduggers, snatch experts, white-slave merchants, yen tasters, hop slingers, boys who play the parlour game over a State line an' the frails who help 'em do it. I have chased everythin' that has committed any sort of mayhem any place in the U.S. jurisdiction—an' a whole lot out of it. I have chased fat guys an' lean ones, boyos who carry the old equaliser an' palookas who rely on a sweet line of gab to get out of a jam.

I have also chased a whole lot of dames for one reason or another. But it has usually been for one reason—an' that is not the one you are thinkin' of, lady. No, sir—the dames I have chased are usually sweet mommas who are so wicked that any time they take a fancy to you it would be better for you to jump in a barrel of sneezin' gas without your gas mask on.

I have also chased dames for other reasons—old-fashioned ones. An' believe it or not, I would like to tell you mugs that it is sometimes a whole lot easier to keep sides up with a wicked blonde from Oklahoma, who has bust every Federal and State law that was ever thought of, than to try a new technique on some honeypot who is so pure that she pulls the bathroom window-blinds down any time she thinks some smart guy is lookin' through the keyhole.

I stand leanin' over a five-barred gate lookin' at the golf course. Just in case you guys should be curious I will tell you that it is July 1941 an' I am in some place called Betchworth, Surrey, England, which is a very nice place and just as good as any other place to be in when you are in the sorta frame of mind that I am in.

It is eleven o'clock at night, but it is still light because of this extra summer-time they have over here, an' the place looks swell. There is a sweet sorta smell of grass an' hay an' what will you. There are long rollin' greens, avenues of lime trees, hills an' everythin' else you could want, if you was the sorta guy who wanted that sorta stuff, I would appreciate this very much more if I was a landscape painter, but as I am merely an F.B.I. Agent with a distorted viewpoint on dames, very little sense of humour left an' a blister on my left heel, I should worry about landscapes.

I give the gate a push but it will not open, which is not very strange when you come to consider that nothing happens the way I want it to. But bein' a guy who does not allow obstacles to stand in my way I put my hand on the top, vault over, catch my foot in a twig on the other side an' bite a large lump outa the English earth. After making a few very cheerful an' bright remarks an' brushin' myself off, I walk up the pathway that leads over the long stretch of grassland towards the avenue of limes.

Believe it or not I am supposed to be havin' a holiday around this dump, an' I have to fall in for this bunch of trouble. One of these fine days I am goin' to get myself inta a frame of mind where I shall lock myself in the back kitchen and play patience just so's I shall not fall inta any set of circumstances which makes me do something I do not wanta do.

The air around here tastes good. It has been hot durin' the day but now there is a sweet breeze. When I get to the top of the rise I can see just on the other side the avenue of limes. I look around for a house but I cannot see any house. I reckon some guy musta moved it outa spite. I lean up against a tree an' light a cigarette. Now I have told you palookas before that I am a poetic sorta guy. I have spent most of my life lookin' for beauty, an' if you ask me what sorta beauty I will tell you the beauty that is usually terminated at one end with a very nice auburn pompadour an' at the other with a pair of four-inch french heels. What is in the middle of these two things has been my hobby for many years, which is one of the reasons why

I am a philosopher who is liable to duck any moment when he sees a blonde advancin' on him sideways. So now you know.

But all this don't mean that I don't appreciate the beauty of an English golf course, which is a helluva place when you look at it. Maybe playin' golf—which is a goddam silly game anyway but which gets a stranglehold on you—is one of the things which enables the inhabitants of this island to sing "Roll out the Barrel" while Jerries are bouncing bombs off the dome of St. Paul's Cathedral, an' the clever guy who said that atmosphere makes character certainly knew his huckleberries.

There are two guys comin' up the fairway from the green below. These guys must be what is generally known as enthusiasts. One of 'em is wearin' Home Guard uniform, with a bag of golf clubs slung over his shoulder. The other guy is carrying the same implements of torture but wearin' a blue shirt an' a bald head. I think maybe I will get some information.

I wait till they get level with me. Then I say to the Home Guard guy: "Maybe you can tell me where Mr. Schribner lives—Mr. Max Schribner? I got an idea he has got a house around here somewhere."

The Home Guard guy thinks. Then he says yes maybe he can. Maybe this Schribner is the guy who lives in the white house on the other side of the roadway past the fourteenth green, about three-quarters of a mile away as the crow flies. He shows me where this place is more or less, an' they scram.

I walk a little way, then I sit down on a tree stump, light a fresh cigarette and wonder what I am goin' to say to this Schribner supposin' I find him. This is one of those jobs where I don't know a thing an' have to guess all the time.

I sit there thinkin' but I find I am not concentratin' on the matter in hand. I am thinkin' about a dame I met up in Omaha about eighteen months ago. This dame was a rare piece. She had everything. She had so much that anything she had not got you could stick in your eye an' not notice it. She was one of those dames. She was blonde in colour, passionate by nature an' had a one-track mind. She was one of those dames who would let you have anything you wanted providin' she did not want something else. I can remember sittin' on the back porch talkin' to this baby on a night rather like this one is. I can remember her sayin': "Lemmy, you are a guy who will always find yourself in it right up to the neck, because any time you were not in it up to the neck you would be so miserable you would jump in the lake. So any time you get into heart trouble don't worry—you'll either get out or somebody will cut your throat an' I'll lay six to four that the somebody will be a dame."

All of which will make you guys come to the conclusion that I am a guy who is clever with dames. Well, maybe I am an' maybe I am not. But no guy is really clever with dames, an' if he escapes from the sweetie with the attractive wiggle and the starry eyes, it is only because he was born under the right star and has a terrific sense of direction at the right moment. Any guy can get inta trouble but it takes a really clever mug to get out, especially where a dame is concerned.

I come to the conclusion that it is no good my thinkin' what I am goin' to say to this Schribner bozo until I have given him the once-over. I throw my cigarette away, get up an' start walkin' towards the fourteenth green. This is on top of a little hill, an' when I get there I can see, stuck away in the valley, with a mist comin' up all round it, a little white house with a red top. I give a big sigh. Anyhow I have found this dump.

I start meanderin' down the hill, across the fairway, towards the white cottage. I start thinkin' about this dame Julia Wayles an' wonderin' just how I am gonna play this business. I begin to wonder what the baby looks like, an' how she walks an' what sort of a line she uses when she talks at, to or with you, because it is all those things which determine just what a dame is goin' to do in life. Whether she is goin' to be one of them nice, quiet janes who stay put an' mend the socks every Tuesday night, or whether she is goin' to get around generally an' start somethin'. I wish I knew which sort Julia was. It might make things easier.

My old mother, who had a very leery eye for dames, an' who was always afraid for me in case I grew up like Pa (who spent the whole of his life in fightin' for some dame's honour an' who discovered too late that when she surrenders the battle has only just begun), usta warn me against anythin' that wore chiffon stockin's an' a winnin' smile. She said that a woman would take me for a ride one day. She was wrong. I been taken for lots of rides *all* my days by a handpicked selection of pieces of overtime that would break your heart to hear about.

Ever since I was seventeen, when I met up with a redhead with a shape that would knock you cold, blue eyes an' a technique that woulda made Messalina look like the dame who does the manglin' every other Tuesday, I been spendin' my life workin' out how to duck from some baby that I have got myself tied in with good an' plenty. I am like that. Either I got an over-developed eye for beauty or I am just one of them guys who is never happy unless he is tryin' out somethin' new. Or maybe I like learnin'. I wouldn't know.

The red-head taught me plenty. I met this dame at a party where they was servin' nothin' but sarsaparilla an' good works, an' when I tell you that I fell for her directly I took a look, I am speakin' nothin' but the truth, an' no kiddin'. She was thirty-five years of age, with no angles an' the correspondin' curves. She had a soft voice an' a way of lookin' at you that made you feel that Adam was only bein' human when he tried to turn over a new leaf.

An' was she good? I'm tellin' you she was *good*. She was so goddam good that she woulda made a Fifth Columnist turn himself inside out an' make a noise like the wind in the willows every time somebody said "Hitler." She belonged to some good-works society that went in for makin' young men stay in in the evenin's. So far as I was concerned the society was successful all right. Because this dame had such an influence on me that I stayed in plenty. I never got away from her for three weeks an' then it was to rush around to the drug store to get somethin' for that tired feelin'. When I went home Ma Caution took one look at me an' then threw a two-quart can of tomato juice at the old man's picture.

Ma was a great believer in heredity.

Well . . . that was my first experience with dames an' from that time I have never looked backwards except to look at some baby with short skirts an' a sweet under-structure climbin' a step-ladder. So now you know. An' you must tell me about yourself sometime.

I push open the garden gate an' start walkin' up the little pathway. It is gettin' good an' dark an' a nice piece of moon is comin' up over a cloud. I get to thinkin' about this Julia dame an' wonderin' what she is like. I reckon she has got to have somethin' otherwise she would not be causin' me to be hangin' around this golf course tryin' to get my hooks on this boyo Schribner when I might be playin' noughts an' crosses with the smart piece of auburn homework I met up with last night, in the American bar at the Savoy.

I ring the bell an' wait. After a minute some guy opens the door. He is a big guy with a fat neck an' he is wearin' a silk shirt with a collar a coupla sizes too small for him. His clothes are good an' he has got a coupla rocks on his fingers that cost plenty. He grins like he was pleased about somethin'. He says: "Can I help?"

I tell him yes. I tell him that my name is Willik—Paul Willik. An' that I am lookin' for some young woman by the name of Julia Wayles. I say maybe he knows some guy called Maxie Schribner. He says sure he does. He says that he is Maxie Schribner.

He stands there leanin' up against the doorpost, lookin' at me like a good-natured porpoise who is tryin' to do somebody a good turn. This guy's face is like a moon. It is round an' fat an' his skin is like rubber. His lips are thick and turned back, but the shape of them is pretty—almost like a woman's lips, a sorta cupid's bow if you know what I mean. The guy has got light blue eyes an' practically white eyebrows. If I had to choose between looking at this guy or last week's leftovers you would find me in the pantry, because this mug has got the sorta face that you look at anything else but.

I say: "Well, that is very nice Mr. Schribner. Now you know who I am an' I know who you are. Maybe you can tell me somethin' about this Wayles dame."

He says: "Sure! Come in."

He turns around an' starts walkin' down the passage-way. I go after him. At the end of the passage he holds a door open an' we go inta a room. It is a nice sorta room, comfortable an' with a shaded light. In one corner is a desk with a lotta papers on it.

I sit down in a big armchair an' he gives me a cigarette. He says: "Well now, what can I do for you? Maybe you'd like to tell me about yourself."

He is smilin' at me sorta old-fashioned, like the headmaster interviewin' the new boy.

I say: "That is easy, Schribner. I told you my name was Willik. I am an operative workin' for the Trans-Atlantic Detective Agency. That's who I am. About this Wayles baby I don't know a thing. All I know is I was over here on a job and my boss sent me a cable tellin' me to try an' find some dame called Julia Wayles, supposed to have come over to this country from New York or somewhere in America three-four months ago. He said if I contacted some guy name of Schribner, who was believed to be livin' at this dump Betchworth, maybe he'd be able to help me."

He says: "Sure!" He gets up an' goes over to the cigar box on the mantelpiece and gives himself a cigar. He goes on: "Well, I don't think I can tell you very much about the Wayles proposition an' I reckon it's sort of funny that my name should come into this. Maybe your people sort of got on to me because I used to know a Julia Wayles one time back in the States, an' maybe my name sort of got mixed up with hers. Though what she would be doing over here I don't know."

I say: "That's fine. So you knew her? What sort of a baby was she? Was she one of those fly-by-nights that you never get a check on or was she a nice steady sort of a dame—not the sort of a dame to go flyin' off with some good-lookin' guy?"

He says: "Oh, so that's the way it is, is it? So your people think she's gone off with somebody?"

I shrug my shoulders.

"If my people knew what she'd done an' where she was they wouldn't be askin' me to find her," I say. "Also if they knew anything about the dame that'd help me they woulda told me when they cabled me. But if you've seen her you know what she looks like, an' if you know what a baby looks like you know a lot about her, don't you?"

He says do you—he hasn't thought of that. It seems to me that this guy is either a first-class mug or he is playin' stupid.

"Look, pal,"—I tell him—"it looks as if you need a lesson in psychology. It stands to reason that if a dame has gotta face like the front page of last week's edition of Home Cookery Hints she is much more liable to be safe than a baby who looks like somethin' that keeps father out at night, who has a shape to dream about an' everythin' that goes with it. Ain't that sense?"

He says yes he thinks that's sense. He says that now he comes to think of it he reckons this Julia Wayles baby comes inta the second class. He talks sorta dreamy like an' I am tellin' you that when this guy looks dreamy he looks like a porpoise that has been washed up on the foreshore—the sorta thing they rail off an' charge a dime to look at.

"Now I come to think of it," he says, "Julia Wayles was a fine looking girl. She was nice and tall and slim but curved mind you—she was curved all right. She had a good complexion and auburn hair and she was a pretty mover. Come to think of it," says he, "Julia was a romantic sort of kid. You never know, she might have got stuck on some guy and taken a powder with him."

"I see," I say. "An' that's all you know about her?"

He nods. "I don't know why she should want to come over here," he says. "Unless some guy brought her over. What I think is—"

I see the door-handle turnin', an' the door starts to open. I look up. When I see the guy who is just comin' in I almost get heart disease. I open my mouth to start sayin' something, but the guy who has just got inside the room talks first. He says:

"Hello, Maxie. What's this punk doin' here?"

I relax an' take a look at him. He is a nice tall feller, broad in the shoulder, thin in the hip. He has got his hands in the side pockets of his jacket and the right hand one is pretty bulky. I reckon he has gotta gun in that pocket. Maxie looks surprised.

"Look. Rudolf—" he says, "ain't you makin' a mistake? This is Mr. Paul Willik of the Trans-Atlantic Detective Agency. He's looking for some young woman called Julia Wayles. He's come over here because he thought I might know something about her."

The other guy starts grinnin'.

"You're tellin' me," he says. "D'you know who this bum is? This bum is Lemmy Caution, the Federal Agent. The bright shining star of the Federal Bureau of Investigation, United States of Justice, Washington, DC. The lousy heel who brought in Willie Kratz and all his bunch eighteen months ago. I reckon this bastard has knocked off more of my pals than I can count. So he's Paul Willik, is he? Hear me laugh!"

"Look—" I begin, but Maxie takes a hand. He says:

"You shut your trap for a moment because I think you have done a very unkind thing, Mr. Caution. You have come musclin' down into the quiet of an old English homestead set in the beauties of the countryside under false pretences, and in doing so you have started something which you will not be able to finish." He draws on his cigar. "Rudolf," he says to the other guy, "what do we do with this heel?"

Rudolf brings his hand outa his right hand pocket an' puts the gun on the table. He sits down in a chair close to it. He says: "Look, Maxie, what is the good of discussin' this business? I don't like this guy anyway. The fact that he's around here tryin' to ease in on this Wayles proposition don't look so good to me either. In fact it stinks! I think we give it to him."

Maxie nods brightly. The guy looks as if he is beginning to take an interest in life. He says:

"Rudolf, I am very sorry about this, but I think you're right. I think we'll have to take care of Mr. Caution." He gets up. He comes over towards me. He says: "Ain't you a mug? If you'd come a little earlier you wouldn't have met Rudolf. If you hadn't met Rudolf you might have gone away again. But you ain't goin' away now. About a coupla miles from here," he goes on, "is a sewage dump. I think we'll stick you in there to-night and you can travel miles an' miles away down to the sea. It oughta be quite interesting only you won't be takin' any interest in it."

I give a big horse laugh.

"Look, Fatty" I tell him. "You don't think you can get away with that stuff around here, do you? This is England an' they get very funny with guys who fog other guys an' throw 'em in the drink. They'll have you before you know what's hit you. Another thing," I go on. "I would like to tell you that you remind me of the inside of a sour elephant an' that you are so goddam low that any time you want to crawl under a slug's belly you would haveta climb up a step-ladder."

"That's O.K., Caution," he says. "Just blow off as much as you like. I got the laugh anyway. You won't be blowin' off any more after to-night. That big mouth of yours will be full of sewer mud an' the eels will be dinin' off your nose. An' how'd you like that, pal?"

I open my mouth to tell this little sweetheart just what I think about his parents, but before I get anything out he smacks me one across the kisser that makes my teeth bounce. I get my hands on the arms of the chair an' give myself a push. But any ideas I had about butting this bastard in the belly are nipped off in the bud. He brings his knee up as I go forward an' I get it hard right in the guts. I go out nice an' quiet.

When I come to I find myself lyin' on a stone floor with my head up against the wall. My hands an' feet are tied with a rope, but the guy who did the tyin' up was not very interested in his business—the knot is one that I can fix with my teeth. I reckon Rudolf musta done the tyin' up. My head is achin' an' I gotta nasty pain in my stomach. I get the rope off my hands an' feet an' lean back against the wall. The place is cold an' damp an' clammy. I reckon I am underground somewhere—maybe in a stone cellar or somethin', but right now I am not interested in geography. I am thinkin' about Rudolf.

First of all I think I oughta wise you guys up that this Rudolf, who did not seem to like me, is nobody else but Charles Milton, which is the reason why I nearly had a fit when I saw him around this dump. He is an F.B.I. Agent workin' in the Oklahoma district, an' it's easy to see why he has taken the line he has. It looks to me like Milton has been put in on this job an' has got himself next to Schribner by pretendin' to be somebody else—this guy Rudolf for instance. Maybe Milton is doin' pretty well, gettin' where he wants to get; maybe he has got himself right into Schribner's confidence— when all of a sudden I comes bustin' in.

Well now, it looks as if Milton might have thought that Schribner knew who I was I reckon he thought that in any event Schribner would try an' pulla fast one on me. So in order to divert suspicion from himself he puts on a big act an' blows the fact that I am Lemmy Caution an' that I oughta be ironed out. This in any event is goin' to sound good to Schribner an' is goin' to make him trust Milton all the more.

I get up and stretch myself. I put my hand in my pocket an' find my cigarette lighter. I snap it on. I am in a stone cellar with a low ceilin'. There is a heap of coal an' logs at one end an' an iron door at the other. I feel in my pocket an' am very glad to find I have still got my cigarette case. I light a cigarette an' relax.

I reckon I am now takin' a bigger interest in this Wayles dame than I was before. If this guy Schribner is prepared to bump me off just so's to stop me finding anythin' out about this Wayles baby, then I reckon she must be plenty important to somebody or other. I wonder who this dame is, what she looks like an' what she does for a livin' when she is not doin' a disappearin' act.

I am right in the middle of these deep ruminations when the door at the end of the cellar opens an' a torch flashes on. It is Milton.

He says: "Hey, Caution . . . are you all right?"

I tell him yes, that beyond the fact that I gotta head that feels like a buzz-saw an' a permanent crick in my entrails, I am perfectly O.K.

He says: "That's swell. Now look—get outa here an' get out quick. Schribner'll be back in about fifteen minutes. When he comes back I'm goin' to tell him that you started raisin' hell here so I bumped you an' chucked you in the ditch. Schribner thinks I am a hot guy from the other side of the Atlantic who is playin' in with this crowd. I want the fat slob to go on thinkin' that. I knew you'd see the way I was playin' it."

"O.K., pal," I tell him. "That's all right with me. But what about you an' me havin' a little meetin' on this job sometime?"

He says: "We got to. This business is goin' to be tough. I don't like it." He asks where I am staying.

"I been stayin' in London," I tell him. "But maybe I better stick around here somewhere."

"That's the idea," he says. "There's an hotel called the White Lion in Dorking. It's a good dump. Go an' put up there. Sometime to-morrow I'll get over an' have a talk with you. But you better bust outa here before that fat guy Schribner comes back. Otherwise there's goin' to be some trouble an' I don't wanta spoil things now."

I tell him O.K. We go upstairs an' I grab my hat an' scram.

It is a lovely night an' the golf course is lookin' swell in the moonlight. I start wanderin' over towards the main road to Dorkin', keepin' in the shadows just in case the Schribner guy is comin' back, but I do not see anybody. I get back on the Dorkin' road an' start headin' towards the town. I light a cigarette an' whistle a little to myself. Maybe this is goin' to be an interestin' job. Anyhow Charlie Milton seems to think so.

Maybe the Wayles dame is goin' to be interestin' too.

CHAPTER TWO
THE GUY LIKES RASPBERRIES

ANY time any of you mugs want to hit the high-spot in gettin' yourselves bored just stick around a hotel bedroom for twenty-four hours an' don't go out. There's nothin' to beat it.

I been sittin' up in this bedroom at the White Lion dump all day. First of all because I am not such a mug as to show my nose around when the Schribner guy might see me an' conclude that I am not dead, an' secondly, I am afraid of missin' Charlie Milton. All this, added to the fact that the hotel people have not got any amount of whisky to speak of—well, not what *I* call any—an' the chambermaid is bowlegged an' squints a bit, an' you have got the whole set-up at your finger-ends. Life can be lousy. But maybe you mugs know that without my tellin' you.

I lie down on the bed an' light a cigarette. I draw the smoke down inta my lungs an' start wonderin' about Julia Wayles. I do this because I have not got anything else to wonder about an' also because wonderin' about dames is a sorta hobby of mine. Maybe you must have tried it too. It's a great pastime. Every time you got nothin' in particular to do you just rest the old carcass on the nearest upholstery an' start wonderin' about dames.

You lie there smokin' an' a long procession of lovelies passes before your mind. There is that sweetie-pie you tried conclusions with back in nineteen hundred and somethin'—the one who took you for a ride, and then, just at the crucial moment, decided that she was stuck on some other guy. Then there was the dame who was so stuck on you that you got bored first, an' the one that you was so stuck on that you knew it couldn't last an' it didn't. Finally, there is the dame that you have always wanted to make an' that you have never got next to because she has not yet arrived. This is the dame that most guys spend their off time wonderin' about. An' the fact that she don't exist don't stop 'em.

Because, as maybe somebody told you when you was young, all guys are gluttons for punishment, an' any time you see some bozo walkin' along the street smilin' you can bet your last dime that (*a*) he has just paid the last instalment on the Buick, or (*b*) she says yes she will . . . she won't say *when*, but she definitely *will*. This guy is smilin' very broadly an' looks like he thinks life is just one big bowl of honeysuckle, an' any time you see him lookin' miserable you will know that it is either because she has kept her promise or because she hasn't. It don't really make any difference.

Lyin' there, smokin', lookin' at the ceilin' an' wonderin' when this Milton guy is goin' to show up I get around to thinkin' about the best dames I have known. The best dames are the ones that come into your life an' go out of it before you got time to satisfy your curiosity. Because every guy is really a born investigator where dames are concerned an' if he has not got anythin' to investigate he just gives up.

Somewhere a clock strikes eleven, an' on the last stroke there is a knock on the door an' Charlie Milton stick his head around it. He has got a siphon of soda an' two glasses in his hand an' a bulge underneath his coat that looks to me like liquor. He comes in an' shuts the door.

"It worked," he says. "When Schribner come back last night I told him you'd got loose an' was raisin' hell in the cellar. I told him that I'd bust you one with a gun butt, dropped you in the river with a brick in your pocket an' put one through your dome just as you was sinkin'. The mug believed it."

He gets the cork outa the whisky bottle.

"O.K.," I tell him. "So I'm a corpse. That suits me. Now maybe you will tell me somethin' about this Julia Wayles proposition."

Charlie pours out a coupla stiff ones. We absorb these an' deal with two more just to keep the germs away.

"It all smells phoney to me," he says. "I'll give you what I know an' that ain't a lot. It's *your* case anyway."

"What the hell!" I tell him. "*My* case. I'm on leave."

"You was," he says. He slings me a big grin. "You was on provisional leave," he says. "You was supposed to keep in touch with the Embassy while you was here playin' around." He takes a big drink an' smacks his lips. "The Director of the Federal Bureau has been cablin' an' telephonin' for four weeks tryin' to get you on to this Wayles business. Well, I was comin' over on a war shipments job an' so they passed it on to me until you showed up."

He lights a cigarette. "Was she nice, Lemmy?" he says.

"I was in Scotland, learnin' to play golf," I say.

"Like hell you was," he says. "Any time I see you on a golf course I'm gonna look out for the blonde that's playin' a practice round just in front of you. When did you get back?"

"Tuesday," I tell him. "I looked in at the Embassy an' got the last cable from the Director. I come down here yesterday afternoon to start lookin' for this Schribner guy. The cable said he was the first contact an' a suspicious one at that."

"You're tellin' me," says Charlie. "Look, here's the way this thing goes: There is some guy called Sigfried Larssen—a Swede—who is a surveyor or somethin' in New York. Well, this guy is tied up with some baby named Julia Wayles. They get around together an' all the time he's worryin' her to get married. But she don't seem in any sorta hurry.

"O.K. Well, this Larssen boyo is not very pleased with waitin', first of all because this dame is so lovely that every time a guy looks at her he starts wonderin' what he's been doin' hitherto, an' secondly because he has got an idea in his head that maybe the dame is stuck on some other guy, an' that this is the reason why she is stallin' him along. He's plenty worried about this, but he stops worryin' when she turns up one day an' says that she is ready to get married next week if he wants it."

Charlie pours out two more shots of whisky. After we have sunk these he goes on: "Little Sigfried is now feelin' very good with himself. He says O.K., rushes out, fixes the licence, gets himself a nice new suit to get married in an' on the stated day rushes round to the City Hall to wait for his little Julia to show up. Well, she don't show up.

"Sigfried waits around for a bit, an' then starts to panic. He goes to the police an' they call through to all the hospitals an' stations but nobody knows anything about Julia. Julia has just disappeared inta thin air.

"After a bit," says Charlie, "Sigfried bounces into the Missin' Persons Bureau an' starts shoutin' his head off. The Missin' Persons Bureau take the case over an' work on it good an' hard, an' they can't find a goddam thing about Julia. An' that's that."

"All this is O.K.," I tell him. "But how does the Bureau of Investigation get inta this? This ain't a job for us. It's Police or Missin' Persons, not F.B.I."

"Correct, Lemmy," says Charlie. "But I'm now tellin' you that this Sigfried person is not such a hick as you might think. He goes to some lawyer an' tells him that he is prepared to pay plenty to have Julia found an' that he does not think the Police or the Missin' Persons Bureau are goin' to be very successful in findin' her. He asks the mouthpiece what is the best way of findin' this dame, an' when the lawyer says that the 'G' men are the guys to do a job like that, little Sigfried asks him how the Federal Bureau can be brought in on the job. The lawyer says that the Bureau can come in if there is suspicion of a Federal offence bein' connected in some way or other with Julia's disappearance, or if she'd been taken over a State line by force, or if there was good an' sufficient reason to believe that she'd been kidnapped. . . ."

"So the mouthpiece got a clever idea," I butt in.

"Right," says Charlie. "The mouthpiece, bein' a smart guy, asks Sigfried about any other guys that Julia was stuck on, an' Sigfried tells him that at one time she was stuck on a mug called Schribner—a palooka who made a whole lot of money runnin' a numbers racket in Detroit.

"The lawyer then tried to find Schribner an' when they can't find him—an' I'm not suggestin' that they looked very hard either— the lawyer an' Sigfried report Julia as bein' missin' an' believed kidnapped by this Schribner guy."

"I got it," I tell him. "So the Federal Bureau of Investigation *have* to come in on the job."

"Right," says Charlie. "They can't help themselves. First of all they start a check up on this Schribner, an' they find that this mug has gone to England. Well, they reckon that the whole business is a bit phoney. They don't think that Julia's been kidnapped at all. They think that she's just got tired of the idea of marryin' little Sigfried an' taken a run-out on him, but they got to do something about it. So the Director sends you a cable. The idea bein' that you, bein' over here on provisional leave an' supposed to report to the Embassy, can handle the job an' combine a little business with pleasure. Instead of which you are neckin' some dame in kilts in the Scotch mountains."

"Which is a goddam lie," I tell him, "because I ain't been anywhere near any mountains an' she didn't wear kilts either. Only her ancestors wore kilts. . . ."

"Yeah," says Charlie. "Well, I don't suppose you'd notice at the time. Anyhow, you can't see a tartan in the dark. Well . . . I was comin' over here on a Lease an' Lend delivery job, an' the Director asked me to have a look at this Schribner an' see if he knew anythin' about Julia. When you turned up—if you did turn up—I was to hand over to you."

"How'd you find Schribner?" I ask him.

"Scotland Yard found him for me," says Charlie. "I went an' saw your old pal Herrick an' he found the guy in three days. I didn't say what I wanted Schribner for. O.K. Well, I got down here three days ago. I found out where Schribner's place was an' put a call through from Dorking. Some dame answered the telephone, an' when I asked if Schribner was there she says: 'Is that Rudy?' I say yes just to see what happens, an' she then gets excited an' tells me to show up pretty quick because Schribner has got the line that the 'G' boys are after him over the Julia Wayles business an' he's got to see me quick. O.K. Well, I stall this dame along an' she then asks me how long I been over here, so it looks to me that this Rudy guy has come over from somewhere. I make a guess that that somewhere would be the U.S. She also asks me to go along an' see Maxie directly he arrives back the next day. She says I'd better telephone Maxie first an' tell him who I am and what time I'm comin' to see him. Which tells me that this Schribner bird has never met this Rudy guy before.

"So I decide to pull a fast one. I wait a day an' then telephone through an' speak to Maxie. I tell him I am Rudy an' that I been here three days an' that I am comin' out to see him. He says O.K. an' that he will drive the car out to meet me on the edge of the golf course an' what do I look like. This tells me that I was right in my guess that he ain't ever seen Rudy before. So I give him a description of myself an' he meets me like he said an' we go along to the cottage. You got all that?"

"I got it," I tell him. I take a little more whisky just to keep my mind clear.

"I'd only been there about three-four hours when you showed up," says Charlie. "I'd just been stallin' Schribner along, lettin' him do the talkin'. It wasn't so difficult because this guy Schribner is a mug. He is so thick that you could pull anything on him. I just let him talk an' I listened. He asks me how the boys are, an' I say they are all swell. He laughs an' says he reckons that Jakie Larue ain't feelin' so swell in Leavenworth; that he never knew a guy to get a not less than fifteen not more than life sentence without feelin' sore. I tell him that Jakie would feel swell anyway, an' I get the idea that this Rudy is supposed to be some sort of mobster. But Schribner don't say a word about the Julia dame. An' I was leavin' the subject alone. I was gonna get around to it later—nice an' quiet. When you showed up an' come bustin' in like you did I didn't like that at all. I reckoned you'd got back from wherever you was got the Director's cable an' come down quick. When Schribner told me you was Paul Willik of the Trans-Atlantic Agency I didn't like it. I knew that Schribner knew somehow that the 'G' service was after him—he'd sort of hinted at it—an' I thought he'd smell a rat. I reckoned that it wouldn't do any harm if I put on an act an' blew who you were. I reckoned that this would get me in with Maxie an' that any jam you got into I could get you out of."

"I got it," I say. "So the position now is that Maxie thinks I'm bein' eat up by eels in the local river on my way to the sea an' he trusts you because you fogged me. Who an' what is the dame that you spoke to on the telephone?"

"I wouldn't know," says Charlie. "I haven't seen anybody except Schribner at the house. This is a lousy case, ain't it?"

"You're tellin' me," I say. "What the hell can we do? First of all we don't know that this Wayles dame has been kidnapped an' we can't pull the cops here in on this job in case we're wrong. Secondly, the fact that Schribner was prepared to iron me out don't mean a thing, because I was never ironed out, an' thirdly, before we can prove that anybody was kidnapped we got to have a body. I suppose you haven't seen any bodies lyin' about—one that's looked like Julia I mean?"

Charlie shakes his head.

"I ain't seen a body for a long time," he says. "Not a real nice stiff one with the toes well turned up, I mean. But maybe I'll come across one yet." He gets up, looks at his wristwatch an' takes another shot of whisky.

"It's all yours, Lemmy," he says. "I'm on my way. I got the heap outside an' I'm hittin' the London road right now. You can think of me to-morrow afternoon, makin' eyes at some socialite dame in London an' telling her that *her* war is *my* war."

"Like hell you will," I tell him. "I would like to hear what else you are going to tell that dame. I thought you was here on Lease an' Lend delivery stuff."

"So I am," he says. "But that ain't no reason why I shouldn't do a little private Lease an' Lend stuff with a dame, is it? After all, war brings us all closer together."

"Yeah!" I tell him. "It ain't brought me any closer to this leave that I ain't gettin'. I reckon this war has only brought me a right royal selection of raspberries."

Charlie grins.

"Which reminds me," he says. "This guy Schribner is nuts about raspberries. He ate a couple pound of 'em raw while I was talkin' to him, an' he got the juice all over them thick lips of his. Maxie is a queer bird."

"So the guy likes raspberries," I tell him. "Well, maybe he'll get a few before this business is over—ones that don't grow on bushes neither."

I grab the whisky bottle before he gets the last shot.

"Well . . . so long, Lemmy," he says. "An' you be very careful of Maxie. Maxie is not a very nice guy, an' any time he sees you around he's liable to think you are a ghost. I'll be seein' you, pal."

He scrams an' a minute afterwards I hear his car go off.

I finish the whisky. An' even that tastes sour.

When I told you guys that I am the onion I was tellin' you the truth all right. At two o'clock in the mornin' I am still lyin' on the bed at the White Lion, smokin', lookin' at the ceilin' an' cussin' generally.

Me—I am the hard luck guy. Anytime some case turns up that hasn't got a beginnin', an' end or a middle, I win it. Anytime some screwy lawyer pulls a fast one just to get a Federal Investigation on some dame who has probably taken a run-out with a boy friend, I get yanked in to elucidate the mystery. I reckon that if that mug Sherlock Holmes hadda been pulled in on some of the stuff they use me for, he would not only have played the fiddle twice as much, an' taken twice as much morphia, he would also have jumped off the end of the pier as well. Because there are moments when life is just too goddam elementary, my dear Watson. . . .

At the same time I reckon this case has got some redeemin' features about it. Me—I am a guy who looks for the funny little things in a case—the incongruities—an' if this Julia Wayles business ain't absolutely stiff with 'em then I am an Indian Princess with kidney trouble.

Look! First of all this Sigfried Larssen, who is engaged to Julia, knows so goddam little about the girl that he ain't really certain that she is gonna turn up to marry him, an' he ain't really surprised when she don't. Instead of thinkin' first of all that she mighta taken a run-out powder with some other boyo he goes around the hospitals an' puts up a police call for her. Then, when the Missin' Persons Bureau has fallen down on the job, an' can't find her, he gets this smart mouthpiece of his to put up some story about kidnappin' that will force the Federal Bureau of Investigation to handle the job, because kidnappin' is a Federal offence an' they *got* to come in on that.

But why does Sigfried think that Julia has been kidnapped? Well, we know that he *don't*. We know that this is just a story put up by him an' his lawyer to get the F.B.I, workin'. That bein' so, what does Sigfried think he is gonna do supposin' the F.B.I, find Julia?

If the dame has gone off with some other guy she is certainly not goin' to return to little Sigfried just because he has got the F.B.I. to find her. No, sir!

Between you an' me an' old Mother Riley this part of the business smells sour to me.

The second thing that smells is that this boyo Schribner is not only a mug but a too trustin' mug, an' crooks are not usually trustin' guys. Maybe he is so goddam trustin' that he oughta have his brains examined. First of all when Charlie Milton rings up, Schribner practically tells him he ain't ever seen him before, then when he meets Charlie he don't ask for any sorta proof of identity. He just takes it that Charlie Milton is Rudy. An' he lets Charlie know who Rudy is. He lets him know that Rudy is some sorta pal to a guy called Jakie Larue, who is servin' a from fifteen to life sentence in Leavenworth. An' all this when Schribner knew that the F.B.I.—the "G" men—was after him! Well, how the hell did he know that?

I sit up on the bed an' light a cigarette. Because it seems elementary to me that the only guys who coulda let Schribner (who was anyway in England) know that the "G" service was after him, was this mug Sigfried Larssen or his lawyer. An' why the hell should they want to do a thing like that?

The third thing that sticks in my sensitive nostrils is the greetin' I got from this Maxie punk. First of all—when I tell him I am Paul Willik of the Trans-Atlantic Agency—he seems quite sorta pleased to see me, but directly Charlie Milton, frontin' as the mysterious Rudy, tells him that I am Lemmy Caution the "G" man, the guy gets all hot and bothered, an' is immediately desirous of bumpin' me an' throwin' me in the local sewage department.

The fourth thing is that he seems goddam casual when Charlie tells him that he has done this. He don't worry about it. He don't want any details. He is quite satisfied to know that somebody has slugged me stuck an iron pill inta me an' sent me floatin' on my way to the sea. Either this Maxie is a very tough as well as a very ugly guy, or else he is just playin' fairies with one an' all.

I give a big sigh. This is just one of them things where you run round in a circle an' try an' catch up with yourself.

I start thinkin' about Julia. I wish I could get a peek at a picture of this dame. I might know somethin' then. I have always found that if you can get a quick look at a dame you know *somethin'* about her. Maybe she has got one of them quiet an' sad pans that spell trouble. Maybe she has a face like a tombstone but a nice line in legs an' a hipline that ain't happy unless it's swingin' on the right angle. Well, that spells trouble too.

Me—I have always found that the main problem in any case you gotta investigate, is the dame in it. The problem of dames is one that maybe some of you guys have concerned yourself with, some time or other, because the question of dames is one that every right-thinkin' guy should consider good an' hard, because a guy who does not spend a certain amount of his time thinkin' about frails has got something wrong somewhere, an' is maybe likely to finish up with an ingrowin' liver or else a thwartation complex that is gonna lead him straight to the local nuthouse.

Because the study of frails, broads, dames, janes, mommas, sweeties, honey-blondes, red-heads, chiffon-slingers, kiss-benders, hip-promoters or whatever you like to call 'em, is one that can last a coupla lifetimes. An' I will go so far as to say that I have known old guys of ninety porin' over the things they have learned when it was all too late, an' tryin' to work out the number of things they coulda done if (*a*) they had had the nerve, (*b*) she hadn't hit 'em across the kisser with a flat-iron, an' (*c*) if her husband hadn't come up the garden path just at the wrong moment, thereby provin' that there is a time an' place for everythin', an' also indicatin' that a fat guy can get through a back window five times too small for him good an' quick, providin' he has the urge to escape bein' hit on the lines of communication with a double charge of buck-shot, or havin' his rear menaced by some infuriated guy usin' the Stalin technique an' the family wood-chopper.

Because all the great scientists includin' Mae West, old man Confucius an' the blonde who runs the corner cigar store, all agree on one thing, an' that is that a guy is either born with dames, acquires dames or has dames thrust upon him. In the first case maybe he will grow out of it with a bit of luck; in the second case he is liable to develop a sweet line in bad tempers through tryin' to muscle in on a controlled market, an' in the third case he gets himself a crick in the neck learnin' to duck. But in any event the poor mug is liable to find himself continually in bad through curiosity, or else get himself all tied up with the wrong dame, just because he was tryin' to see if the technique he used with such success on the red-head in Saratoga last July, is goin' to work out with an outsize in Mexican chiffon step-ins an' the proper curves to fill 'em.

It is about three o'clock an' a nice night. The moonlight is comin' through the windows an' I get to thinkin' that it must look pretty good around the golf course at Betchworth. By now you guys have realised that I am a mug for scenery, an' that nothin' gives me greater pleasure than walkin 'about in the moonlight. Well . . . not a lot of things anyhow.

But thinkin' about this golf course in the moonlight gives me an idea. Anyway, I reckon that it is time I got some action an' started somethin' goin' on this case.

I get up, pull the blinds down, give myself a cold wash-up just to remove the cobwebs, open the door an' find my way down to the hotel hallway. The place is so dark that you practically got to smell your way around.

I find a little room with "Night Porter" on the door, so I give a knock. After a bit some guy says: "Who's there?"

"It's Hitler," I tell him. "I just landed in the High Street by parachute. Give me some quick service an' I will give you a lump of Spain, two islands in the Malay Archipelago, an' a far blonde I tossed Goering for, who can stand on one ear an' play 'We thank our Führer' as a hot number on a jew's harp."

There is a lotta grumblin' an' after a bit some guy who is supposed to be the night porter comes out. I ask this guy where the telephone is an' he shows me. He also informs me that (a) the telephone is practically useless, an' that (b) it is about seventeen hundred to one I won't get through to where I want to, an' (c) if I do get through the guy I want will be either out or dead. I tell him that is O.K. by me an' that I have used English telephones before an' am still alive to tell I the tale. I slip him half-a-crown an' he disappears.

I go inta the box an' I ring Whitehall 1212. Am I lucky or am I? In less than two minutes some guy comes on an' informs me that I am talkin' to Scotland Yard Information Room an' what would I like? I tell him that I would like the private telephone number of Chief Detective Inspector Herrick, that I am Lemmy Caution, accredited Agent of the Federal Bureau attached U.S. Embassy, London, complete with what goes with that an' a raspberry birthmark that I got through my mother thinkin' of fruit on her weddin anniversary.

The guy tells me that I am very lucky because Herrick is workin' on night duty at the Yard, an' he will put me through. Pretty soon Herrick comes on the line.

"Look, Herrick," I tell him, "this is your old pal Lemmy Caution speakin' to you from the wilds of Dorking."

I hear him laugh.

"What're you doing there, Lemmy?" he says.

"I wouldn't know," I tell him. "I just taken over an Embassy job from Charlie Milton, one of our boys. Maybe you remember makin' an inquiry for him about some bozo called Max Schribner?"

Herrick says yes, he remembers. He says they checked on Schribner for Milton an' found out where he was. He says that Schribner is over here on what appears to be legitimate business connected with some metal deliveries from some U.S. Corporation. He asks me why I haven't been in to see him.

I tell him. I tell him I been in Scotland tryin' to learn to play golf, but that I have now started work an' that I will come in an' take a peek at him soon. I ask him if he will do somethin' for me.

He hesitates for a moment, an' then he says:

"Listen, Lemmy. I've got a very soft spot for you and a great admiration for the way you go about things, but the last time you were working over here and supposed to be co-operating with us, we never saw you from the beginning to the end of the case."

I tell him that I know about all that, but that this time it is goin' to be very different an' that when I come to see him in a coupla days I will wise him up to everything that I am doin'. In the meantime, I tell him, I would be very glad if he could do a coupla little things for me.

I hear him give a sigh. He says what are the things?

First of all, I tell him, I want him to get through to the U.S. Embassy night guy an' get a telephone call across to Washington as quick as possible. I give him the message an' he writes it down:

From Lemuel H. Caution, Chief Agent, F.B.I. Code Number 165-43.

To Director Federal Bureau of Investigation United States Department of Justice, Washington, D.C., U.S.A.

Reference Julia Wayles stop Request immediate information reference Jakie Larue serving fifteen years to life sentence Leavenworth stop Also names of his associates visitors correspondents.

Reply care Chief Detective Inspector Herrick New Scotland Yard London who will forward stop Thank you stop.

Herrick says he will get this across to the Embassy night staff as quick as he can, but that he would like to see me as soon as possible just so's he can sorta level things out officially. I tell him that I will be with him as soon as I can make it if not sooner, after which I hang up.

I light a cigarette an' go outa the side door. The moon is up an' it is the sorta night that you expect the Jerries to be comin' over on. But to-night everythin' is as quiet as the local graveyard. I get to feelin' more poetic every minute.

Maybe you bozos, who have heard all the facts in this case, have got some ideas, but if you haven't I will give 'em to you. First of all it looks to me that this kidnap business is phoney. It looks to me it is a set-up on the part of this Sigfried Larssen an' his lawyer. I do not believe for one minute that this guy Larssen believes that Julia Wayles has been kidnapped. I think he just wantsta find the baby for some reason best known to himself. He is so hot on findin' her that he is even goin' to pull in the Federal Bureau of Investigation to help him, an' to do that he has to tell a lotta lies.

For some reason I got an idea in my head that there is a tie-up between this Larssen an' maybe that Maxie Schribner guy—the feller who is so cool, calm an' collected when he hears that I have been bumped off an' chucked in the drink.

Anyhow it is a fine night an' I am goin' to get some action, because I hate stickin' around, an' also because I am a feller who likes to produce a dramatic climax at any moment. So I think I will produce a dramatic climax for Maxie's benefit.

I go back inta the hallway an' find the telephone booth. I get through to "Inquiry," an' after a lotta fandanglin' I get the number of the Schribner house on the golf course. I call through there. After a few minutes some dame's voice answers an' I am tellin' you that the voice is not so bad. It is nice an' low an' even an' cool—one of them sorta husky voices that makes grandpa wish he was two centuries younger.

The voice says hello an' what do I want?

I make my voice sound as much like Charlie Milton's as possible, an' I put a lotta suppressed excitement inta the tone. I say:

"Look, this is Rudy, an' I don't want any time wasted. Is Maxie there?"

She falls for it. She says yes he's takin' a bath an' shall she fetch him.

I say: "No! Go up an' tell him to get outa the bath as quick as he can, get his clothes on an' get down to the bus stop at Holmwood. That's about two miles out on the other side of Dorking. Tell him I will meet him there in twenty minutes' time, an' tell him to be there an' not make any mistakes about it. It's urgent, see?"

She says O.K. She'll do it. I hang up. There is something about this dame's voice I like. Maybe I am goin' to be lucky.

I go back to my bedroom, get my hat an' fill my cigarette case. I light a cigarette an' go out. I start walkin' towards the roundabout on the Reigate road—the road that leads towards the golf course. Just when I get on the other side of the roundabout, a tourin' car with the top down goes by. I give a big grin. The guy drivin' it is Schribner. Anyway, I reckon I got about forty to fifty minutes.

I ease down the road towards Betchworth. I turn up the private road, get over the wire fence they got up to stop the sheep wanderin', an' start gettin' across towards the avenue of limes.

Some wise guy—Confucius or somebody—said there was nothin' like the truth, which is a thing that I believe in—sometimes. Anyhow, I am goin' to try this nothin' but the truth stuff on this dame I spoke to.

What can I lose anyway?

CHAPTER THREE
SEE YOU TAMARA!

IT IS a quarter past three when I get to the Schribner cottage. When I get up to the little white gate I can see that this dump is called "Wild Thyme." I reckon they must have spelt the Thyme part wrong.

I give a knock on the door an' I stand there waitin'. I am thinkin' about the dame I met up with in the American Bar two three nights ago. I think it is too bad that I have hadta break the date that I had with her for to-night, because now I shall never really know just what this sweetie thinks about this and that, an' for the rest of my life I shall be wonderin' about what mighta happened an' whether this particular bundle of blessin's got a system of kissin' that would make grandpa get up an' dance or whether she is one of them quiet ones that just look at you sideways . . . you know the ones.

Because it is always the dame that you didn't know so well that you remember. The old wisecracker Confucius said: "The known charmer is like the book of poems that is well read and without excitement"—which shows that the old boy certainly knew his gherkins, an' I agree with him because when I go in for readin' I like the book to be new an' excitin' an' if the jacket looks good I like the stuff inside it to be even better. An' you too, hey?

Right in the middle of these deep an' serious thoughts the door opens, an' if I was a guy who was given to surprise, I would have gasped like a cuttle-fish with bronchitis.

Because the dame standin' in the doorway, framed against the light in the hall beyond—an' believe it or not this baby is not worryin' about the blackout one little bit—woulda knocked you for six to the boundary.

Maybe you mugs have been stuck on a dame sometime. An' then maybe you've seen somebody you like better an' so on. Well, I'm tellin' you one an' all that if you was to add up all the dames you've been crazy about all your life you would not even be warm when it comes to this one.

She is of middle height an' she has got auburn hair. Her skin is like the cream you skim off the milk in the mornin' an' her eyes are big an' deep blue like the sea. She has got a figure that is a hula girl's dream an' her general style an' set-up are the physician's final instructions. In fact I will go so far as to tell you guys that if I was the Shah of Persia an' had this dame in my harem, I would not even worry to check up on the other five hundred an' forty. No, sir! I would just put up the shutters, order a little soft music and leave a note for the milkman to call every second Thursday.

She stands there lookin' at me. She just don't even blink. Openin' doors to strange guys at a cottage stuck on a golf course at three-fifteen in the mornin' is a business that this honeypot just takes in her stride. She puts one hand on her hip an' the opposite shoulder against the door-post.

She says: "An' what can we do for you?"

An' she sounds just a little bit tough. Not enough to be raspy or anythin' like that, but just enough to be interestin'. This dame is one big eyeful. I'm telling you.

"Lady," I tell her, "I would like to have a spot of conversation with you. There are one or two points that I would like to discuss with you, an' believe it or not you will be a smart dame if you consent without tryin' to duck. Otherwise you will probably regret it."

She don't move. She says:

"Tough. hey? On your way, stranger. We got no vacancies for hired help, an' we don't wanta buy any Christmas cards for next year either. What would I want to talk to you about? An' supposin' I did want to an' didn't, why would I regret it?"

"Here's the reason." I tell her. "My name is Lemmy Caution, an' I got a Federal Bureau of Investigation Card in my pocket an' a great curiosity. First of all I would like to give you some exclusive information that I would not even tell my own mother. Maybe you don't know it but I am a corpse that Maxie Schribner thinks is floatin' about in the local sewage department. Secondly, you are the dame that some guy called Rudy, who is a pal of Schribner's, telephoned to about three quarters of an hour ago. Well, that guy was not Rudy—that guy was *me*. Thirdly, when I heard your sweet an' lovely voice on the telephone I thought you was a baby that oughta be investigated, an' the message I gave you that sent Schribner rushin' out to Holmwood was just hooey. An' fourthly, an' lastly, a collection of figure like you got ought not to be alone at any given moment, because you are very interestin' on the eye, an' although I know that many a sap has left the straight an' narrow roadways because of dangerous curves, I am still willin' to take a chance of rushin' in even if I finish up in a skid. An' thank you for listenin'."

She gives a little smile. I'm tellin' you that this dame is so goddam cool that you coulda used her to ice the Martini with.

"So you're Caution?" she says. "The great Lemmy Caution. Heaven's gift to the Department of Justice. You're just too wonderful . . . aren't you?"

"Think nothin' of it, honey," I tell her.

"I don't," she says. "But come in if you've got to, an' get whatever it is that's on your mind off it. Because I wanta sleep sometime to-night."

"Nuts!" I tell her, steppin' into the hallway with a brisk smile. "Nuts! When I come across a dame wearin' a brown velvet coat an' skirt that fits as well as the ones you got on, two bracelets an' a frill at her neck, to say nothin' of high heeled oxfords, beige chiffon stockin's an' a new water-wave, I know that she is *not* goin' to bed. See? Maybe you was waitin' for somebody?"

She leads the way inta the room where I saw Schribner an' Milton last night. She says:

"I didn't say I was going to sleep in my clothes . . . did I?" She points to a big armchair. "Sit down an' relax," she says. "That is if you Federal Brains Trusts ever do relax. An' excuse me if I appear to be a bit flustered an' het up." She throws me a sarcastic sorta grin. "After all." she says, "I am a very inexperienced girl an' I am not used to meetin' with tycoons like you."

"You don't say?" I tell her. "Where have you been all your life? You never got that line through addressin' women's clubs."

"I know little of men," she goes on, throwin' me a look that was so goddam wicked you coulda lit a cigarette off it. "I have got my experience an' happiness only from good books. . . ."

"Like hell you have, Desdemona," I tell her. "The only happiness you could get from books would be from some guy's cheque book."

She sit down an' crosses her legs. The process is very good for tired eyes. I will not tell you about her line in legs because I have not got the time. But they are definitely legs. I'm tellin' you, an' I *know*.

"All right, Clever," she says. "You think you're doin' fine. You think you got a nice grip on somethin', don't you? O.K. Go ahead, my hero. What's eatin' you?"

"I'll get around to it, Gorgeous," I tell her. "an' you are not so far wrong about the Brain Trust either. Maybe I've got Somethin' on you an' Maxie that can hurt if I want it to."

"An' maybe you haven't," she says. "I heard about you, Mr. Caution. You got a refutation as a quick worker an' for bein' very slick an' very brainy. O.K. Well, I ain't noticed it. Any time your brain works it makes me think of delayed action."

I light a cigarette. "Look, Helen of Troy," I say. "I am gonna advise you to listen to me an' listen hard. Maybe you are tryin' to stall this conversation out till Maxie gets back. But even that ain't gonna help you. because any time I see that guy again, an' I am not in the right frame of mind, I'm gonna paste that fat pan of his until he looks like an ink splash on the carpet. So let's talk."

"Who's stoopin' you?" she says. "Say your piece, you great big beautiful beast. Any time I get bored I'll to sleep."

"O.K.," I tell her. "I'm enjoyin' this. I always was a guy for the company of beautiful women, an' don't you think I'm not havin' a wonderful time baby, because I'm not. First of all what's your name if any?"

"Tamara Phelps," she says. "But my friends call me Tamara."

"I bet they do," I tell her. "O.K., Tamara, let me give you a jugful of information. First of all I am in this country lookin' for a dame called Julia Wayles. This Julia proposition was engaged to a guy called Larssen an' disappeared. The F.B.I, have got an idea that she's been snatched an' I got an idea that Schribner is in on this thing somehow. I also got an idea that you are playin' in with Maxie. O.K. Well, last night I come out here to see Schribner about this baby an' ask him if he knows where she is. I tell him that my name is Paul Willik of the Trans-Atlantic Agency, but some heel who comes in recognises me an' pulls a cannon, after which Maxie orders that I am to be nicely shot an' chucked into the local mill-pond. an' how do you like that?"

"I don't like it," she says. "Maybe it's true an' maybe it's not. But one thing is obvious an' that is that you have not been shot an' that you are not floatin' about in the local ditch, an' I reckon that let's Maxie out on the killin' charge . . . if any."

"Right," I tell her. "But what about the rest of it? If I go shoutin' my head off to the English cops, who d'you think they're goin' to believe—Maxie or me? Why don't you get wise, sister? You're in a bad jam."

"Sarsaparilla," she says. "Any time I'm in a bad jam I'll get scared, but at the moment I'm not even tremblin'."

"Look," I tell her, "I'm tryin' to do you a good turn an' you won't have it I'm tryin' to give you a break an' you're forcin' me to get tough an' hand you out a deal that is goin' to be so raw that you'll probably get yourself stuck in an English penitentiary for about fourteen hundred years. Why don't you get some sense, honey?"

She looks at me for a minute an' then she looks at the floor. She looks sorta pensive an' sad. I'm tellin' you that she has got an expression like a dove that has been handed a raw deal by a passin' eagle. This dame has certainly got somethin'.

Then she says, sorta sudden, as if she'd just thought of somethin': "I don't know that you aren't talking sense . . . You're probably right." She clasps her hands around her knees an' she has the sorta look in her blue eyes that tells me that she is either gonna tell me the story of her life or hand me out a string of boloney that would make the Goebbels propaganda department look like the annual report of the Two Rivers Hot Pickle Corporation.

"Look, Lemmy," she says, "I was sort of attracted to you when I saw you out there on the garden path. You looked like the kind of man that a girl could lean on."

I nod. I am thinkin'. I am thinkin' so goddam hard that you can hear my brain clickin' over. Because when a dame, who looks like this dame looks, starts handin' me out a line of gab like she is issuin', I know that some fireworks are gonna start. When a momma with a sort of "Squeeze me, honey, I ain't indiarubber" eyes that this baby has got, begins to tell me that I am the sorta guy a girl can lean on, then you can bet last year's income to a bad egg that somethin' is going to start good an' quick.

"Yeah!" I tell her. "You can lean on me all right. I am a guy that has been leaned on by janes for so long that I'm practically bent sideways. Shoot, honey . . . the drinks are on me."

The telephone in the corner of the room starts janglin'. She goes over an' grabs the receiver. She says:

"Hello . . . is that you, Maxie? Yeah . . . this is Tamara. No, I haven't seen a soul. Nobody's been here an' nobody's called through. . . . You don't say . . . so Rudy didn't turn up. What do you know about that. Maybe you got the wrong place. Maybe he's waitin' at the bus stop at *North* Holmwood. . . . I would. . . . Yeah. . . . I'd drive along there an' have a look. If he isn't there you come back here. an' if he does call through I'll tell him to come through again later. . . . O.K., Maxie. . . ."

I give a big grin inside. So she has started stallin' Maxie! Maybe I am gonna get some sense outa this dame in a minute. She comes back an' sits down in the chair beside me. She looks sorta pensive. She says:

"There you are. . . . I'm being deflected again. I've stalled Schribner. That gives me another half an hour—" she looks at me an' her blue eyes are misty—"and half an hour is not a long time for a girl to make up her mind in."

"No?" I tell her. "Listen, honeybelle! I have known babies who made up their minds on more important things in about two minutes." I lean forward. "Look"—I tell her—"you have gotta make up your mind, haven't you? You're scared. You know goddam well you either gotta play along with Maxie or with the law—which is me. If you're a wise dame it ain't goin' to take you half an hour to make up your mind about that."

She looks at me sideways.

"That's all very well," she says, "but I don't know that the law comes into this."

"No?" I tell her. "An' what d'ya mean by that one?"

"This is England," she says. "This ain't America. Maybe you might be able to make things pretty tough for me over there but that don't say you can do it here."

"Hooey, Tamara," I tell her. "You know goddam well I have only gotta go to Scotland Yard an' show my F.B.I, identification an' they're goin' to give me all the co-operation I want. Why don't you get wise an' stop stallin'?"

She smiles at me. She says:

"You'd get all the co-operation you want for what? Listen, copper . . . you don't even know that any crime's been committed. You don't know that this Julia Wayles has even been kidnapped. You don't know anything. Before you can get co-operation from the English police you got to have a story to tell 'em. Well, what sort of story have you got? What are you goin' to tell 'em? Are you going to tell 'em that you got Max Schribner's name and address from somewhere, that you came down here; that some guy—a pal of Schribner's—stuck you up with a gun, an' the idea was they were goin' to crease you an' throw you in the river? If it was, why didn't they do it? How is it you got away? Personally, if I was an English copper and you told me a story like that I wouldn't co-operate with you. I'd send you around to a brain specialist."

I light a cigarette just to give myself some time to think. This dame has got somethin' all right, because even an inmate of the local nut-house will allow that the story I *have* got sounds a bit funny, an' even if Herrick was to believe every word I say—an' I have no doubt he would believe it—we haven't got anythin' on these guys—not under English law.

"All right," I tell her. "Well, if that's your opinion, what are you worryin' about? You're sittin' pretty, aren't you? You haven't gotta do a deal with me. O.K. Well, if that is so, what did you stall Schribner for just now? Look, sister," I tell her, "why don't you thrown your hand in? You know goddam well that you're in on somethin' that's pretty funny. You know that there's somethin' behind this Wayles business. You're dyin' to open your mouth. Well, if it's Schribner you're afraid of, don't worry. I'll take care of that guy."

"Maybe you would an' maybe you wouldn't," she says. "Bur how do I know you mean that? You police guys will promise anything to get a girl to do what you want."

"Not me," I tell her. "You'd be surprised! I am a guy who is so truthful that sometimes it positively hurts. Take a look at my frank open countenance an' nice eyes. Why, I am the sorta guy that could we wrecked on a desert island with the top form of the girls' High School an' they'd be so safe you'd be surprised."

"Like hell!" she says. "If I was wrecked on a desert island with you I would give myself up to a crocodile quick. I think maybe that would be safer."

"All right, honeybelle!" I tell her. "You have it which way you like. All you've gotta do is to choose between me an' Schribner." I give a horse laugh. "Schribner! That guy makes me pass out. He is such a goddam mug that if somebody save him a pair of spats he'd try an' get 'em soled an' heeled."

She don't say anythin'. She sits there lookin' inta the fire. I'm tellin' you that she makes a pretty picture. I like the sorta way she's got her shoulders hunched forward. Believe me, when I told you that this dame had a figure I was tellin' you the truth.

After a bit she gets up. She puts her hands behind her back an' she starts walkin' up an' down the room lookin' at the ceilin'. She says:

"I'm in a spot. I don't know what to do." She turns round suddenly. She says: "I wonder if I can trust you?"

I grin at her. "That's one of the things you've gotta take a chance about," I tell her. I get up. I walk over to where she is standin' an' look at her. "The thing," I go on, "is whether *I* can trust *you*."

She puts up her chin. She says:

"You know damn well you can trust me. If you're any judge of character you've only got to look at me once to know that I'm on the up-and-up."

"Maybe," I tell her. "But if I looked at you once or a hundred times, it would not be to see if you was on the up-an'-up."

Her voice breaks a little bit when she speaks. She says: "You're quite right, Lemmy, I'm in a jam. Maybe I want your help to get out of it, and you ought to know that I'm the sort of woman that is going to play ball."

"I oughta know but I don't," I tell her. "My experience has shown me that there are four sorts of women—the ones who play ball an' the ones who don't. You might belong to either of these types."

She raises her eyebrows.

"Oh yes?" she says. "And what are the other two types?"

"They are a sub-division of the first two," I tell her. "They are dames that I divide up inta two classes as regards kissin'. When you kiss a dame," I go on, "she either closes her eyes or she keeps 'em open. You can tell a lot about a dame after you've kissed her."

She smiles. She shows a very nice set of very fine, very white little teeth. She comes very close an' puts her mouth up. "I never minded being examined as to what sort of a girl I was," she says.

I am just goin' to open my mouth to say somethin', but before I can get a word out she has got her arms round my neck an' in another second her mouth is on mine an' she is kissin' me like it was her last night on earth. This baby is certainly a thruster. Then she steps back. She says: "Now what sort of a woman am I?"

"I wouldn't know," I tell her. "I didn't notice whether you had your eyes open or shut. Maybe sometime we'll try it out again. I'll be more observant."

"Maybe," she says. She gives a little sigh. Then she walks over to the chair in the corner, picks up my hat. She comes back an' gives it to me. "Where can I find you?" she says. "I want to talk to you but I can't talk now. Schribner's got to be back soon. I wouldn't like him to find you here."

"Why not?" I say. "It might be a good thing. Although maybe it wouldn't be so good for him."

"Never mind," she says. "Schribner doesn't matter right now. The thing is I've got to talk to you. It's important. I'm going to trust you."

"O.K.," I tell her. "I'm stayin' at a dump here called the White Lion, but I'm checkin' out to-morrow mornin'. I'm goin' up to London. You'll find me at 726a Jermyn Street—here's the phone number. Unless the Jerries have blown the place up in the meantime."

I write down the telephone number an' give it to her.

"Now, look, kid," I tell her. "Let me give you a tip-off. Don't try any funny business. Maybe you think you're gettin' rid of me nice an' easy, but if you don't cash in like you said I'll make things very tough for you."

"I'll cash in, Lemmy," she says. "Somehow I don't think I'll mind talkin' to you. There's something about you I like."

I grin at her. "You don't say?" I tell her. "There's somethin' about you I like too."

"Yes?" she says. "Well, you try an' get it. Now you get out of here. I won't let you down."

"O.K.," I tell her.

She opens the door an' I go out an' along the small hallway. Outside, the golf course is bathed in moonlight. I get a sorta feelin' that if I had a notebook an' a pencil I might even write some poetry. I believe I have told you bozos I am a poetic sorta guy.

"So long, Tamara," I tell her. "You be a good girl an' don't get lookin' outa any high windows. You might fall out. an' don't forget I'll expect to be seein' you."

"I'll be there," she says. "So long."

I go down the garden path an' open the little white gate. Lookin' back I can see her standin' in the doorway. I blow out on the pathway an' just as I am movin' off she says: "Hey, Lemmy . . . you wanted to know whether I was one of those dames who keep their eyes open or closed when they're kissed. I can tell you."

"Yeah?" I say. "An' what do you do?"

"Well." she says, "when I was kissin' you I kept 'em open—I was so bored I was afraid of falling asleep. Good-night, dewdrop!"

I walk across the green with the tee box that has got fifteen painted on it, down the long fairway an' towards the avenue of limes. I am doin' some very heavy thinkin', because you guys must not make any mistake about me. Just because I indulge in a little persiflage now an' again it does not mean that the old brain is not tickin' over. Maybe you think I have been a mug about this Tamara dame. Well, maybe I have, an' then again maybe not. Because in any event whatever she does, whichever way she plays it, she's got to do one of two things. She's either gotta take Schribner for a ride or she's gotta take me for a ride, an' whichever she does we'll still find somethin' out.

When I get through the avenue of lime trees, I can see the Reigate road. Comin' along towards me is a pair of headlights. I reckon this will be Maxie comin' home. Maybe Maxie is not feelin' so happy, an' he certainly won't be happy when he finds the guy he thought was Rudy has disappeared. Maybe Charlie Milton's act is goin' to be more useful than he ever thought.

I light a cigarette an' go on my way. I start whistlin' an old song—"Life is just a Bowl of Cherries."

An' who says it ain't?

CHAPTER FOUR
CONFUCIUS HE SAY . . .

I STAND lookin' outa the window of my apartment on Jermyn Street, lampin' the women as they go past, an' ponderin' on this guy Confucius. Maybe you have heard of this palooka. This guy is a smart Chinese fella who was so good at wise-crackin' that if he hadda been alive to-day they woulda got him signed up as a script writer in Hollywood, after which he would probably have forgot to be funny.

O.K. Well, Confucius is a palooka that usta think about dames considerably. Also he was a bozo who had been over a bit of grass in his time, because what he didn't know about frails coulda been stuck underneath a canary's toenails an' the canary wouldn't even have known. One of the things the boyo said was: "A snake strikes without an embrace. But a woman strikes at a man whilst her arms are about him." Which tells you all you wanta know, an' even if the Chinaman did pinch the idea from Issy Shank the scriptwriter, who said in his book *Advice to Young Women in Love*—"Cuddle 'em first an' crack 'em afterwards"—it shows you that the old boy had the right idea.

All of which brings me around to Tamara Phelps (I reckon Tamara is a sonsy sorta name—a dame with a name like that is liable to go places very quickly if she wanted it that way), Maxie Schribner an' anybody else who is takin' a hand in this little parlour game. I got an idea that before this business is all over Charlie Milton is gonna be sorta sorry that he was so goddam glad to hand this case over to me an' scram back to his lease an' lend delivery job, because everything about the whole set-up smells of right royal skulduggery to me an' I don't mean perhaps.

The sun is shinin' an' if it wasn't for the barrage balloons you could kid yourself that there wasn't even a war on—if you could get any cigarettes that is. On the other side of the road there is a very well dressed honeypot gettin' out of a car an' showin' more than the regulation twenty-four inches of leg while she is doin' it. But maybe this is because the sun is shinin' an' she is feelin' sorta reckless, or maybe it is because there is an Air Force Pilot on the sidewalk, watchin' her with that hawklike expression he got through peerin' at Messerschmitts. The dame takes a look over her shoulder, gives a little wiggle an' goes inta the scent shop on the other side of the road, an' before you can say knife the airman goes after her. Maybe *he* wants some perfume too.

Well I hope the dame is clever. I hope she's done a course in aerial combat, because if she ain't maybe that air guy is gonna get on to her blind flyin' side an' before she can say hey, he will be doin' a Victory roll an' she will be seen disappearin' behind a cloud with black smoke pourin' from her fuselage.

I wonder what Confucius woulda made out of Tamara Phelps. Maybe the old Chink woulda thought the same as I do. I think Tamara has the makin's. I also think that she is a baby who knows how many beans make five an' that she has got a good nerve besides all the other physical attractions. Also I think she is a bit scared, which shows me that she has been playin' in some set-up that is not so good an' that she thinks she might be better out of.

Schribner is another proportion. That guy might be anything. Maybe he wasn't such a mug as I thought. Maybe he is a tough guy an' would think nothin' of ironin' me out an' throwin' me to the fishes. A guy with a pan like Maxie's can just be anything at all. You don't know until he gets inta action.

I light a cigarette, snatch myself just one little shot of rye whisky out of the last of a dozen bottles I brought over with me, grab my hat an' scram. Outside I get a cab an' tell the guy to go to Scotland Yard.

Herrick is lookin' just the same. A bit greyer around the temples maybe, but with the same quiet thin an' relaxed pan that would not even show any excitement if he had pulled in Adolf Hitler on a charge of pinchin' a baby's rattle. I give him the works. I tell him that I am tryin' to find this Julia Wayles dame but that the department is not really very excited about the job; that it is just one of those things.

He says he remembers about it. He says Charlie Milton gave him the outline when he was down at the Yard askin' for a check-up on the Schribner guy. I ask Herrick what he knows about Schribner. He smiles.

"I don't think he's a kidnapper," he says. "He's over here on a survey job for the U.S. Government. Everything about him seems to be in order. He's in England for two or three weeks and then goes to Northern Ireland on the U.S. construction works in Londonderry. He's taken the cottage near Dorking for a month or two."

He lights his pipe an' looks at me through the flame of the match. He says: "I wonder why you're playing this job down, Lemmy. After all, if the Federal Bureau thinks there's nothing in it, why do they put *you* on to it. Why didn't they ask us to make the usual inquiries."

I shrug my shoulders. "I wouldn't know," I tell him. "But I got an idea that I won this case because I happened to be over here on leave—that's all."

He blows a smoke ring. "Well, we'll do anything we can to help," he says. "If you want any co-operation you've only got to ask for it. But there's just one thing . . ."

"Which is what?" I ask him.

"Which is that you don't start any funny business over here unless you let me know what you're doing," he says.

I look surprised.

"I wouldn't do a thing like that," I tell him.

He grins at me.

"Of course you wouldn't," he says. "You couldn't dream of such a thing, could you?" He takes his pipe outa his mouth an' points the stem at me. "D'you remember the last case you were on over here," he says, "—that Whitaker Dive Bomber case? Well, you made a fool out of us over that case. You stalled us the whole time. We never knew what you were doing until the thing was all over. That didn't matter so much, but some of the methods you used were hardly the sort that the Commissioner of Police likes in this country. This isn't America you know, Lemmy."

"You're tellin' me!" I say. "But don't you worry your head, Herrick. I wouldn't do a thing to annoy you guys. You're much too swell. an' right now there's only one little thing I would like you to do for me."

He asks what it is.

"I want the name of a good firm of private inquiry agents over here," I tell him. "A firm that has got some brains an' knows how to use 'em. I reckon this Julia Wayles thing is not of sufficient importance for me to make a police job of unless it develops, an' I don't wanta tie up a coupla your boys to hang around an' do nothin', because I reckon you're good an' busy right now."

He says that's true enough. Then he smokes for a bit.

Then he says: "There's a firm called Callaghan Investigations, in Berkeley Square. An organisation run by Slim Callaghan. They're about the best people I know. Callaghan's got brains . . . too much brains sometimes. . . ."

I say thanks a lot an' I take the address an' telephone number of the Callaghan firm, after which I shake hands an' scram.

When I get to the doorway I take a look back at Herrick. He is puffin' at his pipe an' lookin' at me very old-fashioned.

I reckon he is wonderin' whether I am gonna pull another fast one on him.

Well . . . you never know.

I find the Callaghan office in Berkeley Square an' go up in the elevator. I open the office door an' take a quick look at the dame who is poundin' the typewriter.

I reckon the mug who found her was a detective all right. She is so goddam good-lookin' that it almost hurts. She has got red hair an' green eyes an' a pair of ankles that woulda forced King Solomon to decide that four hundred wives wasn't enough. He'd just haveta have had the odd one. She looks at me an' says Yes? in a quiet sorta voice.

I tell her I would like to have a word with Mr. Callaghan an' that my business is private. She calls through on the telephone an' after a minute shows me into an inner office.

The Callaghan guy is sittin' behind a desk in the corner. He is a cute lookin' bird. He has got a lot of black hair an' a thin face with a pointed chin. He is wearin' very good clothes an' looks bored. He gives me the impression of bein' a very tough guy in a controlled sorta way.

I tell him who I am. I tell him that I am over here on leave an' have interested myself in a bit of funny business that I have come up against. I say that I would like a little help from him.

He lights a cigarette an' hands one to me. He says;

"Such as?"

"I want a guy to give me a little assistance," I tell him. "Chief Inspector Herrick of Scotland Yard is an old pal of mine. He put me on to you. What I want is a clever guy to do a little tailin' for me. To keep an eye on one or two people an' just get around an' be helpful, if you know what I mean."

He says he knows what I mean. He rings the bell on his desk an' the cute baby from the outer office comes in an' stands there with her notebook in her hand waitin'.

"Effie," he says, "tell Nikolls to come here."

She goes out.

"My own personal assistant—Windemere Nikolls—isn't on anything in particular at the moment," he says. "And as I would like to do anything I could for Herrick I'm going to turn him on to you. You'll find he knows most of the answers, and his knowledge of London is considerable. He's a Canadian."

The door opens an' a big bozo comes in. He has got a round face with twinklin' eyes, an' runs to a little bit of belly. He stands nice an' square on his feet an' looks as if he could be plenty useful in a rough house. He says:

"What's doin', Slim?"

Callaghan says: "This is Mr. Caution. He wants you to do a job for him. He'll tell you what he wants."

"O.K.," says the Nikolls guy. He pulls out a packet of Lucky Strikes an' throws one over to me. I ask him where he gets 'em.

"I gotta place," he says. "Maybe I can put you on to it." He looks at me an' grins. "I know another place where they got the straightest bourbon that ever come outa Kentucky," he goes on. "But maybe that wouldn't interest you."

"It would," I tell him. "Maybe you can lead a search party around there an' we can talk at the same time."

He says that is O.K. by him. I grab my hat.

"This costs you seven guineas a day an' expenses," says Callaghan "The office will send you an account when you're through with Nikolls. You might give Miss Thompson your address."

I say O.K. an' so long, an' we go outside an' fix it with the red head. The Nikolls any outs on a fedora just over one eye, an' we go out on this bourbon party.

By the time we got through one bottle I begin to like this Nikolls guy. The funny thing is that he usta work for the Trans-Atlantic Agency one time—which is a good recommendation for any guy.

I start leadin' the conversation around to dames just to get this boyo's reactions; but I needn't have worried. Directly I say the word his eyes light up.

"I'm sorta interested in dames," he says. "I reckon that every guy in the detective business oughta make a study of 'em. I'm writin' a book about 'em. I gotta theory." He gives a big sigh. "I started writin' that book ten years ago in Toronto." he says, "an' I ain't got it finished yet. Some baby has always stopped me finishin' it."

He looks at me an' grins. I reckon this Nikolls has got a sense of humour all right. I am beginnin' to think that maybe I can use this bozo for a little idea I got.

He goes on: "I got another theory about hip lines. I reckon you can always tell anythin' you wanta know about a jane by her hip line."

"Yes . . ." I tell him. "Especially if she is sittin' on your knee."

"I don't mean that way," he says. "I mean by just lookin' at 'em. You take a dame with a thin hipline an' hip joints that stick out. In nine cases outa ten this baby has got a discontented husband, no hope an' an acid nature. Whereas the well an' truly rounded dame has a bright an' hopeful viewpoint an' is never surprised at anythin'. The more streamlinin' she has got the earlier her old man gets home from the office because he has already sensed that the guy across the road is interested in streamlinin' too. Am I right or am I?"

"You are so right you'd be surprised," I tell him. I order a couple more shots of rye. "Look Nikolls," I go on, "here's what I want you to do an' I don't want any slip-ups because this business is rather urgent. See?"

"I don't go in for slip-ups," he says. "We don't recognise the word in Callaghan Investigations."

"O.K.," I tell him. "But you gotta be careful because the baby I am goin' to put you on to is no sap. This dame has got so much brains that they're practically stickin' out of her ears."

"What's she like?" he says. "an' what does she call herself? You can tell a lot by the name a dame has."

"Maybe," I tell him. "an' you can tell a lot more by listenin' to what her boy friend calls her when he's steamed up over somethin'. O.K. Well, this one is called Tamara Phelps."

"That's a swell name," he says. "Tamara Phelps. . . . I reckon a frail with a name like that has got sufficient to get around with."

"Right once again, Nikolls," I tell him. "She's got plenty—an' everythin' properly distributed an' under control. She's a looker. She's got them dreamy eyes that can change to steel blue any time she wants. She's so graceful when she walks around that you just wanta watch her. She's got a figure that would make a sculptor throw a lump of clay at his favourite model, an' she's cute."

"She sounds a nice dame," he says. "an' what do I have to do to her?"

"I am not certain about this baby," I tell him. "I think that maybe she's tryin' to play me along. Also I got an idea that I'm goin' to hear from her pretty soon. I think she's goin' to call through to me at my apartment on Jermyn Street. O.K. Well, if she does I'm goin' to get her to come around an' see me. Maybe she will an' maybe she won't. If she does I'm gonna call you on the telephone an' I want you to get along an' tail her when she leaves my place. I want you to find out where she goes, what she does an' anything else you can get. You got that?"

"I got it," he says. "It sounds easy."

"All you have not got to do is to let this dame know that I'm havin' her tailed," I go on. "I want to get her confidence an' if she knows I'm havin' her watched she is likely to take a run-out an' bust the whole works."

"O.K.," he says. "I got it. She won't know a thing. When I tail a dame she *stays* tailed."

We have a couple more shots of rye an' he tells me about some of the dames he has known around the world. This guy certainly seems to know his cornflakes an' the only thing that surprises me is that he has had any time to do any detectin'. There have been so many janes in this guy's life that I calculate he ain't safe anywhere except in one small spot in Iceland.

After a few more drinks, I say so-long to this Nikolls guy. I got his telephone number so's I can ring him when I want him, an' I give him my number an' address so's he'll know where to pick up Tamara if she shows up. I reckon he is the right guy for the job.

I go back to the Jermyn Street dump, take off my coat an' waistcoat, light a cigarette an' lay down on the bed an' relax.

It is six o'clock when I wake up, an' it looks like a very nice evenin' an' I hope it is goin' to turn out that way too. I stick around, light a cigarette an' help myself to just one little shot of bourbon just to get the old headpiece workin'.

Me . . . I am not dissatisfied with this case. I got an idea that in a minute somethin' is goin' to bust an' we shall get started. I reckon that Tamara Phelos is scared an' the next thing—after that baby decides to talk, that is if she *does* talk—is to throw a scare inta Maxie Schribner an' see if we can get him to open up.

At the same time I cannot see why there should be such a hullabaloo about this Julia Wayles jane. Dames have disappeared before an' the Federal Bureau don't get excited about 'em. But maybe she's somebody's sister or somethin'—somebody who matters.

There is a knock at the door an' the service guy comes in. He gives me an envelope an' scrams. I bust open the envelope an' it is the reply to the telephone cable that Herrick sent to the Department in Washington. It says:

From Department of Director Federal Bureau of Investigation Washington D.C.

To Lemuel H. Caution Chief Agent F.B.I. Code Number 165-43 care of Herrick C.I.D. Scotland Yard London.

Reference your inquiries stop Jakie Larue is Indianapolis gun-man and snatch racketeer serving Leavenworth sentence for kidnap conviction His main associate is Rudy Zimman still at

*large stop He has no visitors Zimman suspected of maintaining
and running Larue gang pending attempt escape on part of Larue
severed attempts already made stop Nearest associate of Rudy
Zimman is Tamara Phelps stop Phelps has served four terms
for harbouring and assisting in kidnap attempts stop Phelps is
considered dangerous stop Is under observation at present time
stop Good luck stop.*

Well, well! So we are gettin' a little bit warmer. I reckon this
message gives me plenty food for thought an' I am just doin' a little
bit of heavy concentratin' when the telephone lines I go over an'
grab it off. It is Tamara.

"Hey, Tamara," I tell her, "I'm glad to hear you talkin'. So you
decided to come across."

"Yeah." she says. "I thought it over an' what's a girl to do anyway?
I'm goin' to blow the works, Lemmy, but you got to look after me."

"Don't you worry, kid," I tell her. "Where are you right now?"

She says she is talkin' from the subway call box in Piccadilly
Circus.

"O.K.," I tell her. "Well, you come across here right now an' have
a little drink an' a cigarette, an' talk to Uncle Caution like a good
girl an' maybe I'll forget an' forgive."

"All right," she says, "I'll come over. an' I hope a girl can be safe
in your apartment."

"Look, baby," I tell her, "with a face an' figure like you got the only
place you would be safe would be in the ice-box. So hurry along."

She says she'll come right over. I hang up, wait a minute an'
then ring through to the Nikolls guy.

"Look, Nikolls," I tell him, "that Tamara Phelps dame is on her
way here right now. She's just called me from a Piccadilly telephone
booth. O.K. Well, she'll be here talkin' for a little while. Get over
here an' stick around in the doorway on the other side of the road.
She won't see you there. When she leaves here tail her an' don't
leave her. Directly she stays put some place give me a call through
an' tell me all about it. You got that?"

He says O.K. he's got it. He says he'll get action right away.

I hang up an' give myself another little drink. I got a feelin' that this case is gonna start right now. You'll see why in about two minutes if you stick around.

I have just sunk the liquor when there is a knock on the apartment door. I go across the hallway an' open it an' there she is.

I'm tellin' you mugs that this baby is a sight for a guy who likes lookin' at dames. She is wearin' a sapphire blue linen coat an' skirt that matches up with her eyes. She is wearin' no stockin's but her legs are tanned just the way a dame's legs ought to be. She has got on little white kid court shoes picked out with blue, an' she is carryin' in her hand a soft white straw hat an' a white kid handbag ornamented with blue leather.

"Tamara," I tell her, "what have I been doin' all your life? You look so good that you just couldn't be wicked. Come in."

She comes in an' I shut the door behind her. She walks inta my sittin'-room an' stands in front of the fireplace, lookin' at herself in the mirror an' arrangin' a curl. Maybe she knows her figure looks good that way.

I push the big armchair forward for her, get a box of cigarettes. She sits down sorta languid. Lookin' at her outa the corner of my eye I don't think this baby is as scared as she makes out to be.

"What about a little tiny drink, honey?" I ask. "A shot of straight bourbon just to cement the fact that you an' I are goin' to be friends from now on."

She says she don't mind if she does. I get the bottle an' pour out two little drinks. I watch her while she drinks it. The way she sinks that drink is just nobody's business. It looks to me like she's a dame who has met bourbon before. I light a cigarette an' sit down in the other chair.

"Now, look, Tamara," I tell her, "you tell me this: How is it between you an' Maxie Schribner? Would you be his girl?"

"Don't be silly," she says. "I'd rather be tied up to an alligator. That punk makes me sick."

"That's O.K. by me," I tell her. "Because he makes me sick too. All right, baby, shoot an' let's have the works."

"Well," she says, "maybe I'm goin' to get myself in a spot tellin' you all this. Maybe I'm a fool. But there's something about you I go for, Lemmy, and I sort of trust you."

"That is nice news," I say. "You're making me blush all over. But go on!"

"Well," she says, "about this Julia Wayles, it's a snatch all right. And Schribner's in on it."

I blow a good-lookin' smoke ring an' watch it as it sails across the room.

"So it *is* a snatch, hey?" I say. "Who fixed it?"

"I wouldn't know," she says. "All I know is it was arranged somewhere in New York Somebody—I wouldn't know who—wants to snatch this Wayles dame, an' they snatched her."

"So that's it, hey?" I say. "What was it done for—money? Has she got a lotta dough? I've never heard about any Julia Wayles who had a lotta money."

"I wouldn't know what she's got," she says. "But I reckon girls have been snatched for something else except money before now."

I cock my eyebrows at her.

"Have they?" I ask her. "Well, I never knew a dame who was snatched just because she was good-lookin' before. I have known dames snatched because somebody wanted to get a ransom for 'em; I have known dames snatched because somebody thought they knew somethin' an' wouldn't come across; an' I have known dames to be snatched because somebody thought they knew too much an' wanted to shut their mouths up permanently. But I have never known a dame snatched for any other reason except one of those three."

"Maybe you're right," she says, "but I wouldn't know."

"I get it," I say. "So somebody in New York wants Julia Wayles snatched. That's all right. Well, who snatches her?"

"I don't know," she says. "All I know is that she has been snatched, an' that she's over here in England."

"Well, how did she get over here?" I ask. "I suppose she didn't walk."

"Right first time," she says. "I can tell you definitely she didn't walk. She was brought over here. She was brought over here on a boat. How they managed it I don't know."

"I see," I tell her. "In a minute I shall really begin to know somethin' about this. Well, how does Schribner come inta this business?"

"Schribner's got something to do with it this end," she says. "I believe Schribner knows where she is. I believe Schribner's working in with the mob who snatched her, but I'm not certain."

"I see," I tell her. "This is one of them cases where nobody knows anythin' about anybody else. Well, you tell me somethin': What are *you* doin' in on this job?"

"Well Lemmy," she says, "you know how it is. Things haven't been too good for the mobs in the States, not since Mr. Hoover turned the heat on an' this war started. Everybody's got too goddam patriotic to have time for gangsters. Why," she says, "some of the tough eggs on Broadway are gettin' themselves into the army just to have a bust at that guy Hitler."

"I see," I tell her. "So things was bad, hey?"

"That's right," she says. "I was sorta stickin' around an' not doin' much. Well, one day I met a girl friend in Moxsie's Bar. She asked me if I wanted a job—a nice job with some nice easy jack on the end of it and not too honest. When I asked her what it was she says there is some dame over in England; that this dame wants lookin' after an' that the guys who was lookin' after her at the moment have got an idea in their heads that they'd like to have a dame around."

"I get it," I say. "A sorta nurse, hey? In case Julia Wayles was to be sick or somethin'?"

"I wouldn't know that either," she says. "Maybe these boyos over here want to have some valid reason for holdin' her. Maybe they'd even suggest she was a mental case or something like that. Anyhow I don't know because I never ask too many questions."

"I see," I say. "So you didn't ask this dame too many questions. How did you get over here?"

"She fixed me up," she says. "She gave me some jack, fixed my passage and told me to report here to Schribner. Well, I came over here an' went down an' connected with Schribner at the dump near

Dorking. It was when that guy Rudy turned up that I began to smell a real life-sized rat."

"Oh yeah?" I tell her. "So Rudy got you thinkin', did he? An' what did Rudy make you think?"

"Well," she says, "I take one look at him an' I know who he is. He's a guy called Rudy Zimman—a very tough hombre. This boyo used to blow around with a mob that went in for snatchin' guys in the States. Directly I saw him I knew that Julia Wayles had been snatched."

"O.K.," I tell her. "So there it is. You believed somebody in New York has Julia Wayles snatched, stuck on a boat an' sent over here. You believe that rat Schribner is waitin' for her; you believe that Schribner has either got her stuck some place or knows where she is. O.K. Well, after this business has been done they feel they've gotta have a dame to look after her. So they look for a really tough dame—a dame as tough as Tamara Phelps. They give you some jack an' send you over here, an' you report to Maxie Schribner.

"The next thing is that Rudy Zimman turns up. So directly Rudy Zimman turns up you know it's a snatch because he is a guy you know was in the snatch game. O.K. Where do we go from there? Where is this Wayles baby?"

"I don't know," she says. "Maybe Schribner's not too keen on trustin' anybody yet. But he's got to talk to me some time, hasn't he?"

"I get it," I tell her. "He's gotta talk to you some time, an' when he talks to you, you're goin' to tell me, hey?"

"That's right," she says. She gives me a long sidelong smile. "You're a clever guy, aren't you, Lemmy?"

I give a little grin.

"Maybe I am an' maybe I'm not," I tell her. "But you tell me one thing: What are you gettin' scared about? You was in on this thing when this dame, who put this proposition up to you in New York, fixed your passage an' gave you some jack to come over here. You knew the game wasn't on the level, didn't you? O.K. Well, what's happened since you've been over here to make you scared? Ain't Schribner treated you right? What made you suddenly decide to talk to me?"

"I'm not quite certain," she says. "But I'm scared all right. First of all it was something that Schribner said. He sort of suggested that the 'G' men were in on this job." She shrugs her shoulders. "I don't like 'G ' men," she says. "Those guys are too hot and when they send you up they send you up for a long time and you stay put There aren't many guys get out of Federal prisons on parole, an' I don't like the idea of losin' my beauty looking through a prison grating for two years."

I nod my head.

"So that's it?" I tell her. "And you had to get to Dorkin', England, before you realised that. You couldn't think a little thing like that comin' over on the boat?"

She gets up. She stands lookin' down at me. Her eyes are sorta misty.

"Maybe you don't believe me, Lemmy," she says. "Maybe you don't think I'm tellin' you the truth?"

I grin at her. "You go an' sit down, baby," I say.

She goes back to her chair.

"Look, honey," I tell her, "what's the matter with you? You remind me of the dame who was so ignorant that she thought the Dumb Friends League was a club for blondes."

"Oh yeah?" she says. "an' what do you mean by that one?"

"I mean this," I tell her. "You are as much Tamara Phelps as I am Old King Cole. Maybe in a minute you'll be tellin' me that I am Santa Claus. Look, whoever you are, you brown snake, you're the lousiest liar I have ever met in my life, an' if you think I'm fallin' for any of this hooey you have got something comin' to you."

"Say, what the hell?" she says.

"Listen, honey," I tell her. "Maybe you thought I was sponge cake above the ears. Well. I'm not. Maybe it would surprise you to know that the guy that you recognised as Rudy Zimman was nobody else but Charlie Milton—a 'G' man—who four-flushed himself on you an' on Maxie Schribner as Rudy. Just because Schribner was mug enough to let him know that some guy called Rudy was comin' over. Well, you just told me that you recognised this guy as Rudy Zimman—a member of a snatch mob. That told me that you are a first-class liar. That told me that you've never seen the real Rudy

Zimman, or if you have it suits your book to make me think he's over here.

"O.K. For the same reason you're callin' yourself Tamara Phelps when you're not. Directly Charlie Milton told me that Schribner had mentioned the name of Jakie Larue to him—Jakie Larue bein' a guy who is servin' a from fifteen years to life sentence at Leavenworth, I had a telephone call put through to the F.B.I, at Washington.

"All right, sweetheart. Well, I gotta reply to that. Not so long ago Rudy Zimman was head man for Jakie Larue. Rudy Zimman's girl was a girl called Tamara Phelps. She's under observation now in the States. an' how d'ya like that, sweetheart?"

She looks at me with her mouth open.

She says: "I don't like it."

"O.K.," I tell her. "Well, havin' discussed this little bit of business so far, maybe now we can talk some real business. You tell me somethin': Who are you? an' don't give me any more fairy tales, sister."

"Look, Lemmy," she says, "maybe I've made a fool of myself. Listen—I'm going to tell you the truth now—an' you'll know it's the truth. Look—I'll prove it to you. . . ."

She flips open her handbag, puts her hand inside an' brings out a very pretty little pearl-handled .32 automatic. The muzzle is pointin' right at my navel. It almost gives me a stomach ache to look at it.

"O.K., wise guy," she says. "Just take it easy, an' don't start anything, otherwise this cannon is going to go off."

I shrug my shoulders.

"That's O.K., honeybelle," I tell her. "So you came heeled? You was prepared for a show-down, hey?"

"I'm always prepared for a show-down," she says. "And I'm not always unlucky, although I was a little bit unlucky over this Rudy Zimman-Tamara Phelps business. It looks as if I picked the wrong name, doesn't it?"

"You certainly did," I tell her. "an' now we come to mention it, what is the name?"

"Santa Claus to you," she says. She gets up an' walks over to the door. "Look, pal," she says, "I'm going. If you take a tip from me, you're going to stay in that chair till I'm out of this flat. Otherwise I am going to let a little daylight into you." She backs across the hallway, puts one hand behind her an' opens the door. "So long, copper," she says. "Maybe I'll be seein' you—and maybe I won't." The door slams behind her.

I give a big grin. I light myself a cigarette an' pour out one little shot of bourbon. It tastes good to me.

An' why not!

CHAPTER FIVE
TOO MANY RUDYS

WHEN the clock on the mantelpiece strikes ten I am still sittin' there with my feet up smokin', drinkin' a little spot of bourbon an' just thinkin' around this case generally. One fact is as obvious as a stick of liquorice on a white carpet, an' that is that somebody has been takin' this guy Schribner for a ride. Work it out for yourselves an' tell me if you don't agree with me.

O.K. Here we go: First of all let's assume for the sake of argument that this Julia Wayles baby has been snatched. Somehow or other she has been got away from New York over here to England. What happens to her when she gets here or where she is we do not know, an' for the moment we do not care. But Schribner has got somethin' to do with her. Maybe the phoney Tamara Phelps was tellin' the truth for once when she said Schribner was the guy who was supposed to look after Julia while she was here an' that he knows where she is.

All the indications seem to show that Julia was snatched by some guys who are members of Jakie Larue's old gang, an' this idea is supported by the fact that Schribner talks about Larue bein' in Leavenworth at the time that Charlie Milton, pretendin' to be Rudy, says all the boys are feelin' pretty good; to which Schribner says Larue won't be feelin' so good because he is doin' a fifteen year stretch in Leavenworth.

The idea is again supported by the fact that both Rudy Zimman an' Tamara Phelps—the real ones I mean—usta be pals of Jakie Larue, an' Schribner is expectin' these two to come over an' contact him for some reasons connected with this business.

But Schribner don't know Rudy an' he don't know Tamara, which looks as though, *if* he is workin' in with Larue's old gang, arrangements about this Wayles snatch an' Schribner receivin' this dame over here, have been made through the post or somehow. Because if Schribner *had* known Larue, or knew the members of his mob who've pulled this snatch, he would know Rudy an' he would know Tamara.

But there is somebody else in on this business. There's got to be. There is somebody else in on this business *who knows that Schribner don't know Rudy Zimman an' don't know Tamara Phelps.* This wise guy, whoever he may be, for some reason best known to himself, lets Schribner know that this Rudy Zimman is comin' over an' also that Tamara Phelps is comin' over.

O.K. Well, the baby who just stuck me up with a gun an' got outa here quick, an' who is not Tamara Phelps, comes over to this country, kids Schribner that she is Tamara Phelps an' settles herself in at the house at Dorkin'.

While she is down there Charlie Milton rings through. She thinks it is Rudy Zimman. who obviously she don't know, an' suggests the fact to him. Charlie, bein' a wise guy, jumps in an' says he is Rudy.

So we now arrive at two interestin' decisions, an' we've got some sweet questions to ask ourselves The first one is who was it put in the phoney Tamara Phelps; who was it that knew the real Tamara Phelps was due to come over here, an' why did they wanta put in the dame I have met in her place? The second interestin' thing is that there is no doubt that the real Rudy Zimman an' the real Tamara Phelps are either here or on their way here. When these two real guys meet Schribner some fun is goin' to start, because that guy is goin' to realise that somebody has taken him for a ride.

That's the way I see it, an' I think you guys will agree with me that this is the real set-up. It is also the sorta set-up that I like, because once you get enough guys mixed up—all wonderin' what the hell the other one is at—all you gotta do is to sit back an' let them sort themselves out, because in nine cases outa ten while they're at it, they'll sort the case out for you too, an' although maybe this is not the real Sherlock Holmes technique, it is one that works a darned sight better an' stops you rushin' around with a double-barrelled magnifyin' glass lookin' for clues under the edge of the dinin'-room sideboard, an' only findin' a lump of chewin' gum that somebody stuck there three weeks ago.

It is a quarter past ten when I get up an' give myself a warm shower. First of all I think I'll get inta bed. Then after a minute I think no maybe somethin' will happen. So I dress an' have one little snifter just to keep the germs away.

At half-past ten the house telephone goes. The janitor from downstairs rings up to say that there is a gentleman by the name of Nikolls to see me. I say O.K. send him up.

A coupla minutes afterwards Nikolls comes in. He shuts the hall door behind him an' hangs his hat up on the hallstand. He takes a pack of Lucky Strikes out of one coat pocket, a wax vesta outa the other an' strikes it on the seat of his pants. He lights the cigarette an' relaxes in the big armchair. I got the idea it would take a lot to disturb this Nikolls guy.

He looks at the bottle on the table.

"I could use a little of that," he says. "I find I always think better on rye. I told you I was writin' a book on the art of bein' a detective, didn't I?"

"You don't say?" I tell him. "I reckon it's goin' to be good, ain't it? What does that boss of your—Callaghan—think about it?"

Nikolls spreads his hands.

"Oh *him*!" he says. "Well, he's got a different technique to me. Maybe he's a little bit jealous."

I nod. I pour him out a shot of bourbon which he sinks in one gulp. He draws a big mouthful of tobacco smoke an' blows it out through his nostrils. Then he says:

"I expect you wanta know about this Phelps baby, don't you? I picked her up when she left here. I think I hadda bit of luck about that baby."

"Yeah?" I tell him. "How lucky?"

"She took a cab at the end of Jermyn Street," he says, "an' she went out to an apartment block—Mayfield Court—this side of Hampstead—a nice place. I went behind her in another cab. When she went in the block, I went in after her. The place is one of them dumps with a long corridor. I could see her walkin' ahead of me.

Presently she stopped an' rang the bell at the door of an apartment on the ground floor. She went in.

"I hung around until I found the liftman. I slipped him a quid and told him I was doin' some private inquiry work in a divorce case; asked him who owned the apartment that Tamara had just gone into. He told me it was owned by some dame named Owen—a Mrs. Owen. Just then Tamara came out. I stuck around the corner. She called the liftman an' asked him if it was possible for him to fix with a taxi to drive her out to Dorking at about a quarter to twelve to-night. He said he didn't know but he's find out an' let her know. She went back inta the apartment.

"The lift guy went off to visit the local taxi rank. When he came back he told me he'd fixed it. A cab was goin' to call for this Tamara baby at a quarter to twelve an' take her out to Dorking. I can't give you the address they're goin' to—he didn't know so he couldn't tell me. I guess she'll tell the cabman when the time comes."

"That's O.K., Nikolls," I tell him. "I reckon I know the address she's goin' to." I pour him out another drink. "Look, Nikolls," I go on, "when I pulled you in on this job I told your boss I just wanted you to do a little tailin' an' nothin' else. Well, maybe I can use you again, but it might be a little bit tough this time. Does the idea sort of appeal to you?"

He looks at me an' he grins.

"If you knew anything about Callashan Investigations." he says. "you'd know you've sot to be plenty tough to string along with that guy Callaghan. I just been brought up bein' tough. I usta work for a firm of private dicks in Chicago in '35. Would that mean anything to you?"

I grin. "It would mean plenty," I tell him. "'35 was a right royal year in Chicago an' any private dick who went around the windy city those days was liable to find himself in the gutter with a lead slug in his belly any day in the week. If you managed to survive that epoch you're O.K., pal."

He puts his hand out an' grabs the rye bottle. He pours himself another slug.

"Anythin' you want just let me know," he says.

I do a little quiet thinkin'. Then I tell him:

"Look—when this dame, that we think is Tamara Phelps but isn't, goes out to this Dorkin' dump to-night I'm goin' after her. I got an idea she's goin' out to see a guy called Schribner an' tell him a little fairy story. All right. Well, you're not concerned with the fairy story. I'm goin' to give that dame long enough to tell Schribner what she wants; then I'm goin' to bust in that dump. The joke is I ain't goin' to have a gun. I'm goin' to be easy meat for anybody. This guy Schribner has tried to get rid of me once. He don't like me. Maybe he's goin' to try it on again."

"I got it," he says. "an' where do I come in? I suppose I clock him at the crucial moment?"

"Oh no," I tell him. "What you gotta do is this: You get down to Dorking at about twelve-thirty. When you get there drive out of the town along the Reigate road. About two hundred and fifty yards past the Dorkin' roundabout you'll find the golf course. There's lots of places you can park a car there where nobody will see it.

"O.K. You get over the wire fence an' you start walkin' across the sixth fairway till you come to an avenue of limes. Follow the avenue of limes uphill an' when you get to the top where the trees stop just stick there in the shade an' wait for me."

"I get it," he says. "I oughta be there round about a quarter to one."

"That's O.K.," I tell him. "If the phoney Tamara leaves Hampstead by cab at a quarter to twelve she's not goin' to get out to the dump she's goin' to, which is on this golf course, until about one o'clock. That gives us plenty of time to fix things up. You got all that?"

"O.K.," he says. "I'll be there. There's only one thing. If anybody's goin' to get hurt on this job—I mean if I've gotta hurt somebody—I'd like to do it nice an' quiet. My boss Callaghan don't like any sorta publicity about sluggin' guys."

I grin at him. "Don't worry," I tell him. "I don't want any publicity myself. If we've gotta slug anybody we'll do it nice an' quiet."

"O.K.," he says. He looks at his watch. "It's a quarter to eleven," he says. "I reckon I got a half an hour before I leave—just time enough to see a cutie I know with a nice hip-line. Maybe she'll sorta inspire me for a little night work with you. So long."

He strikes another match on the seat of his pants an' lights a fresh cigarette. He puts his hat on an' scrams. This guy Nikolls is nice an' quiet an' easy on his feet although he is a big man. I reckon he might be good in a rough house.

I take off the telephone an' I ring through to the U.S. Embassy. I speak to the night secretary an' give him my name an' code number. I tell him I want a car round here in Jermyn Street at eleven o'clock an' can he fix it for me. He says O.K. He'll send one of the Embassy cars round. The driver'll park it outside an' leave it. I tell him thanks a lot. I tell him also I'd be very glad if he'd have the Embassy diplomatic badge taken off the car, because I don't wanta start another war down in Dorkin'. He says O.K. he'll do that.

"By the way, Mr. Caution," he goes on, "I'm glad you're back in town an' workin'. We've been wonderin' where you were."

"Yeah?" I tell him. "Well, you oughta know. I was supposed to be on leave. I was in Scotland. Didn't they tell you I love scenery?"

I hear him chuckle. "I've heard about you," he says. "I think I can make a guess at the sort of scenery you were looking at. Good-night."

A clock is just strikin' half-past twelve when I get over the wire fence just off the Reigate road an' start wanderin' across the grass towards the avenue of lime trees. It has got a bit cold an' there is a spot of rain fallin'. There are big clouds in front of the moon an' I get the sorta feelin' that this is the sorta night that somethin' happens on. I hope it is gonna be something good.

I walk up the middle of the avenue. Away on the right is a fairway with a helluva lot of sheep stickin' around. Some of 'em have gone inta the trees for shelter an' some of 'em—the mugs—are standin' out on the fairway lookin' at the ground. I reckon sheep are like people. Some duck when the trouble starts an' some don't.

Somebody says: "Hello . . ." I look around an' there is the Nikolls guy. He is leanin' up against a lime tree smokin' a cigarette, shieldin' the end with his hand.

"Hello," I tell him. "How was the hipline? I hope it wasn't difficult for you to drag yourself away."

"Oh no," he says. "I never mind. You can always find another one—if you look."

He hands me a Lucky Strike an' holds up his lighter. The smoke tastes good.

"Well," he says, "how do we play this—whatever it is—an' do I get back to London before to-morrow or am I turn in' rustic?"

"You . . ." I tell him, "are a guy called Rudy Zimman. You are a bad guy. You usta get around with a boyo named Jakie Larue who is stuck inside Leavenworth at the present moment servin' from fifteen years to life for snatchin' somebody. You got that?"

"I got it," he says. "An' what have I been doin' since Larue's been inside? Just rollin' around—or have I been committin' some more crimes?"

"I reckon you've done practically everything" I tell him. "I reckon you are so bad that you don't even like yourself sometimes. Maybe you've been doin' a bit of white slavin' lately. . . ."

"I see," he says. "I been doin' that just for a nice change, I suppose?"

"Somethin' like that," I tell him. "Well, anyhow, somebody I don't know gets in touch with you in New York an' tells you to come over here an' make a contact with a guy called Maxie Schribner. This guy lives in a white cottage—not a bad sorta little house—a coupla miles or so from here. I'll show you where the dump is. You got all that?"

"I got it," he says. "Tell me some more. I'm sort of interested in my life's history."

"Some dame has also been sent over to contact this Schribner guy," I tell him. "Her name is Tamara Phelps, but she is not the one we know. That one is a phoney one. But Schribner thinks the phoney one is the genuine article. Well, this dame don't know Rudy Zimman. She probably knows he is comin' over here but she don't know him. She's already taken some other guy for him."

"So I'm going to meet her, am I?" he says. "It looks like it's goin' to be an interestin' session."

"You never know," I tell him. "Anyhow . . . I got an idea in my head that this phoney Tamara is comin' out here tonight to tell Schribner some story an' duck. She's scared, see? She's scared because of the little talk she an' I had in my apartment before you tailed her to Hampstead."

"I got it," he says. "The phoney Tamara thinks that things are gettin' a little bit too warm an' wants to duck."

"Right," I tell him. "I reckon she's gonna tell Schribner some story to keep him quiet an' then she's gonna fade. Well, I want you to show up before she does. I want you to knock on the door of Schribner's place an' when you get in you tell him that you are Rudy Zimman an' that you just arrived here in England an' came out as soon as you could. The guy is then gonna get scared an' say what the hell is this; that he has already met up with one Rudy who has disappeared. You say that's right; that the Rudy he has met is nobody else but an F.B.I, operative called Charlie Milton, who is the guy who let Lemmy Caution—the other 'G' man—escape, an' that this Milton guy is all set to make things good an' hot for Schribner.

"Schribner then gets scared, an' then you ask who the dame is. Schribner is gonna have another surprise because Rudy Zimman oughta know her. He is gonna say what the hell again, an' you are goin' to tell him that this dame is not Tamara Phelps any more than you are old King Cole. You are also gonna tell him that there has been a darn sight too much funny business goin' on an' too many outsiders musclin' in on this job, an' that you are goin' to start some cleanin' up beginnin' with the phoney Tamara. You are goin' to suggest that you are goin' to give it to her.

"Well, I reckon that Schribner will fall for this line. Maybe he's gonna suggest that you crease this dame an' throw her in the local sewage, which was an idea he had about me. So you got to take that dame off. You gotta sell the idea to Schribner that you're gonna bump her. When you get her outside you march her across to the heap you come down in, an' take her back to my apartment on Jermyn Street. Maybe she'll do some talkin' an' maybe she's goin' to be quiet. If she talks remember what she says. Anyhow, I'll be along some time an' I'll talk to that bird."

"O.K.," he says. "That's all right by me. Are you goin' to be stickin' around on this little party?"

"Maybe an' maybe not," I say. "I wouldn't know right now, but you just go ahead with the schedule as arranged."

"That suits me," he says. "an' what time is Rudy Zimman supposed to arrive at this cottage?"

"Blow in around half-past one," I tell him. "an' don't be surprised what happens. This is not an ordinary business."

He gives me a grin. "I didn't think it was," he says.

I tell him where the cottage is. I leave him leanin' up against the lime tree blowin' smoke through his nose.

It is as dark as hell. The moon has scrammed an' a fine rain is fallin'. It is one of them nights when you oughta be discussin' the war with somethin' in a pink negligee an' a nice frame of mind. I get a ripple on. I ease over the wet grass an' wish they wouldn't make these golf courses so big. I also wish that things would look the same at night as they do in the day.

When I get to the cottage there is nothin' to see or hear. I open the white gate, an' gumshoe along the path. I listen at the front door, an' then ease around to the side an' look at all the windows an' try an' hear if anythin' is stirrin'. All the windows are blacked-out an' it is not easy to work out whether there are any lights on or not.

I am just comin' back to the front of the cottage when I hear: the noise of a car. Away down the road that cuts the golf course in half I can see a coupla dimmed headlights comin' this way. I get a hunch that maybe this is Tamara's taxi. An' I am right. The guy pulls up as near to the cottage as he can get.

I ease around the back pronto. While I was checkin' up a few minutes before, I passed the back door. If Max Schribner is the only guy in the cottage an' he is openin' the front door for the dame here is my chance to do a quick bust in at the back.

I try the door. It ain't even locked. I open it an' slip inside. From the front of the cottage I can hear voices—one of 'em a man's. I reckon that is Schribner.

I light my cigarette lighter an' shield it with my hand. I am in a kitchen an' there is a door on the other side. I snap off the lighter, open the door a bit an' take a look. The door opens on to a passage that runs from the front door right inta the kitchen. Down the passage I can see Schribner an' Tamara just goin' into the sittin'-room on the left.

I go back inta the kitchen an' stick around. I reckon I will give these two a chance to get settled. After a bit I take another look

through the door. I can hear 'em talkin'. I ease down the passage
until I get up against the door of the sittin'-room. The door is a little
bit open an' I can hear the dame we call Tamara beefin' off in that
low distinct voice of hers.

"Listen, Maxie," she is sayin', "we're in bad an' the sooner we
realise it the sooner we're goin' to get out of what looks like a first-
class lousy spot. Maybe you're the brave guy; maybe you don't scare
easy. Well, I don't either, but I'm scared right now. . . ."

Schribner starts in to say somethin', but she shuts him up an'
goes on.

"Where's Rudy gone to?" she says. "He's scrammed out of it,
ain't he? He's got out while the goin's good. An' this bastard Caution
knows he's got out. He had to know that because he ain't shot an'
chucked in the ditch like you said he was to be. That means that
Caution was able to throw a scare inta Rudy that made Rudy let
Caution scram an' then take a run-out powder. See?"

I give a big grin. Because you will realise as well as I do that this
Tamara baby is playin' some game of her own. She knows goddam
well that the Rudy she is talkin' about wasn't Rudy at all but Charlie
Milton. She knows goddam well that it was Charlie Milton who let
me outa the cellar, but for some reasons best known to herself she
is kiddin' Schribner that Rudy *was* Rudy Zimman an' that he let
me go because I threw a scare inta him, an' that afterwards the guy
scrammed an' got out while the goin' was good. I wonder what this
baby is playin' at.

Schribner says: "I don't like it. I don't like it at all. What the
hell's goin' on around here? An' why should Rudy do a thing like
that? Rudy ain't supposed to be like that. I've always heard that that
guy is so tough that he'd rather burn than do a deal with a lousy
copper. I don't like it."

I grin some more. You bet he don't like it. He would like it still
less if the silly punk was to know that the dame who is handin'
him this line of spiel ain't even Tamara Phelps like he thinks she
is. An' he wouldn't be a little bit happy if he knew that I was lurkin'
outside the door listenin'.

But Schribner don't sound scared. I got to hand him that. He
sounds worried but not scared.

She says: "Look—why don't we play this thing the right way? Why don't we grab this Wayles dame an' stick her somewhere where we got a chance to do a deal with Caution or anybody else if we want to? Where is the dame anyway?"

Schribner gives a little laugh. "That's my big secret," he says. "an' I ain't gonna tell anybody. That's just a little somethin' I'm keepin' up my sleeve. See, Tamara?"

"O.K.," she says. "You play it your own way if you want. But it looks to me that if you don't do somethin' definite in a minute you won't have any sleeve to keep anything up. It looks to me like this Caution sonofabitch is gonna line you an' me an' everybody else up. But if you want to be brave you be brave. I don't feel that way."

Schribner says in a nasty voice: "Well, what are you goin' to do? You ain't suggestin' that *you're* gonna talk, are you? You ain't suggestin' that even if this bum Rudy has been yellow enough to let Caution get away an' scrammed himself, that he's mug enough to open his trap an' talk. If he has I wouldn't like to be that guy, because he's liable to get himself a hot paraffin bath. You ain't suggestin' that you'd like one too, are you?"

"Don't be a sap, Maxie," she says. "You oughta have heard better things about me than that. Why don't you use some common sense? If I wanted to scram out of this business would I be here talkin' to you like this? I would have scrammed out of it, wouldn't I? I would have taken a run-out a long while ago. Why don't you be your age?"

"All right . . . all right . . . !" says Schribner. "Maybe that's sense, but I don't like this business."

I hear him get up, an' then I hear the clink of a bottle at the sideboard. I reckon he's pourin' out drinks. I'm right. He says:

"Well, let's have a little snifter an' think this out. We gotta think something out. Something's gotta be done."

I take a look at my wrist-watch an' the luminous hands tell me we're gettin' somewhere near the time when this guy Nikolls oughta do his act. I gumshoe along the passage, back through the kitchen an' outa the back door. I walk around the side of the cottage an' stand in the shadow of the bushes watchin'. After about five minutes I see Nikolls comin' across the fairway. As he starts to cross the road towards the cottage gate, I scram back inta the house, go through the kitchen an' stand up against the wail in the passage. From here I can hear what is goin' on at the front door. After a minute there is a knock on the door. Then I see the light in the passage as Schribner opens the sittin'-room door an' comes out. He walks along to the front door an' opens it.

He says: "Yeah? An' what can I do for you?"

By the dim light that there is in the hallway near the door I can see Nikolls' face. He is grinnin' nice an' easy. This guy Nikolls is an actor all right. He says:

"What d'you think you can do for me? My name's Rudy Zimman."

There is a pause. I hear Maxie Schribner suckin' in his breath through those fat lips of his.

"For Jeez' sake!" he says. "What d'you mean by that?"

"What d'you think I mean?" Nikolls says. "That's plain English, ain't it? My name's Rudy Zimman. If you don't know what I've come over here to see you about you oughta. An' I've come a long way too, an' the idea wasn't to stand around here in the doorway talkin' about who I am. You're Schribner, ain't you?"

Schribner says: "Yeah, I'm Schribner all right. But there is quite a lotta things I don't get. You better come inside."

He turns away from the door. He stands with his back to me holdin' the sittin'-room door open for Nikolls to go in. Nikolls goes in an' Schribner goes after him. I'm very glad that he just pushes the door behind him an' don't quite close it. I ease along the passage an' stand by the doorway.

Nikolls says: "An' who might this be?"

Schribner says in a funny sorta voice: "Listen, d'you mean to say you don't know this dame?"

"How should I know her?" says Nikolls. "I've never seen her before in my life. What's goin' on around here?"

Schribner says: "I'm beginnin' to get it. So the guy who comes here some days ago an' said he was Rudy Zimman an' then scrammed, was some other guy. An' this ain't Tamara Phelps?"

Nikolls laughs:

"Don't be a goddam lug," he says. "I oughta know Tamara Phelps, oughtn't I? I don t know who this name is."

There is a little pause; then I hear the baby we know as Tamara say in a funny sorta voice:

"Listen, you guys. . . ."

But Schribner says: "Shut up, you lousy jane. You keep your trap shut. When we want you to talk we'll tell you."

Nikolls says: "So there's some funny business been goin' on, hey? Well, what about it, Schribner? This don't look so good to me. So you met some other guy who told you he was Rudy Zimman, an' you believed him?"

Schribner says: "Yeah, that's how it is. I believed him. Am I the mug or am I? But what was I to do? Look," he goes on, "I ain't ever met up with Rudy Zimman in my life. I get a cable from the other side tellin' me that Rudy Zimman is comin' over here, that he'll contact me. An' so will a dame called Tamara Phelps. O.K. Well, this frail blows in. She tells me she's Tamara Phelps. I believe her, don't I? All right. Then she tells me that Rudy Zimman is comin' along, an' some fella who says he is Rudy comes along an' I believe him. Why shouldn't I? If there was any doubt in my mind about it, he'd got a good way of puttin' it right."

"What way?" says Nikolls. "What the hell are you talkin' about?"

Standin' there by the doorway I give a grin. This guy Nikolls certainly knows how to do his stuff. I like the way he handles this situation. It looks like this Callaghan guy knows how to pick assistants.

Schribner says: "Well, not so long ago, while this Rudy mug was takin' the air, a fella comes here. He says his name's Willik—Paul Willik. He says he's a private dick workin' for an American Agency, tryin' to find a dame called Julia Wayles. Well, I think that's fairly normal. That sounds O.K. I think maybe the Wayles family have got some private dicks on to try an' find this dame. So I get ready to stall this mug along.

"When Rudy comes in, the first thing he tells me is that this Willik is not Willik at all, but Lemmy Caution, a 'G' man. Well, that looks pretty good. If I have any doubts about this Rudy I wouldn'ta had after that."

"I see," says Nikolls. "An' what happens then?"

Schribner says: "We chucked this fella in the can downstairs. Rudy is goin to give him the heat an' chuck him in the local sewage dump. Well, I haveta go out an' when I come back Rudy says he's fogged Caution an' dropped him in the river with a brick in his pocket. Rudy then scrams an' I ain't seen him since."

"You bet you haven't," says Nikolls. "The trouble with you, Schribner, is you're dead from the neck up. Your head's just fulla lead. Anybody could take you for a ride, an' it looks to me like they've taken you plenty. First of all, let me tell you something. This guy that you thought was Rudy Zimman was nobody else but Charlie Milton, an F.B.I. agent—another 'G' bastard—who comes here an' four-flushes himself on to you.

"An' then Caution turns up. Well, what does Milton do? Milton thinks he's gotta get Caution out of a jam, see? An' he's clever. He puts on a big act an' tells you that the guy who says he's Willik is nobody else but Caution an' that he'll bump him off. Then what does he do? He lets Caution go an' he scrams."

I hear a sound that I recognise as being that made when Nikolls strikes a wax vesta on the seat of his pants.

He goes on: "But there's somethin' more important than that. What about this frail here? Can't you see the set-up?"

"I got it all right," said Schribner. "This dame is workin' in with Charlie Milton an' this Caution guy. Milton come here frontin' as Rudy, an' she's come here frontin' as Tamara Phelps. I got it."

"You bet you've got it," says Nikolls. "Well, there's something gotta be done, an' there's no time like the present."

The jane pipes in. She says: "Listen here, Schribner. . . ."

Nikolls says: "Shut your trap, sister. You're all washed up." His voice is pretty grim. He says to Schribner: "Look —before I do anything else—before I talk to you—I gotta get something off my mind. It looks like the Milton mug has got away with it. It looks like Caution has got away with it. But there's one dame who is not goin' to get away with it, an' that is this dame."

Schribner says: "You're tellin' me?" An' when he says it he sounds plenty ominous. "How do we play this?"

Nikolls says: "Have you got a gun?"

"Sure," says Schribner. I hear a drawer bein' opened an' shut. I reckon he's passin' the gun to Nikolls.

Nikolls says: "Look, this is one of the nicest golf courses for this sorta job I have ever seen. I'm not wastin' any time with this dame. I'm goin' to give it to her now. Then we'll know she's right out."

"That suits me," says Schribner. "Look—maybe I can give you a tip. When you get outa the cottage, if you cross over the roadway, turn right when you get on the fairway an' follow it, you'll come to the thirteenth hole." He gives a cackle. "That's goin' to be an unlucky number for somebody. Right at the back of the green are some bushes an' on the other side of the bushes is the river. If somebody tied a brick round this jane's neck they'll never find her for weeks. Nobody knows she's here anyway."

"That suits me," says Nikolls, "an' it's a nice night for it. Come on, sweetheart."

She says: "You can't get away with this. . . ."

Nikolls gives a little laugh.

"You watch me," he says. "Now look, sister, I'm talkin' sense to you. Maybe they've told you there is more ways than one of killin' a cat. Well, they was right. If you like to come along nice an' quiet maybe it'll be quick. If you don't I'll give it to you where it will take you quite a few minutes to hand in your dinner pail. Now you have it which way you like. Come on, sweetie-pie."

There is a pause. I ease back down the passage inta the kitchen. Then I see the door open. Nikolls comes out. He's got hold of the dame's left arm with a hand that's almost as big as a leg of mutton. In the other hand I can see the automatic. He pushes her up against the wall while he opens the front door. Then he takes her out. The door shuts behind him.

Inside the sittin'-room I can hear the clink of the glass as Schribner pours himself out another drink.

I reckon he's feelin' good.

CHAPTER SIX

THE DAME HAS TEETH

I STAND there in the passage thinkin' what the next move in the game is goin' to be. After a bit I hear some more clinkin' from the sittin'-room, so it sounds like Schribner is havin' another little drink just so's he can sorta get things straightened out after the shock of meetin' Rudy number two. Maybe Schribner is not feelin' quite so good.

Anyhow it looks to me like these guys are desperate guys. Bumpin' somebody off—whether it's me or the dame he thought was Tamara—don't seem to worry 'em a lot. Which means that the stakes they are playin' for are pretty high, because even a heel like Schribner don't go litterin' up the countryside with stiffs unless the game is gonna be worth it.

But I reckon that I am gettin' a little bit tired of this boyo, so I ease along the passage nice an' quiet an' push the door open a little bit more an' take a peek.

The mug is sittin' in the big chair set at an angle to the door. He can't see me. He is slumped down in the chair smokin' a cigarette, with the whisky decanter on the floor by his side an' a glass in his hand. It looks like the big brain is at work on some campaign plan.

I stick there for a minute lookin' at him, an' then I give the door a smack an' walk in.

"Hello, pal," I tell him. "I was passin' an' thought I'd look in just to see bow you was makin' out."

He says: "Oh Jeez . . .!"

His face looks like pork drippin'. An' some little beads of sweat come out on his forehead. Then he takes a pull at himself an' forces a weak sorta smile across his thick lips. On the end of the mantelpiece I notice a bag of raspberries. The bag is open an' they look like nice plump fruit. I remember what Charlie Milton told me about this guy bein' crazy about raspberries. Maybe I can give him some more.

He says: "Well . . . if it ain't Caution. I was just thinkin' about you."

"Of course you was," I tell him. "You was thinkin' what a nice feller I am an' that you was all washed up, an' that it was time you made a deal with me. Ain't that what you was thinkin'?"

"Yeah . . ." he says, "I was thinkin' that way. I reckon I know when I'm beat."

He heaves himself up outa the chair an' starts walkin' towards the sideboard. He puts his hand out to get hold of the bottle of whisky that is standin' there.

I grin at him. Because there is whisky in the decanter where he was sittin'. An' I also notice that there is a drawer in the sideboard. I take a quick step towards him an' bust him a smart rap on the snoozle that makes a noise like drawin' a champagne cork. He flops over an' sits up on the floor lookin' at me sorta hurt.

"Look, you right royal bastard," I tell him. "Maybe you think I am quite absent above the forehead, but if you think I'm gonna let you play games with me you think some more." I flip open the drawer an' inside is a little .25 special. I drop it in my pocket.

He says: "You got me wrong. I was goin' for the whisky. It's better than the other stuff. You don't haveta get rough."

I put my foot on his face an' give him a push backwards. His head hits the edge of the sideboard an' he lets go a howl. When he brings his hand away from his head there is blood on it. His pan goes even whiter than it was before. He lies there lookin' like a porpoise that has been smacked in the belly by a passin' U-boat.

I pick up the decanter an' give myself a short one. The stuff is good. This boyo Schribner certainly knows his liquor. I sit on the edge of the armchair an' look at him.

"Look, love-child . . ." I say, "you an' me are goin' to have a little conference, an' my advice to you is to talk good an' plenty. An' watch your step. First of all I think that you are such a goddam liar that you would make Ananias look like George Washington sayin' his favourite piece on Sunday afternoon, an' secondly I don't like your pan. Thirdly, I think you are such a goddam mug that any time you say anythin' the conversation practically ceases to exist. Havin' got these points into that lousy dome of yours, take a tip from me an' open up, otherwise I am gonna split you up from the navel downwards just to see what makes a greasy, raspberry stuffin' sonofabitch like you tick over. Savvy."

He don't say anything. He sits there, propped against the sideboard, lookin' like the last days of Pompeii.

I think maybe he needs a little help so I go over an' drop a few spots of whisky on his ugly pan. The raw spirit starts ticklin' an' he puts his hands over his eyes.

"O.K., hero," I tell him. "Just relax an' listen to what I got to tell you. First of all I wanta know where Julia Wayles is, an' secondly I wanta know why that dame was snatched—that is if she *was* snatched."

He takes out his handkerchief an' begins to wipe his face. I'm tellin' you mugs that little Maxie is beginnin' to look like somethin' the cat has found an' dragged in.

He says: "Can I get up?"

"Why not?" I tell him. "Maybe you'd look better in a perpendicular position, but let me tell you, brother, that any time you try to start anythin' I'll do somethin' to you that would make bein' boiled in petrol a real pleasure compared with. You got that?"

He says he's got it. He says he is gonna play ball. He gets up an' grabs the decanter. He gives himself a good swig an' does a fancy shudder. Then he stands leanin' up against the wall.

"I don't know a goddam thing about Julia Wayles," he says. "I ain't ever seen her. I wouldn't know her if somebody was to produce her right now. I wish to Christ I'd never even heard of the dame."

"Well, that's somethin'," I tell him. "So you've heard of her? Well, what didya hear?"

"She was supposed to come over here," he says. "But whether she has or whether she hasn't, I wouldn't know. When she got over here I was to look after the dame. Well, by the way things are goin' I'd rather be janitor in a bughouse. I'm gettin' tired of that one."

"Maybe," I say. "But how was she gonna contact you? How was this dame goin' to get in touch with you when she did get here?"

"Rudy Zimman was supposed to tell me that," he says. "Rudy was supposed to be in charge of the job, an' some other baby—Tamara Phelps—was supposed to look after her. Just so's nobody got at her I mean. Well, you know what's happened? Some bastards have put a phony Rudy Zimman in to jig up the works, an' it looks as if the dame who was callin' herself Tamara Phelps is also some more boloney."

"Well, she's paid a nice price for pretendin', hasn't she?" I say. "I was lurkin' about outside when your pal Rudy took her out to give it to her. I reckon right now she's floatin' about the bottom of the river behind the thirteenth green with a brick round her neck an' Rudy's kind regards written all over her in lead. You're a nice guy, aren't you, Schribner?"

He looks like death. He says:

"Jeez . . .! So you was here then? You was here an' you didn't try to stop it. You coulda stopped Rudy . . ."

"Like hell I could," I say. "An' why should I? What does one more or less phony Tamara mean in my young life? She muscled in on this business an' now Rudy has muscled her out again. That dame bein' bumped is maybe goin' to simplify matters."

"How?" he says. "From your angle, I mean?"

"I got a murder charge on you," I tell him. "I got a murder charge on you an' Rudy. An' that is one of the reasons you an' Rudy are goin' to tell me what I want to know."

"He can tell you," he says. "I can't. I've told you everythin' I know about this goddam business." He thinks for a minute an' then he begins to brighten up. He looks like he has got a big idea.

"Another thing," he says. "I don't know that you got anything on me. I never bumped that dame. Rudy done it. An' you was here when he took her off an' you never did a goddam thing to stop it. O.K. Well . . . about this Julia Wayles jane. . . . Well, what about her? I ain't done nothin' to her, have I? I ain't even seen her. I just been paid to come over here an' stick around to wait for a dame who is comin' over because she wants a sea voyage. You can't do anything to me for that. What the hell . . .?"

"You don't say," I tell him. "Just fancy that now, Schribner," I go on. "You are like a big lump of suet studded with raspberries. You look like a performin' seal an' you gotta brain like a one-way street with a traffic block at the end. You are so goddam unconscious that it somebody was to hit you on the dome with a cokehammer you'd never know."

He says: "You go to hell, copper." His voice is sorta surly. "You go to hell, You can't get to work on me here. This is England, an' they don't have any third degree around here."

"Oh, they don't?" I say. "Just wait a minute, pal, an' I'll give you a little demonstration."

I get what is in this bum's mind. He is stallin' along, waitin' tor the guy he thinks is Rudy Zimman to come back. He reckons that as Rudy has bumped the dame, he'll haveta take care of me as well, an' that he can still slide out from under.

This Schribner is a punk all right, an' I can even believe him when he says that he don't know anything much about the Julia dame. Why should he? Any mob that is aimin' to pull somethin' is not goin' to use a yellow heel like Maxie to do anythin' that really matters. They have probably used him as a stooge—a guy who ain't ever done anything sufficiently bad to give him a police record, a guy they could send over here an' who would stick around an' do the donkey work until Rudy Zimman an' Tamara Phelps—who I reckon are the real dyed-in-the-wool mugs—arrive. That sorta matches up with Schribner an' the way he is standin' up to a little trouble.

I take another swig at the decanter. One thing is plain to me an' that is that I have gotta get rid of this heel somehow while I am investigatin' into this Tamara piece again. I reckon by now Nikolls has got her in the car an' is takin' her around to my place on Jermyn Street. Maybe he's doin' a little investigatin' himself. Still, I don't suppose it's gonna do any harm even if he is interested in her particular brand of hipline. It might even help. You never know with dames.

"Look, Schribner," I say, "you gotta nice stone cellar around here somewhere, an' you're goin' in it. You're goin' to stay there nice an' quiet until I got some other use for you. The question is are you goin' quiet or are you goin' to try an' get tough?"

He says: "I ain't gonna do anythin'! I'm stayin' right here."

I go over to him an' I take hold of him by the lapel of his coat. He just stands there lookin' at me like a cock-eyed sheep. But his eyes are sorta smoulderin'. I reckon this lousy mug could be cruel if he wanted to.

"One of these days," he says, "I'm gonna have a chance to do somethin' to you an' then I'm gonna do it."

"Why don't you try now, pal?" I ask him. But I don't wait for any answer. I bust him one. A nice easy short-arm jab that contacts with his jaw an' sounds like somebody choppin' wood. He goes out like a light.

I go over him. I find a notecase with some English money in it an' some pictures of some dames—the sorta pictures that you would expect a guy like Maxie to have on him—an' a bunch of keys.

I take the keys an' a flashlamp that I find on the end of the mantelpiece an' start to take a look around the cottage. I don't reckon that Schribner is goin' to be interested in anything for quite a bit.

It don't take me long to find the cellar. On one side of the kitchen there is a door with a circular flight of stone stairs that leads down to the cellar. It strikes me as bein' a bit peculiar for a one-storey cottage to have a cellar—an' a stone one at that. I reckon that maybe these guys thought they'd have a use for that cellar. Maybe they was goin' to store the Julia dame in there. Who knows?

I go back, stick Schribner across my shoulder, take him downstairs, prop him up against the end of the cellar wall an' lock the door. Maybe I'll come back some time an' let him out—maybe not. If I don't he can amuse himself eatin' coal.

Then I go upstairs, take a little swig of whisky just to help me relax, an' start lampin' around this place. I don't find anything interestin' inside except there is a big basket of raspberries in the kitchen. I reckon this Schribner must spend a lotta time an' trouble gettin' supplies of raspberries in, because you know as well as I do that the fruit market ain't so good in England these days.

After a bit I go outside. Outside the kitchen door is a little garden railed off with white palin's like the front of the house is, an' over on the left-hand side is a shed. This looks to me like the garage. The door is closed but it is not locked. I go inside an' take a look. There is a big Benz car inside—a fancy sorta car that was never built in this country. I flash the torch inside an' I see the upholstery is raspberry coloured, so I reckon this car is Maxie's all right.

An' then I see somethin'. On the passenger seat, where you couldn't help seein' it when you look in the car, is a piece of paper, an' written on it is: *"Where the hell are you? Sometime, when you're not busy, you might look in at The Waterfall, Capel."* The note is not signed.

I fold it up an' put it in my pocket. Then I go back inta the cottage, sit down in the big chair in the sittin'-room, have a little more whisky an' light a cigarette.

Things are beginnin' to move.

It is a quarter to three when I start walkin' across the fairway towards the avenue of limes on my way to pick up the car that I left stuck in some little lane off the Reigate Road. I wonder what this Waterfall dump is—whether it is an hotel, an inn or one of those fancy night places they've got out in the country. Anyhow I reckon I'll have a look.

I start up the car an' drive in towards Dorkin'. It's pretty good an' dark an' I can't see a soul. But out on the other side of the town I meet a cycle cop. I ask him if he can tell me where Capel is. He tells me it is not very far away. I then ask him if he knows a dump called The Waterfall. He says yes, but that he thinks they'll be closed now. He's lookin' at me in an odd sorta way. I think maybe he's heard somethin' about this dump.

I say thanks a lot an' go on my way. Pretty soon I get to this Capel place. It is a nice little place, but bein' dark I don't appreciate the scenery very much. I leave the car behind the hedge an' start walkin' through the iron gates up the avenue the cycle cop told me about that leads towards The Waterfall.

This Waterfall is one of those places that have been converted inta whatever it is from an old-time country mansion. As I walk towards it the moon comes out from behind the clouds an' I can see the place is a pretty swell sorta dump—the sorta place that requires guys in wigs an' silk an' satin clothes an' swords an' all that sorta stuff. There is a portico entrance an' some steps leadin' up to it, but everything is dark an' quiet.

After a bit I come to the conclusion that I don't like the front entrance to this place, so I get around the side an' see what I can find there. Around at the side there are more doors but no life. I get around to the back an' find another door. I stand there listenin'.

From inside very softly comes the sound of some music an' it sounds hot to me. I knock on the door. I stand there with my hands in my pockets waitin'. After two or three minutes the door opens a little bit. There is no light inside. I reckon maybe they got a blackout curtain behind the door.

Some guy says: "Yes?"

"Good-evenin'," I tell him. "I thought maybe some friends of mine was here."

He gives me a funny sorta grin. "Well, I can't say yes until I know who you are, can I?" he says.

I grin back.

"Oh, that!" I tell him. "Well, I wonder if it would mean anything to you if I said I was a pal of Maxie Schribner's?"

"It might," he said. "Who do you want to see?"

I give him another beautiful grin.

"So she is here, is she?" I tell him.

"She might me," he says. "What's her name?"

I take a chance. "The name is Phelps," I tell him, an' I can see by his face that I am right. "What are we wastin' time for?" I say. "Don't you know that Miss Tamara Phelps is expectin' a caller?"

"O.K.," he says. "Come in."

I close the door behind me an' he hold aside the blackout curtain so that I can go in. We go across a big kitchen, through a place that looks like a servants' hall an' along a passage. We pass by a doorway where I can see a coupla guys cookin', then we go up some stairs. The music is comin' from somewhere up there. When we get to the first floor some good carpets start. Everythin' is bright an' well-furnished. All the windows are very carefully blacked-out and curtained. I reckon this is one of them places all right.

We go along a long wide corridor that's got old pictures on either side of it. At the end are a coupla foldin' doors. When he pushes them open I can see the sorta sight that you see in any big city in the world—a dance floor with tables round it an' a five-piece band playin' on a platform at the end. Would you believe it? Here you are stuck away in the country thirty miles outside London, an' you get, even in war-time, the same old imitation of a night club that guys all over the world have just gotta have—war or no war.

It looks as if they are just packin' up. Two or three of the band guys are puttin' their instruments away an' about a dozen people are movin' from the tables to the doorway. The guy who has led me in starts walkin' across the room. Away on the right-hand side of the band platform is a table by itself an' sittin' at this table eatin' is a dame. So this is Tamara—the real one. Boy!

Maybe I have told you guys before that whenever you get mayhem you get beautiful janes. Maybe a lotta you mugs have wondered why it is that when I am in on a case most of the frails in it have certainly got somethin' to sell. Maybe you wonder why we don't have some ugly dames now an' again. Well, the reason is not far to seek. It is not the ugly baby who leaves the farm an' scrams up to the big city because she needs a little excitement. No, sir! It is always the good-lookin' one who thinks she is not gettin' a break where she is an' that when she gets in the big city she'll get a little appreciation from guys. Once she gets there she finds things not so good. Sometimes she slips.

An' it is always the dame with looks that falls to the guy who is in some racket or other. I never heard of a mobster usin' an ugly dame for anythin' yet. So when I tell you that this Tamara has got somethin' I mean it. Not only has she got somethin', but she knows how to sit an' she knows how to dress. I could spend hours lookin' at this dame—if I was that sort of a guy.

I follow the guy towards, the table an' all the while I am tryin' to take what they call a mental picture of this baby, tryin' to get some idea as to how I can play her along the way I want. An' I come to the quick conclusion that it ain't gonna be easy.

This one has style an' looks an' every other goddam thing an' she also looks demure. Maybe this last thing don't mean a lot to you, but I am a guy who is scared of demure dames. They always pack a load or trouble, I have always round that janes are either brassy, tough or demure. The tough ones you know about, but the demure ones keep you guessin'. You never know whether they're really like that or just frontin'. An' you very seldom make a sap out of a demure dame. Well—not often.

In all my time I only knew one guy who ever took a demure lookin' baby for a ride up the garden path. This guy was so goddam ugly that if he had been hit in the face by a cannon ball it woulda been a great improvement. O.K. Well, he was stuck on some demure lookin' baby an' he reckoned he was gonna marry the dame by fair means or foul. So he got himself introduced to her during an air-raid practice when everythin' was black an' she couldn't see his pan. After which he arranged to call around an' see her.

Directly he arrived around at her place he took a quick jump at her an' started kissin' her like mad. Bein' the demure kind she turned the light off, after which she never got a chance to look at the guy until they was married—an' then it was too late. I reckon if that guy Confucius hadda known about this he'd have thought up another wise-crack. Or maybe not.

Any demure dame is dangerous because if she's that way natural then you gotta watch your step, because a really demure baby is one of them guaranteed virgins. An' there ain't a steam whistle you ever heard that could make a noise like a guaranteed virgin makes when she gets necked by accident. If she ain't really demure an' is merely puttin' up a front then she is twice as dangerous, because she is a dame who knows all the answers an' is pretendin' that she don't for reasons best known to herself. You get me?

Me—I have always been a guy who likes a jane to know her vegetables an' not conceal the fact, an' in this idea I am in good company because old man Confucius said: "The woman who pretends purity seeks to disguise guilty knowledge." All of which will show you mugs that old Confucius woulda held his own with any blonde that come out of Ma Licovat's love parlour on fourteenth at Barrel alley—that is if he coulda got out his notebook an' found the right proverb in time.

This dame Tamara is a pip. She is sittin' there all alone eatin' sorta slow an' very nice. She is wearin' a tight black lace dinner frock that advertises her figure, beige silk stockin's an' black georgette shoes with four-inch red heels. Around her shoulders an' over her hair is a sorta mantilla of powder-blue georgette.

Her hair is blonde an' *real*. That colour never came outa any bottle. She has got a swell skin an' a mouth that a guy would go mad over. It is one of them beautifully chiseled mouths that drive you nutty because you want to look at it all the time, which sorta makes it difficult to keep to the business on hand. The dame had also got a swell foot an' a nice way of puttin' it on the ground. You know what I mean, sorta neat an' graceful an' tidy.

When she puts a piece of bread in her mouth I can see she has nice hands with long fingers an' that the tight fittin' sleeves of her frock have got little tiny turn-back cuffs of the same powder blue georgette.

I give a sigh. One of these days I am gonna meet up with a dame who looks like this an' is on the side of law an' order—which will be a nice change an' almost impossible.

The boyo who has took me over says: "This is somebody from Maxie Schribner." Then he scrams.

She takes a look at me an' when I say she takes a look I mean she takes a *look*. She has got eyes that are limpid an' blue as they can be an' she casts 'em down to my feet an' then lets 'em ride. An' do those eyes ride? They come up—slow as slow right up my legs an' up the front buttons of my waistcoat until they get to the top of my head. Oh boy! I'm tellin' you I got a new sensation an' I didn't know it was possible. Bein' looked over by this dame is like bein' undressed to slow music by Helen of Troy an' the Queen of Sheba, with Sweet Nell of Old Drury holdin' the score card just to keep the game straight.

I just stick around an' say nothin'. I'm waitin' for this baby to start talkin'. I'm waitin' to see if her voice matches up with the rest of the outfit. But I don't haveta worry. When she speaks she talks very soft an' drawls a little bit, an' the words sorta drop out of her mouth like cream bein' spilt on rose leaves. I'm confidin' to you mugs that this dame is the ultimate berries an' I don't mean perhaps.

She says: "Hello, pal. . . ." Her lips break into a little smile an' she stays put, lookin' at me with a bit of roll between the fingers of her right hand half-way up to her mouth.

I sit down. I don't say a thing. I think maybe I'll let her talk a bit more. It might be easier for me that way.

She says: "So you're from Schribner. I suppose he came back an' got the note?"

"Yeah," I tell her. "Somebody left a note on the seat of Maxie's car. Maxie figured he'd come around while there was nobody at the cottage an' left the note so's to make a quick contact. He asked me to come right over."

She gives me a long look. She says:

"You look to me like the sort of *hombre* who could dance. You ever heard of the *conga?*"

Is this dame surprisin' or is she? Right in the middle of a whole set-up of crime an' what-have-you-got she has to know if I can dance the *conga*.

"Lady," I tell her, "I practically invented the conga."

She nods. She looks up an' signals to some guy in a tuxedo on the other side of the room. He comes over.

"Tell the boys to get back on the stand an' play a *conga*," she says. "I want to dance."

They get back an' they start to play. She gets up an' so do I. She comes over to me an' just slides herself into my arms just like nobody's business—an' can she dance?

There is nobody else on the floor an' the band is not so bad. She cuddles inta my arms an' we get goin'. I have danced the *conga* before an' maybe shall dance it again, but it won't ever be like that time. This dame has one of them figures that don't even need a wrap around, an' dancin' with her is an education in itself. I just forget everythin' an' go to town.

They played five numbers before we packed it up an' went back to the table. While we have been away they have brought a bottle of whisky. She opens it an' pours a stiff one. She puts in a little soda an' hands it to me.

"What's your name, handsome?" she says. "An' what're you doin' with Maxie Schribner?"

"I'm Willy Careras," I tell her. "I usta get around with Margoni's boys in Chicago. Then it got a little hot. I got a tip that a holiday would be good for me. So I come over here a year ago. I just been hangin' around . . . see? Then I met up with Schribner. I've known him a long time in New York an' he said I could stick around an' maybe help him a little. He's got some business on—I don't know what it is. I'm just a sorta stooge. If you get me?"

She says: "I hope he pays you plenty. You're some stooge. . . ." She slings me a little smile that says a lot. "I could use a stooge like you," she says.

I hand her a wicked look that woulda made Casanova look like the farmer's boy.

"Go ahead, Tamara," I tell her.

"I meant for runnin' around an' answerin' the telephone," she says, still smilin'. "That's all." She raises her blue eyes an' looks at me. Her lips twitch a little. She says sorta demure: "I wouldn't like you to think anything wrong . . . Willy. Please don't think I'm the sorta girl you can make in a hurry. I'm a very cold person. . . ."

I grin at her.

"O.K. If you say so," I tell her. "But if you're cold I'm gonna use ice cream for hot packs, an' whoever taught you to dance the *conga* like you do musta been an expert in . . ."

"That's different," she says. "I like dancin'. But that's as far as I go. . . ." She drops her eyes on her plate.

"Maybe," I tell her. "But one day you'll feel different." I sling her another wicked grin. "Maybe you haven't met the right kind of guy," I go on.

"Perhaps," she says. She sighs. "I think I'm a Yes woman who's never had an opportunity to say anything but No. . . ."

She puts out her hand an' takes my glass. She puts it up to her lips an' just drinks a little tiny drop. Then she hands me the glass back.

"I wanted to taste it," she says. She opens a gold cigarette case an' takes out two cigarettes. She puts 'em both in her mouth an' lights 'em. Then she hands me one. When I put it in my mouth I can just sorta sense a touch of perfume. Maybe from her handbag. It's pretty good scent too. I take a quick look at her. I start thinkin' that this baby is so goddam lovely that she could become a habit almost before you knew it.

She gets up. The powder-blue georgette mantilla around her hair an' shoulders makes her look like a nun. *Some* nun! She says: "O.K., Willy . . . just you run back to Maxie an' tell him that Rudy'll be contactin' him to-morrow. Good-night, handsome." She picks up her handbag an' goes. She goes over to a door on the other side of the floor.

I finish my drink. When I look around the guy who brought me up is waitin' for me. He shows me the way down.

When I get outside it is rainin' a little an' dark. So I am not too pleased with anything. I still haven't got next to anything an' the dame I have just met has stalled me along the way she wanted to. Maybe she's waitin' for Rudy Zimman—the real one—to turn up. Maybe that's it.

I get down to the end of the carriage drive where I left the car. Right behind it is another car—a big tourer. I am just openin' the door when somebody puts a hand on my arm. I spin round. It is the dame.

"Well . . . well . . ." I say. "I'm glad to see you again, Tamara. It's a long time since we met."

She gives a little soft laugh. By the light of the parkin' lights on the car behind us I can see she has got on a persian lamb coat, an' she has tied the mantilla arrangement around her hair. She is standin' close to me an' I can smell the same perfume that came off the cigarette.

"Look, Willy," she says, "just remember this. Maybe you're gonna be busy with Schribner. Maybe he's going to have a lot of business. But when you've time come an' see me. I'd like to talk to you."

"Yeah . . .?" I tell her. "An' why, Lovely?"

She laughs—a little low soft laugh, right down in her throat. "You remind me of a pet canary I had one time," she says. "I'm staying at the Grange apartments, in Mount Street, London. Look in some time."

"I'll be there . . ." I tell her.

"That's going to be *very* nice," she says.

She puts up a hand that has a white kid glove on it an' she takes my lower lip between her finger an' thumb. She pulls my head down an' puts her face up an' she kisses me just like that. I'm tellin' you mugs that this Tamara is electric *plus*. Boy. . . .!

She stands away from me. She says in a cool sorta voice:

"I'm inclined to be crazy about you. God knows why. But I am. Well . . . so long, Handsome. . . ."

She gets into the tourer, starts it up an' backs down the drive. I stand there lookin' after the tail light.

*

I roll the heap back towards Betchworth nice an' easy. I got plenty to think about an' a lotta time to do it.

The rain has stopped now an' a bit of moon is showin'. The road wanders around corners like it does in this country an' I'm not even unhappy. Just sorta curious.

This set-up is goddam funny. Whichever way you look at it there ain't any beginnin' or endin'. Nothin' makes much sense—but then interestin' things never do.

I start thinkin' about this Tamara dame. That one certainly knows her cereals. She knows which way she's pointin', all the answers an' then quite a lot. That dame is no mug. Maybe nobody in this job is a mug except me.

I wonder how the guy Nikolls is gettin' along with that other dame. I wonder what *her* name is. I wonder what the hell *she* is playin' at, an' I wonder who the next dame is gonna be. Because things always come in threes. An' that goes for dames. I never met up with a case yet that produced a coupla lookers like the first dame an' Tamara without producin' a third one. Maybe we'll get a third one with a homely pan. It would be a nice change.

I park the car along a quiet lane on the side of the golf course an' start walkin' over the fairways to Schribner's dump. I have made up my mind about one thing an' that is that this Schribner mug is gonna talk even if I have to hold a cigarette lighter under his nostrils. That guy is through with bein' close. He's gotta open up.

I go in the back way an' ease downstairs to the cellar. I unlock the door an' go in. He has put an electric light on. He is lying up at the far end propped up against the wall, smokin' a cigarette an' he has got a lump on the side of his jaw where I clocked him.

He looks at me. He looks at me like I was the devil. Maxie has got a definite idea that he don't like me.

There is an old chair leanin' up against the wall. I take it an' stick it down a few feet in front of Schribner. I sit down on it an' look at him.

"Look, Schribner," I tell him. "The time has come when you an' me have gotta do a little talkin'. We gotta talk sense, see? It's gonna be sensible for you to talk because if you don't I'm goin to make you talk, an' if I can't do it one way I'm goin to do it another."

"Oh yeah?" he says. "Ain't you interestin'! I reckon you must be very popular with your friends, you . . ."

I grin at him. "Take it easy, pal," I tell him. "You ain't gonna get nowhere by losin' your temper."

I light myself cigarette.

"Here's the way it goes," I go on. "After I slung you down here I had a look around the garage an' found a note in your car. The note was sorta sarcastic. It said that when you got back you might like to look in at The Waterfall, at Capel, a dump on the other side of Holmwood. I reckon it was Rudy Zimman that wrote that note."

"What the hell do you mean?" he says. "Rudy Zimman was here. He . . ."

I hold up my hand. "You don't know the first thing," I tell him. "The guy that was here an' took off that dame was no more Rudy Zimman than I am. That bird was a guy I got workin' tor me. We pulled a fast one."

He says: "Jeez . .! I don't do nothin' but meet phonys."

"Right," I tell him. "That is the sorta guy you are. Everybody four-flushes you. There have been so many Rudy Zimman s kickin' around in this business that you could practically start a nudist colony with these guys. But don't worry," I go on. "The palooka who wrote that note an' left it in the car was the real one all right."

He says: "If that other guy was workin' for you then he didn't bump that dame."

"Right again, Brain-Trust," I tell him. "He did not bump that dame."

"I wonder who the hell *she* was," he says.

"Wouldn't you know?" I ask him. "Look, Schribner, why don't you make it easy for yourself? Why don't you spill it an' let's get down to cases? First of all it's as plain as the Naragansett Lighthouse that somebody put this dame in to get next to what you mugs are tryin' to do over here with this Julia Wayles dame. Somebody on the other side who was wise to everything. Now you tell me somethin'. You tell me who that somebody would be."

"I don't know," he says. "I don't know a goddam thing. Maybe somebody was tryin' to muscle in. Maybe some mob has got wise to somethin'. . . ."

"Sure," I tell him. "Maybe you're right. It wouldn't be the first time that somebody has tried to hi-jack in a kidnap game. I suppose that somebody thought if they could snatch the Wayles baby offa your friends they'd be in the market for some jack. Maybe they thought your pals would pay 'em to return the dame. I reckon that dame has got somethin' valuable."

He shrugs his shoulders. He don't say anythin'.

I light a fresh cigarette.

"Look," I tell him, "it ought to be plain to you that you are right on the wrong end of the market. I got this dame who come over here an' four-flushed you inta thinkin' that she was Tamara Phelps. I got her. I'm gonna make her talk. I'm goin' to find out from her just who put her in an' what's goin' on at that end of the stick. Then I'm goin' to make you talk. An' then I'm goin' to make Rudy Zimman talk—the *real* Rudy Zimman, after which I'm all set."

"You don't say?" he says. "an' how're you goin' to make Rudy Zimman talk? We don't even know where he is."

I grin at him.

"I went over to Capel to-night," I tell him. "I went to this Waterfall dump. By the look of it most of the guys there are friends of Rudy's. Maybe he's got an organisation over here. I suppose you wouldn't know that either?"

"I told you I don't know a thing," he says. "Not a goddam thing. . . ."

"All right," I tell him. "We'll come to that in a minute. Well . . . when I get to this Waterfall dump they ask me who I want. I take a chance an' tell 'em Tamara Phelps. So they take me along to see her. Then I pull one on her. I tell her I am Willy Careras, a mobster who usta get around with the Margoni mob in the old days in Chicago. I sorta suggest to her that I'm over here for my health an' that I run inta you an' that you're usin' me as a general sorta stooge—that I don't know anythin' about what you're at, but that I'm a sorta handyman around the place. See?

"Well, she falls for this line. It sounds sense anyhow an' I reckon that she knows goddam well that you are such a lousy heel that you just gotta have somebody to do any dirty work that's goin'. Because even if Rudy Zimman an' Tamara haven't met you they know plenty about you, don't they? They got to. If they didn't know you was a dyed-in-the-wool thug they'd never have had you in on this game."

"Nuts," he says. "I'm tellin' you that I ain't done a thing up to date that the law can put a linger on me for. Not one goddam thing."

"What do I care?" I tell him. I slip him another big grin. "I reckon I'm gettin' hold of this situation," I tell him. "I reckon I got you an' this Rudy an' little Tamara just where the hair is short."

"What are you gonna do?" he asks.

"Just this," I tell him. "I'm gonna stick around here. I'm gonna wait for Rudy to show up. An' I'm gonna keep you down here. You ain't going to see that bird. O.K. When he shows up I'm gonna tell him that you're sick, that you're in the local nursing home or somethin' an' that you've told me as much as you wanted to about this business an' that I am O.K. to act as your deputy. Well, Tamara has probably told him about me. She has told him that I am Willy Careras, an' he will know that name. He will know that Willy Careras is so goddam bloodstained with crime of all sorts an' shapes that he would make Satan look like the dame who distributes tracts around San Diego port when the Navy comes in. So he's gonna trust me, ain't he? He's gonna talk. Maybe he's gonna tell me where Julia is. After which I can go to town on this case."

He don't say anythin', but he looks not very happy.

I get up an' stretch. Me—I am feelin' pretty good. I am thinkin' that I sorta got things well in hand.

"Schribner," I tell him, "I am now goin' to leave you in order to give myself a little snifter up in the sittin'-room. An' let me tell you this. Let me hear one crack outa you an' I am comin' down here to give you such a bust on the schnozzle that you will look like you run inta a tank. *Adios, caballero. . . .*"

I lock the cellar door an' I go upstairs. Maybe this ain't gonna be such a difficult business after all. If I can pull a fast one on this Rudy when he shows up, an' if I can make that dame that Nikolls is keepin' warm for me talk, I reckon I got the whole thing in the bag.

I stop at the top of the stone steps to light another cigarette; then I ease along the passage an' go inta the sittin'-room. When I get inside I stop.

There is a guy sittin in the armchair. He is a tall, slim, rangy sorta guy. His clothes are custom made an' he is wearin' a silk shirt that cost fifty dollars. Everythin' about this boyo is tops. He has got a pan like death. His face is dead white an' his mouth looks like a slit cut with a razor; his hair is black an' sleeked back.

He takes a platinum cigarette case outa his pocket an' lights a cigarette. He looks me over nice an' quiet an' casual. When he talks his voice is nice an' soft an' easy, but sorta bitter—if you get me.

"I'm Rudy Zimman," he says. "I suppose you're Willy Careras. Where's Schribner?"

"Sick," I tell him. "He's got some disease—measles or somethin'. They rushed him on to the hospital at Guildford. He told me you'd be comin' over an' to take care of anythin'. I got the note you left in the car an' went over to Capel, but I reckon I missed you. . . ."

"Yeah," he says. He puts his hand inside his coat an' he pulls out a Mauser pistol. He points it at the pit of my stomach. He starts smilin'. The guy does not look at all nice. "O.K., Caution," he says. "You can cut out all that neat stuff. I'm wise to you, You're in a spot, pal. I'm gonna rub you out, see?"

"I see," I tell him. "It looks to me like the day-dream is over."

He goes over to the sideboard an' pours one. He drinks it nice an' easy, leanin' up against the sideboard, lookin' at me. He don't blink at all an' his eyes are sorta red. I don't like this boyo at all.

From outside there comes the noise of a car stoppin', an' just for the moment I think that maybe I'm gonna get a break—but not for long.

The sittin'-room door opens an' Tamara comes in. She looks at Rudy an' hands him a nice smile. Then she moves over to where I am. Did I tell you that when this dame walks it is a treat to watch her. She just floats, an' the guy who invented hip control musta been thinkin' of this baby.

She stands just in front of me an' opens her persian lamb coat. She takes off the mantilla arrangement she has got around her hair. Her fingers are long, an' she has got pink enamelled nails. I reckon her hands woulda kept a sculptor awake at nights. Rudy stands leanin' up against the sideboard watchin' her. He is grinnin'. This Rudy is the cruellest lookin' cuss I have ever seen.

"Hello, handsome," she says in that nice low voice of hers. "So you thought you was gettin' away with something, did you? You thought you'd pulled a little one on Tamara." She turns around to Rudy. "Isn't he sweet, Rudy?" she says. "Isn't he the cutest thing? Look at those shoulders an' that thin waist an' hips."

She comes up close to me.

"I think you're marvellous, big boy," she says. "The only thing about you is that when they stuck that nice mop of hair on your head they forgot to put any brains underneath. He's sweet, isn't he, Rudy?"

"I think so too," says Rudy. He pours himself another drink. He grins at her. "Why don't you give him a kiss?" he says. "If you're so stuck on the guy why don't you show him a little affection? If I was gonna be shot through the belly like he is I would like a little kiss off some dame first."

She says: "You're so kind, Rudy. That's what I like about you. You're nice an' thoughtful."

She turns around to me. Rudy moves so that his gun is still sighted on me. She puts her hand up to my mouth an' pulls my lower lip down. Her fingers are nice an' cool. Then she puts her mouth up to mine. "Sweet bastard," she says nice an' soft. "I could eat you."

She bites right through my lower lip, then she stands away. I can feel the blood tricklin' down my chin, an' the tears are rollin' down my cheeks. I call her a rude name.

"Didn't you like it, honey?" she says. "Didn't you like bein' kissed?" She throws me a long smile.

I can hear Rudy laughin' in his throat.

"O.K., Tamara," he says. "Stand aside. I'm gonna give it to him. Where do I let him have it?"

"Please yourself, Rudy," she says. "Personally I think round about the navel is a good place. I haven't seen a guy wriggle for a long time. But if you got any better idea let me know."

Rudy starts to say somethin'. Then the telephone rings.

There is somethin' extraordinary about a telephone bell when you ain't expectin' it—it sorta makes you jump. An' these guys wasn't expectin' it. Tamara swings her head around an' looks towards the corner of the room where the phone is, an' Rudy's swings round after hers.

I chance it. I take one dive for the electric light standard. As I hit it an' it goes over, I throw myself sideways. The room goes dark an' Rudy starts loosin' off. I can hear the shells hittin' the fireplace; then Tamara's voice as cool an' as low as ever:

"You wouldn't shoot me, would you, Rudy?" she says.

I am down on all tours, like a runner waitin' to get away, on the right of the fireplace. There is a silence; then the telephone bell jangles again.

Rudy says: "Come over here while I crease him."

I say: "Like hell!"

I take a jump an' shoot straight forward. I go right through the bay window, blackout frame an' everythin'. A lump of glass cuts my face, but I should worry. I land on the top of my head on the lawn outside, but that don't worry me either. Julius Caesar, takin' a grab at the earth of Britain when he arrived here, has got nothin' on me. I get up an' I scram—over the iron fence on the other side of the road an' on to the fairway. When I get to the avenue of limes I ease up an' mop my forehead. My lip is still sore from that hell-cat's teeth an' I have got a cut cheek that is bleedin' plenty.

I sit down on a tree trunk an' I give voice. I say the whole book. The things that I call that guy Zimman an' his lady friend Tamara woulda made a Marine sergeant, who has been rolled for his wallet by a hare-lipped blonde, sound like the Tiny Tots Hour on the radio.

One of these days I am gonna get topsides up with that Tamara babe an' when I do she is gonna remember me.

An' I do not mean perhaps!

CHAPTER SEVEN

FUNNY BUSINESS

I FIND the car where I left it. I get inside the drivin' seat, light myself a cigarette an' start a little quiet rumination on this business. Because it looks to me that somethin' which started as an ordinary sorta snatch is gonna end up in somethin' bigger than anybody thought.

But one thing is stickin' out an' that is that the dame that Nikolls has got waitin' for me up in my apartment—the phoney Tamara—has gotta talk She has *gotta*. An' if she won't do it by fair means then I'm goin' to put the screw on.

Because this baby has to know *somethin'*. Whoever put her in to pretend to be Tamara an' come over here an' get next to Max Schribner probably knew the whole works. Either that guy was somebody plannin' to snatch Julia Wayles from under their noses as a sorta hi-jack to make 'em pay good an' plenty or for some other reason that we don't know about. Well, we gotta know. An' once I get an idea as to who this bozo is an' what he wanted to do it for then I gotta chance of gettin' a ripple on.

An' I reckon that the dame is gonna talk without a lot of pressin'. I reckon she was plenty scared when Nikolls took her outa the cottage an' she thought she was goin' to get herself nicely creased out an' chucked in the river. An' she has had plenty of time since then to think over what's gonna be good for her.

Besides which that guy Nikolls has probably gone to work on the dame. An' I reckon that boy knows his stuff.

It is half-past four when I start the heap an' get on my why back to London. The moon has come out now an' it is a good night. I roll along thinkin' about the people in this case ah' wonderin' what's goin' to happen to 'em before the job is over, because I got an idea at the back of my head that this Julia Wayles business is one of them phony rackets that gets more odd as you go along.

At a quarter-past five I pull up outside my dump in Jermyn Street. I go in an' press the elevator button, but nothin' happens. I reckon the night janitor has gone to bed. I walk up the stairs an' stop at the top a few yards from the door of my apartment to light a cigarette. I'm pretty good an' tired, but at the same time I am lookin' forward to the interview with this dame who is inside with Nikolls. I told you I have made up my mind that this baby has gotta talk.

I walk along the corridor, open the door an' go in. I stand in the hallway sorta surprised, because the place is dark. It feels sorta empty. I walk across the hallway, push open the door of my sittin'-room, snap on the light. There's nobody there. I take a peek inta the other rooms; then I go back to the sittin'-room. I wonder what this means. I wonder if Nikolls is workin' some idea of his own.

I wait a minute—then I get an idea. I grab the telephone book an' look up the number of Callaghan Investigations. Maybe Nikolls has got in touch with them about somethin' or other. Maybe they might know where he is. I grab the telephone an' dial the number. After a minute some guy answers. I ask him who he is. He tells me he is the night porter. I ask him to put me through to Callaghan Investigations. He says he can't—there ain't anybody there but that if I like an' it's important he will put me through to Mr. Callaghan, whose flat is above the office. I say O.K. An' hang on. After a bit I hear Callaghan's voice on the line.

"Look," I tell him, "this is Caution speakin'. It's about that guy of yours—Nikolls. This bozo is supposed to meet up with me here at my apartment on Jermyn Street. Well, I just arrived an' he ain't here. I thought maybe you might know somethin' about it."

He says he doesn't know a thing, except that Nikolls phoned through to him about an hour before an' asked if he'd have a dictaphone sent around to Jermyn Street. That's all he knows. I say thanks a lot an' hang up.

Now what the hell does this mean? Where is this guy Nikolls an' what would he want with a dictaphone around here? I think maybe he's left a message with the night janitor. I go downstairs an' ring the elevator bell again but nothin' happens. I stick around for a bit, then I go down the stairs to the basement where the janitor's place is. It is pretty dark down there an' at the bottom of the stairways I trip up an' fall over. I get up, take out my cigarette lighter an' take a look. I don't wonder why the janitor didn't answer the elevator bell! He is lyin' there in a corner right out. There is some blood on his forehead an' I reckon somebody has given him a smart rap on the dome with what is usually described as a blunt instrument. It looks to me like things have been happenin' around here.

I prop this guy up against the wall an' go back to my apartment. I take a look around. Away over in the corner by the window is a little table an' lying across this table is a raincoat. I reckon it is the one Nikolls was wearin'. I get an idea. I go across an' lift it up. Underneath is the dictaphone. I turn the switch over an' after a minute I hear Nikolls' voice sayin':

"Come on, baby—you gotta talk. You can take it from me you gotta talk, an' you better talk to me rather than wait till that guy Caution comes back. He's a tough *hombre*, that one. Maybe he won't be so nice to you as I'm bein'."

Then I hear her voice. She says:

"Well, it looks as if I'm in a jam. I've tried to be clever in this business, but maybe I'm nor so good at being clever as I was. Here's the way it goes: First, part of that stuff I told Caution was true. I was hanging around in New York an' I hadn't got very much to do. It's like I told him. Things have been pretty bad since the war started, an' J. Edgar Hoover's been ridin' the mobs pretty hard. I was looking around for any sort of job providing it was the sort of job I wanted to do. O.K. Well . . ."

All of a sudden the pitch of this dame's voice alters. She goes on in a sorta shriek. She says:

"Say . . . what the hell!"

Then I hear Nikolls' voice say: "Take it easy, kid."

Then the record sorta trails off. I switch off the dictaphone. I go to the big armchair an' I sit down. I reckon I get this. It looks like we have been caught short again. I light another cigarette. I told you guys before that I was the onion in this job. Well, it looks like I still am.

I reckon Rudy Zimman musta been hangin' around outside Maxie Schribner's cottage when Nikolls came in. I reckon he was hangin' around while Nikolls was havin' that scene inside with Maxie and the phoney Tamara while I was standin' out in the passageway listenin'. An' Rudy wasn't alone; he'd got somebody with him. When Nikolls an' the dame came out Rudy stuck around, but whoever it is is with him tails 'em. They got a car an' they go after Nikolls an' Tamara an' they tail 'em back to my apartment on Jermyn Street.

I go out an' find the note in Schribner's car. I go over to The Waterfall at Capel an' meet up with Tamara Phelps, but when I get there she knows who I am. She knows I'm Caution all right. Then I go back to Schribner's place. While I am on my way Zimman comes through to her; tells her what's happened. He tells her he's goin' straight to Schribner's place an' she's to come on after.

When he gets there he comes inside an' finds nobody there because that is the time I'm having my seance with Schribner down in the cellar. Then I have my scene with him, an' Tamara arrives, after which he tries to fog me an' I get away.

But now Zimman knows the fat's in the fire. He knows goddam well that I'm goin' to start somethin'. He knows that I'm goin' to put the heat on that dame who has pretended to be Tamara an' find out something which is goin' to put me in on this business. I reckon Rudy makes up his mind he's goin' to head me off, so he gets on the telephone to the guy who's tailed Nikolls an' the dame, an' tells him to crash inta the apartment an' grab off the dame.

O.K. In the meantime Nikolls has gotta big idea. He's persuaded the dame he's got with him to talk, but he's too goddam lazy to write down what she says, so he telephones through to Callaghan an' gets him to send a dictaphone round. The dame is just beginnin' to say her piece when somebody busts the door in an' walks in with a gun. The dame gives a shriek an' Nikolls, thinkin' it might give me some sort of idea when I get back, chucks his raincoat over the dictaphone. So there you are!

Well—this don't look so good. I give myself a final cigarette an' just one little shot of rye; then I take a warm shower an' get inta bed. Because I have always discovered that it is a very good thing when you don't know anythin' to go to bed, because bed is a very safe place—well . . . sometimes! An' in any event even if you can't do anythin' very constructive you can't make many mistakes.

I wake up an' look at my watch. It is eleven o'clock an' I can see the rain drippin' on the window pane. It's just one of those days, an' believe it or not I feel just like the weather looks an' that is lousy.

I lay there lookin' at the ceilin' an' doin' a little quiet rumination on the skulduggery that is goin' on over this Julia Wayles business. But my thinkin' is not very constructive, because if you wanta be constructive you have gotta have somethin' tangible to think about, an' anybody who says this case is tangible oughta go an' have their brains examined by one of these long-faced specialists who give you a smart rap on the dome with a silver hammer an' then charge about five hundred bucks for tellin' you that you are nuts—a fact that has probably been obvious to everybody else for years an' which they have told you plenty times—for nothin'.

I get up an' take another shower. I then ring down to service an' tell 'em to send me up some breakfast an' a lot of coffee. When the guy arrives with the tray I ask him about the night janitor an' what happened to the guy.

He tells me. He tells me that the night janitor has been around to the local hospital an' got himself some stitches put in his scalp. Beyond that he is fairly O.K.

Last night—or early this mornin' to be exact—the breakfast guy tells me, a guy comes inta the block an' rings the elevator bell. The elevator is down on the basement floor. The night janitor brings it up to the ground floor an' opens the door. The guy outside says that he wants to see the bozo who is waitin' for him in Mr. Caution's apartment. The night janitor tells him that my apartment is on the first floor an' starts the elevator goin'. As soon as it is movin' the other guy produces a rod, sticks it in the night janitor's navel an' tells him to take the elevator down to the basement floor—that is if he wantsta stay in one piece.

The janitor takes the elevator down. He is good an' scared because he says that the guy with the gun looks like business—nasty business. When they get down to the basement the janitor opens the gates an' stands aside for the guy to get out, an' just when he is doin' this he gets a smart rap over his brain box with the butt end of an automatic. He decides to go nice an' unconscious an' that is all he knows. When he comes to he is lyin' propped up against the wall—where I left him.

I say thanks a lot to the breakfast guy an' slip him a five-spot. He scrams an' I have my breakfast, followed by one little shot of four fingers of the old Kentucky brew just to keep the cold away, an' get the old headpiece workin'. I then sit down at the writin' table an' take a piece of paper an' start a little fact chasin'.

I write down all the things that I know about this Wayles business—an' that ain't much. At the same time it is a good idea to sorta get things down in black an' white, because very often this way you get an idea. Anyway this is what I write down, an' if some of you mugs are clever maybe you'll get some more information outa this stuff than I do.

Here are the facts:

1. For some reason or other Julia Wayles—who is a dame that we do not know very much about—leaves U.S. and comes over to England. She does this for one of two reasons:

(a) That she wants to come for some reason that nobody knows, or (b) That she is snatched.

For the sake of argument we will take it she was snatched.

2. This snatch has somethin' to do with Jakie Larue—a guy who is servin' a fifteen to life term in Leavenworth an' who has already tried to make a prison break two or three times. We believe this because pals of Larue—Rudy Zimman and Tamara Phelps (who are a pair of mobsters who are stuck on each other) are definitely connected in some way with the Wayles disappearance.

3. Somebody sends Max Schribner over here to get ready to take over Julia when she arrives. But he says he ain't seen her an' wouldn't know her if he did. It may sound funny but I believe this guy.

4. After Julia has disappeared, her boy friend, a guy named Larssen—gets a smart lawyer to pull the F.B.I. in on this job after the Missing Persons Bureau have failed to find out where she is.

5. The F.B.I., not being able to contact me, put Charlie Milton on the job and tell him that his first contact is Schribner. Well, they musta got this information from somewhere, so it looks as if they got the Schribner tip either from Larssen or his lawyer.

6. Schribner is told by whoever it is is behind the snatch that Rudy Zimman and Tamara Phelps are coming over to England and that he will get his instructions from them.

7. But somebody else begins to muscle in on this business. Some guy or guys who know that Rudy Zimman and Tamara Phelps are tied up in all this bezuzus, get some dame (whose name we don't know yet) to come over here fronting as Tamara Phelps, and contact Schribner for the purpose of—what? We don't know this.

8. By a lucky chance I find out that this dame is a phoney. I pull a fast one with Nikolls and pick up this dame—who is our star witness at the moment because she must know something about what is going on—and then both the dame and Nikolls get snatched again by somebody working for Rudy. They have to snatch Nikolls as well even if they don't really want him. And I don't reckon they want him. They want the dame. They want to make her talk. They want to find out who it is in U.S. was wise to their game and was trying to get in on it.

Well . . . there you are. There is the set-up the way I see it, an' it looks to me as if there is only one thing—or *two* things maybe—to be done. An' I reckon I'm gonna do 'em—good an' quick.

I give myself another little drink just in case there are influenza germs lurkin' in the undergrowth, after which I proceed to dress myself in a very nice grey pinhead suit with a blue silk shirt an' collar an' a navy barathea silk tie. I stick a brown fedora over one eye, take a quick look in the glass an' register satisfaction. Maybe they told you that I am not a bad-lookin' guy even if the old pan is a bit scratched. I stick a little bunch of violets that are in a vase on the mantelpiece in my buttonhole, an' scram.

Outside in Jermyn Street I pick up a taxi. I tell the guy to drive me around to Mayfield Court out at Hampstead an' I tell him to step on it.

I sit back in the cab an' relax. I light myself a cigarette an' do a little fancy smoke ring blowin'.

I have told you guys before that things always go in threes—an' that goes for dames too. Well . . . we have had a coupla dames in this case—first of all the phoney Tamara who is a looker all right, an' second the real Tamara who is somethin' to make you blink—even if she is so goddam full of mayhem that she would make a really bad dame look like the local Sunday-school marm.

O.K. Well, now let's see what this one is gonna be like.

An' I hope she's gonna be good . . . even if she don't look it.

By the time I get to the Mayfield Court dump it has stopped rainin' an' the sun is beginnin' to come out. This makes me feel good for no particular reason that I can think of, because I am not one of those guys who are only happy on a sunny day or when they are cockeyed. Because I am the sort of poetic guy who can be happy very easy. All I need is a little chicken farm way down where the blue grass grows, about sixty gallons of straight Kentucky an' a dame with a nice line in figures an' tempers. This is what the politicians call wishful thinkin' an' maybe when I get around to havin' all these things I shall be so goddam old that I will not know what to do with 'em, which brings me back to that smart guy Confucius who said: "All things that are beautiful belong to youth." Which, bein' translated by my old friend Issy Smack the Hollywood scriptwriter is said to mean "The old may be bold but it don't get 'em no place with frails."

I take a look around the hallway of this Mayfield dump an' I see an indicator that tells me that Mrs. Lorella Owen is livin' in suite No. 5 on the ground floor. I ease along the passageway, find No. 5, ring the bell. After a minute the door opens an' I find myself confronted by a maid who is so goddam smart that she looks as if she had just jumped out of the chorus in a leg show.

She says do I want anything an' I tell her that I am Mr. Caution an' that it is most necessary that I should have a little conversation with Mrs. Owen pronto. She then gives me a quick once-over an' havin' come to the conclusion that I am not the guy who goes around pinchin' gas-meters she says will I come in. I follow this baby across the hall into a very nice sittin'-room. She tells me to stick around an' that she will tell Mrs. Owen.

I sit down an' twiddle my thumbs for about five minutes an' then the door opens an' a dame comes in. She is grey-haired an' she has got a very nice figure that woulda looked good on a baby half her age. She has got a nice skin an' she walks sorta pretty. On one side of her face is a lump that looks as if somebody had hit her a sweet one with a rollin' pin when she was a baby. But the shock comes when she starts talkin'.

This dame has a voice on her that is so goddam awful that it makes you wish you was in Siam. She is one of them nasal dames. Everything she says comes to you through one nostril an' sounds like a jew's harp bein' played off-key.

Well . . . I thought it was time we got a dame who is not so good to look at.

She says: "I am Mrs. Owen an' can I do something for you?"

I tell her yes. I tell her that I would be very much obliged to her if she would sit down an' listen very carefully to what I am goin' to say to her an' that if she does this she might save a lot of trouble for all concerned.

She looks a bit surprised but she says "Of course" an' sits down.

"Look, Mrs. Owen," I tell her, "I am Lemuel H. Caution, an' I am a Special Agent of the Federal Bureau of Investigation who is over here lookin' for some frail by the name of Julia Wayles. The idea is that this Wayles dame has been snatched an' got over here somehow. You got that?"

She says yes she has got it.

"O.K.," I go on. "Well, in tryin' to find out where this Wayles proposition is I run inta a tough *hombre* that is bad medicine by the name of Max Schribner. Stringin' around with him is a good-lookin' baby who is pretendin' that she is Tamara Phelps—another hot number from the States. Well, for reasons that we don't haveta discuss, I come to the conclusion that this dame is not Tamara Phelps at all but some other dame an' I wanta find out just what she is playin' at. So I get her to come around an' see me.

"Well, she comes. But when I tell her that she is tryin' to pull a fast one an' that she is *not* Tamara, an' ask her what the hell is goin' on around here, she gets all hot an' bothered an' pulls a gun on me. After which she makes a very dignified exit, leavin' me knowin' no more than when I started in. Have you got that, Mrs. Owen?"

She says yes, she's got that but she doesn't quite understand . . .

I interrupt her. I say: "Look, lady, let me give you a straight tip-off, an' that is please do not try an' pull any funny stuff on me about not understandin'."

She looks dignified. "I really don't know what you mean, Mr. Caution," she says in that terrible voice of hers.

"I mean this," I tell her. "When that dame left my apartment what she didn't know was that I had got a tail waitin' for her outside. An' when I say tail I do not mean the thing that monkeys have. I mean a guy waitin' to follow her to see where she went to. Well, he saw where she went to. She came right here an' she saw you an' she had some talk with you before she went back to Max Schribner's place at Betchworth."

I stop talkin' an' take a quick look at her. She is sittin' quite calm an' collected with her hands folded in her lap. I look at her hands. They sorta fascinate me. They are swell hands with long, supple fingers an' very nice fingernails. I reckon I am *very* interested in this Lorella Owen proposition.

"So that's the way it is," I go on. "An' you will now realise what I am doin' here. It is stickin' out like a Roman nose that you know plenty about this dame who was frontin' as Tamara Phelps. It is stickin' out that she rushed around here after she pulled that gat on me an' did that fadin' act to see you about it. You got that?"

She says: "Yes . . . I understand what you mean, Mr. Caution, and I also understand that to a man of your profession such a procedure must have seemed rather suspicious."

"You don't say," I tell her. "Rather suspicious is good. I would go a bit further than that. I would say the idea stinks an' that if you know what's good for you you're gonna come across an' tell me the whole works. See?"

"That sounds a little like threatening, Mr. Caution," she says, claspin' an' unclaspin' her nice fingers. "I don't like being threatened. I'm a person who doesn't react to threats."

"Ain't that just too bad?" I tell her. "So you don't react to threats. Well . . . well . . . well. . . . Let's see how you react to this one. I'm gonna give you five minutes to make up your mind to let me in on what is goin' on around here or else I'm gonna slam you into a taxicab an' take you down to Scotland Yard. An' when I get you there I'm gonna ask 'em to hold you on a charge of obstructin' a Federal Officer who is operatin' in this country in the legitimate discharge of his duty under the American Government, an' how do you like that, pal?"

She says: "I don't like the sound of it at all. Would you like to smoke a cigarette?"

I tell her yes an' she gets a big silver box an' hands it to me. The cigarettes inside are Lucky Strikes—a favourite brand of mine.

She takes one herself an' I light it for her. She sits there smokin' an' lookin' out of the window. She looks to me like a dame who is tryin' to make up her mind about somethin' serious.

I don't say a word. I just look at her an' do a big grin inside. Maybe this baby is goin' to tell me another one of those fairy stories, an' maybe she's gonna tell the truth. You never know with dames.

After a bit she says: "Mr. Caution, I'm in a very difficult position. I want to do what is right and I believe I shall best do that by telling you everything. Also, I shall be a great deal happier. When a woman gets to my age she should be beyond lies and insincerities. That is what I think."

"Me too," I say. "But that don't mean that a dame of any age can't do a bit of lyin' when she feels like it. In fact I would go so far as to say that the older they are the better they tell 'em . . . sometimes. Mind you, I don't mean that sorta personal."

I slip her a happy little smile. One of them charmin' smiles that breeds confidence an' sympathy an' what-have-you-got-to-day stuff.

"Look, lady," I say, "you just go right ahead an' talk. But before you say anythin' let me give you a tip-off. Don't tell me any fairy stories—because I am a guy who does not believe in Santa Claus. Another thing is this: If you give me the low-down on this job maybe I'll be able to get some action. Then if you've done anythin' that ain't quite legal maybe I'll be ready to forgive about it. But if you give me a phoney line of talk an' I find you out—an' I should find out—I'm goin' to make it hot for you."

She gives me a little winsome look. This dame looks as if butter wouldn't melt in her mouth. She says, in that terrible voice of hers: "Mr. Caution, I have already told you that I do not like threats. I'm going to tell you the truth because I believe it's my duty to tell you the truth."

She gives a little sigh.

"I expect you'll say I've been rather foolish," she says.

"I wouldn't know," I tell her. "You tell me what you've gotta tell me an' then I'll tell you whether I think you've been foolish or not. Get goin', baby."

She throws me a sharp look. "I'm not a baby," she says, "and I don't like being talked to like that."

"I never thought you was a baby," I tell her. "Didn't they tell you 'baby' is a term of endearment used among sailors, an' don't tell me now that I'm not a sailor—just go ahead. . . ."

"Well," she says, "first of all you'll want to know about this mysterious woman—the woman who pretended to be Tamara Phelps." She looks serious. "I must say," she says, "that she rather exceeded her instructions in threatening you with a gun, but I expect she felt she had to get away."

I bring her back to the point.

"Who is this dame?" I ask her.

"She's a woman who was mixed up with a rather unsavoury crowd in New York," she says. "The sort of person you'd probably describe as a 'frail.' She used to travel around with mobs.

"Well, I'd better tell you first of all that my name's Mrs. Lorella Owen; that I'm a widow; that I'm a very old friend of the Wayles family. I used to know Henry Wayles—the father—a long time ago," she gives a little simper—"and that at one time it was thought we might be married. So that naturally after he died I was very interested in his two daughters.

"When I heard that Julia had disappeared I was terribly upset. Some time after that I heard from a friend of mine who is employed in the Missing Persons Bureau in Chicago that they'd had a nation-wide check up to try and find her and failed. Then by some extraordinary coincidences which don't really matter I met this woman—Dodo Malendas. She told me she was certain that Julia Wayles had been kidnapped; that she was in England—being held there. She told me that the kidnap had been engineered by two people—a man called Rudy Zimman and a woman called Tamara Phelps, and that they were going over to England in order to contact the man who was holding Julia, whose name was Schribner. This woman suggested that as Schribner had never met either Rudy Zimman or Tamara

Phelps, she should go to England, find Schribner, pretend that she was Tamara Phelps and find out where Julia was."

She gives another bashful sorta smile. She looks plenty soppy to me. Then she goes on:

"You see, Mr. Caution, there's never been very much adventure in my life and I must say I was rather thrilled at the idea of rescuing Julia. So I agreed. I told Dodo Malendas that I'd come over too, and that when she found where Julia was we'd go to the police here and get Zimman, Phelps and Schribner arrested. Well, it seems it hasn't worked out as I hoped it would."

"You're tellin' me," I say. "It hasn't worked out at all like that. Another thing, lady," I go on, "any time you feel you wanta get some more thrills you'd much better go an' tackle a sleepin' tiger than go an' get yourself mixed up with a mob like the Zimman bunch. Didn't they tell you that those guys get tough sometimes? If they got their hooks on you they'd do all sorts of things to you."

"Do you think they would, Mr. Caution?" she says sorta hopeful.

"Yeah," I tell her, "they would." But I gotta mental reservation about this. When I look at the lump that this dame has got on one side of her pan an' when I listen to that goddam awful voice of hers, I reckon that the only thing that Rudy would do to her would be to take her outside an' give her the heat. I reckon directly he heard her talk he'd wanta croak her. In point of fact I don't know that I don't wanta croak her myself. She gives me a pain in the neck.

"O.K.," I tell her. "Well, that sounds as if it might be the truth. But your friend Dodo has got herself in a nice jam. She went back to Schribner's all right. I suppose she went back there to have a last try to find out where Julia was. I grabbed her outa there an' had her sent along to my apartment on Jermyn Street. Now it looks as if the Zimman bunch have wiped her up again. Maybe they've fogged her by now."

"Oh dear," she says. "How terrible! And she was such a nice looking woman too."

"Nice lookin'?" I tell her. "This Dodo baby was more than nice lookin'. She was beautiful."

It seems to me that this Mrs. Owen is a cool sorta cuss. She don't get very excited at the idea of Dodo bein' ironed out by the Zimman bunch, but maybe that is because she is lookin' for adventure.

"Listen, Mrs. Owen," I tell her, "you tell me somethin' about these Wayles sisters. There was two of 'em you said—Julia an' another one? What was her name?"

"She was Karen Wayles. She was a year younger than Julia. They were both very nice girls—both very beautiful and attractive to men—at least that's what I've been told." She looks at me archly. "I wouldn't know about that, Mr. Caution," she says, "not being a man. But there was one big difference between them. Julia was an extremely clever girl—almost brilliant, I mink. One of those rare cases of brains and beauty combined; whereas Karen I am sorry to say was really rather stupid."

"Yeah!" I say. "Just how was she stupid?"

"She was one of those young women who was always falling in love," she goes on. "She thought she was in love with every good-looking man she met. But I'm glad to say she's taken a turn for the better in that respect now she has a job. She's working at W.P.A. in New York and doing very well, I believe. I think it is good for a young woman to have a job to occupy her mind, don't you, Mr. Caution?"

"I wouldn't know," I tell her. "From what I know of dames they always find somethin' to occupy their minds, an' I haven't known a job keep a dame who wantsta get inta mischief out of it."

I get up. "Well, thanks a lot, Mrs. Owen," I tell her. "I suppose you'll be stayin' here?"

"Oh yes," she says. "Of course I shall. And will you be very good and let me know if you can what's happened to Dodo?"

"I'll let you know," I tell her.

She gets up. "Good-bye, Mr. Caution," she says. "I wish you the best of luck. By the way," she goes on, "I suppose you wouldn't like a glass of elderberry wine before you go? I brought three bottles of it from America. It is my grandmother's recipe."

"No thanks, lady," I tell her. "I'm one of those guys who got an anti to elderberry wine. Any time I drink it I come out in green spots."

She holds out her hand an' I take it in mine. I told you this dame had got nice hands. Her fingers are soft an' supple to touch. I think it is a pity that the rest of her don't match up with her hands an' her figure.

I say good-bye an' scram. The neat-lookin' maid lets me outa the front door. As I go out I sling her a sideways look. I think maybe I'd like to talk to that baby sometime.

I walk along the corridor an' outa the entrance. Outside I get a cab an' tell him to drive me to Jermyn Street, but when we get around the corner I rap on the window an' stop him. I pay him off an' walk around the back of the block until I am on the corner facin' the entrance of the Mayfield Court. Just along the road is a little coffee shop—the sorta place that is kept by a couple of old ladies an' a cat. I go in there, order a cup of coffee an' light a cigarette. From the table where I am I can see the entrance to Mayfield Court.

Me—I am not very satisfied with this Mrs. Lorella Owen. There is somethin' about a dame like that. I get to thinkin' about her. It's funny how nature can be unkind to a woman, but maybe you thought that before. Here is a dame with a figure that you could write a poem about, lovely hands, a bulge at one side of her face, a swell complexion, grey hair and a voice that is so goddam awful that you wouldn't think it possible.

Wait a minute! Maybe that voice is not possible! Now I know why I was so struck with this dame's hands. Mrs. Owen is a phoney all right. Her figure is young, an' so are her hands—soft an' white an' supple. The only old things about her are her hair, the shape of her face an' her voice. Well, I don't reckon anybody was ever born with a voice like that. Maybe we got somebody else puttin' on an act.

I drink my coffee an' order another. When I have smoked three more cigarettes I see somebody come outa Mayfield Court, an' it is Mrs. Owen. I couldn't make a mistake about that figure or those ankles. An' I was right or was I? Because this dame has not got a bulge in her face an' she has not got grey hair. I can see the auburn curls stickin' out under a smart little hat she's got over one eye.

She walks along the road an' goes up to the cab rank. Directly she gets inta the cab I nip along an' grab another. I tell the driver to keep on the tail of her cab an' not lose it. Then I sit back in the corner, relax an' smoke another cigarette.

We go back to London. We go down Oxford Street, away along Regent Street, down by the Admiralty. I get another surprise. Her cab pulls up in front of Scotland Yard. She gets out an' goes in. Well. . . well . . . well. . .!

I pay off my cab, lean up against the wall, doin' a little quiet thinkin'. Then I get an idea. I think I'll try a fast one. I walk along the street until I come to a phone box. I go in an' ring through to Scotland Yard. I get onta the Information Room. When some guy answers I say:

"I'm sorry to trouble you, but my name's Rackets. I'm a friend of Mrs. Lorella Owen. I believe right now she's with Chief Detective Inspector Herrick. Would you mind puttin' me through to him."

The guy tells me to hold on for a minute. Then he says O.K. he's puttin' me through. A minute later I hear Herrick's voice on the line sayin' hello. I make my voice sound very low. I say:

"Is that Chief Detective Inspector Herrick?"

He says yes, what can he do for me?

"I believe my friend Mrs. Owen is with you," I tell him. "I wonder if I could speak to her for a minute."

He says all right, hold on.

I don't. I hang up and ease outa the telephone booth. I start walkin' back towards Charing Cross. What the hell is goin' on in this case, an' what the hell is this Lorella Owen dame doin' dressin' herself up with false lumps in her face, grey wigs an' all the rest of it an' then rushin' off an' havin' conversaziones with Herrick directly she has pulled a lot of stuff on me! An' Herrick is the guy who don't want me to do anythin' behind his back. Herrick is the guy who was grumblin' because of the way I handled my last case over here in England.

Somebody is bein' clever with me. Well. . . . O.K. From now on I'm gonna be so smart that I ain't even goin' to tell *me* what I'm doin'. . . .

That is if I know myself. . . .

So now you know.

CHAPTER EIGHT
SLUG PARTY

I EASE along to a hash house on Regent Street an' get myself a salad an' some rolls. When I tell you that I am a very thoughtful guy I mean it. I'm doin' so much concentratin' that any time I look at anythin' I practically see double. But one thing is stickin' out an' that is everybody around here is takin' me for a ride an' I'm goin' to find out why. I've been in some funny businesses in my life, but I reckon I have never struck a case stuck so full with phoneys as this one is.

First of all there is this Dodo Malendas, pretendin' to be Tamara Phelps, an' now we've got Mrs. Lorella Owen, with a lump on her face, grey hair an' a voice that sounds like a cannin' factory, tryin' to pull another fast one, an' all the time she is as good a looker as any of the other dames an' maybe as bad.

I finish my lunch an' go back to Jermyn Street. I give myself a coupla stiff ones just in case I get a touch of rheumatism some time an' I go to bed. Directly I get my head on the pillow I fall asleep, because as I have told you mugs before I am a guy who is nearly always content with any situation that happens any time, because if you don't like a situation you can always do somethin' about it . . . sometimes!

It is ten o'clock when I wake up. It is gettin' pretty dark. I take a warm shower, dress myself an' stick the old Luger in the shoulder holster under my left arm. It sorta makes me feel good. Then I grab off the telephone an' ring through to Scotland Yard. Herrick is not there but they give me his private number. After a bit I get him on the line.

"Look, Herrick," I tell him. "I'm a bit worried about this Wayles case. I thought I'd like to talk to you about it."

"I'm sorry to hear that," he says. "Can I help in any way? I thought you weren't taking it very seriously." There is a little pause—then he goes on: "Didn't I put you on to Callaghan Investigations? Haven't they been able to give you the help you want?"

"Oh yeah," I tell him. "They've given me plenty help. As a matter of fact I got a swell guy workin' for me by the name of Nikolls. He's O.K. It's not them I'm worry in' about."

"Well, what is it?" he says.

"Well," I tell him. "I sorta can't get a grip on anythin' in this case. There seem to me to be a lotta guys rushin' around in circles without anybody doin' anythin' really definite. But there is one thing I thought you could do for me."

"What is it?" he says.

"This guy Max Schribner," I tell him. "The boyo who is livin' down in Dorkin'. It looks to me as if this palooka was the boy who was supposed to take charge of Julia Wayles when she was got over here. Well, I thought it would be a good idea to knock off that guy."

There is another little pause. Then he says:

"Ye-es! Have you got any charge against him?"

"Oh, shucks!" I tell him. "Surely you can frame somethin' on that bozo. This guy is a thug an' I think he oughta be knocked off."

"That's as maybe," he says, "but in this country you've got to have a charge before you can arrest people."

"All right," I tell him. "How'd you like one of attempted murder? Supposin' I tell you that this guy tried to fog me. What about that?"

"Yes," he says, "it might do. Did he try to kill you himself?"

"Well, not exactly," I tell him. "But he sort of arranged it with some other guy."

"I see," he says. "And who was the other guy?"

I tell him. I tell him the other guy was Charlie Milton. Herrick gives a big sigh. "Look, Lemmy," he says, "you ought to know better than that. You know you can't charge Schribner for telling Milton to kill you. Milton wouldn't have done it in any event."

"That's as maybe," I tell him. "But Schribner didn't know that Milton was Milton. He thought he was another guy who *would* kill me."

Herrick says: "Have a heart, Lemmy. Just imagine a Court listening to a story like that."

"O.K. O.K.," I say. "I get it. An' you told me you wanted to co-operate."

"I do want to co-operate. I want to co-operate as much as possible. But I don't see I'm going to do any good arresting Schribner on a false charge. The murder charge is no good—you take that from me, Lemmy. Now is there anything else I can do?"

"I don't think so," I tell him. "If I want you I'll ring you."

"Do that, Lemmy," he says. "You know I'm only too glad to help you any time."

I hang up. I give a big grin. I reckon Herrick has told me all I wanta know. Maybe I'm a mug some of the time, but believe it or not I'm not a mug all of the time. I light a cigarette an' start reviewin' all the big personalities in this case.

Dodo Malendas who is a tough baby, who suddenly decides that she will work for Mrs. Lorella Owen tryin' to find Julia Wayles. Mrs. Lorella Owen who is a friend of the Wayles family an' who is so stuck on tryin' to find Julia that she employs a moll like Dodo Malendas to do it, an' takes the trouble to come over here an' sorta supervise things. Not only does she do that, but directly I show up an' do a little straight talkin' she runs around to Herrick at the Yard just as if she had a tiger after her.

An' Herrick is stallin'. Herrick always had a big grouse about cases I have worked on over in this country, an' that is that I have never let him know what I am doin'. I have gone behind his back.

But here is one case where I *do* wanta co-operate with that guy an' all he does is to duck. I got an idea in my head. Maybe it is a wrong idea but I should worry. I'd rather get action an' do somethin' with a wrong idea than sit down an' go to sleep on a right one. So here we go.

I pull the car inta a little lane not far from the Waterfall at Capel, light a cigarette an' do some thinkin'.

I am tryin' to get the idea of this place. First of all there are lots of road-houses with bands an' bars an' a bunch of city slickers stickin' around in this country—in normal times I mean; but these ain't normal times an' I am curious to know just what sort of business a place like this Waterfall Inn does.

Think it out for yourself an' you'll see what I mean. A place like this is O.K. when people with jack have got the cars an' the petrol to get out from the big city. But in these days who's got the petrol?

This place might easily be a dump that Rudy Zimman is runnin' for his own purposes. It might be a front an' the band boys an' other mugs supposed to be workin' around the place might be playin' in with him on some scheme or another. Anyhow whether I am right about this or not I'm gonna take the chance on it.

I get outa the car, throw my cigarette away an' ease over the roadway an' along the drive that leads up to the house. I skirt around it till I come to the door I went in by last time I was here.

I give a knock on the door an' stand waitin'. After a few minutes I hear somebody comin'. The door opens a few inches an' the same voice that spoke to me before says: "Yes, what is it?"

I say: "Look, pal . . ." an' while I am sayin' it I shoot my hand through the crack in the door an' grab. An' I'm tellin' you it is a lucky grab. I get hold of the bozo by the hair an' before he can let outa yelp I yank him forward an' hear his face do a smart smack on the edge of the door.

I kick the door open an' get my other hand in. I get it around his neck an' yank him outside; then I put a Japanese arm lock on him an' start a whisperin' campaign on this guy. "Look, punk," I tell him "I want just one crack outa you. Just one. An' what I'm gonna do to you is nobody's business. You got that?"

He says he's got it.

I take the Luger outa its holster an' stick it into his ribs.

"Start walkin', fella," I tell him, "an' don't stop, an' don't talk. You an' me have gotta do some business."

He don't say anything. I march this boyo down the drive across the roadway an' down the little lane where I have parked the heap.

It is as dark as hell an' there is a little rain fallin'. This is the sorta night when things happen.

I open the door of the car an' push this mug inta the back seat. Then I sit sideways on the drivin' seat facin' him. I get out a shaded torch that is in the dashboard locker an' shine it on him. He is the usual sorta punk with a weak good-lookin' face an' he is scared sick. I reckon this baby is not gonna be difficult.

"Look, handsome," I tell him. "You listen to me for a minute an' then make up your mind. This car we're sittin' in belongs to the U.S. Embassy, see? Well . . . maybe when I go back to town to-night

I'm goin' to ring through to the local cops an' report it as pinched. I'm gonna tell 'em that I left it outside my rooms on Jermyn Street while I went in for a coat an' when I come down it was gone.

"O.K. Well, then they're gonna look for it. They'll find it to-morrow. They'll find it along here at the bottom of the chalkpits on the Reigate Road an' they'll find *you* inside it. You won't be pretty to look at either. . . ."

He says: "What the hell do you mean?"

"Just this, mug," I tell him. "You're either goin' to talk an' talk fast, or I'm goin' to give you a bust over the dome with this gun. Then I'm gonna stick you in the front seat an' run you along to the road that runs around the top of the chalk pits. Then I'm gonna stick you in the drivin' seat, push some raw liquor inta your mouth, so's they think you was cockeyed when they find you, put the car in gear an' scram out of it just before it goes over the edge. You can finish the drop on your own."

I blow a coupla smoke rings at him.

"The idea is easy," I go on. "They'll think you found the car parked and pinched it, that you drove out here for some reasons you got, that you found the flask of liquor in the dashboard an' got cockeyed an' that when you got onto the chalkpits road you was so high you didn't know what you was doin' an' drove over the edge . . . the drop's two hundred feet they tell me . . . you oughta have a long time to think while you're fallin'. . . ."

He says: "Do you mean that?" His lower lip is tremblin'.

"Take a look at me," I tell him, "an' answer the question for yourself."

"Whaddya wanta know?" he says.

I give him a grin.

"So you're gonna play?" I say. "Well, you're wise. O.K. First of all, who are the bunch around at the Waterfall? How many of those guys are English guys?"

"Two," he says. "The rest are American."

"How long've they been over here?" I ask him.

"About two months," he says.

"An' Rudy Zimman arranged for 'em to come over?" I ask. "An' he had this Waterfall dump ready-eyed? It was all ready for 'em to walk into and the road-house business is a front, hey?"

"Somethin' like that," he says. "If legitimate people came around in the day we served 'em food. After dark we said we was shut."

"What was goin' on there?" I ask him.

"I wouldn't know," he says. "Honest . . . I just draw my jack each week an' don't ask any questions. I'm a wise guy. All I do is look after the door."

"You wouldn't hand me any funny stuff, would you, pal?" I ask him. "Because I am a very bad-tempered guy an' if I thought you wasn't tryin' I'd just as soon see you ridin' over the edge of the chalkpits as look at you."

"I'm not tryin' any stuff," he says, "I'm givin' you what I know an' if it ain't much, that ain't my fault. Why don't you pick on some of the other guys?"

"That's a good idea," I tell him. "Maybe I will when I've done with you. O.K. Well, tell me this. Is Tamara Phelps over at The Waterfall?"

He shakes his head.

"No," he says. "She comes in sometimes but she ain't been there to-day. I beard she was in town."

"An' Rudy Zimman?" I ask him.

"He's away—somewhere near Liverpool," he says. "They don't expect him back for two-three days." .

I nod my head.

"Did you know who I was when I come here the other night?" I ask him. "Did you know I was Caution?"

He says yes. He knew that after I'd scrammed. He says Tamara Phelps was beefin' about who I was an' that she didn't seem to give a cuss.

I grin at him.

"Maybe that dame thinks she's on somethin' that's foolproof," I tell him. "Maybe they got to the state of mind where they ain't even afraid of a 'G' man any more. Maybe you're feelin' like that?"

He says No. He says he ain't feelin' that way at all. I ask him why not.

"Well," he says, "I don't like this business. I don't like it because I don't know anythin' about it. I like to *know* what I'm doin'."

I tell him I think he is a wise guy. I stop talkin' an' light a cigarette. While I am doin' it I am watchin' this guy. He is beginnin' to look a bit better an' not so scared. Maybe he thinks he's gonna be better off playin' along with me than with the Zimman bunch.

I blow a smoke ring across the car an' get to considerin' the psychology of mobsters. This guy is like the rest of 'em. They're O.K. until somethin' happens. They're one hundred per cent while the goin' is good but when it gets a little rough they start lookin' around for a chance to duck. He says: "Can I smoke?"

"Sure," I tell him. I give him a cigarette an' light it for him.

"Look, pal," I say, "I'm thinkin' of givin' you a break. An' I ain't doin' that because I like your ugly pan either. It just might suit me the way things are goin', that's all."

"Yeah?" he says. "What break? An' how do I know it's on the up-and-up?"

"You don't," I tell him. "You don't know a thing. You just have to be a trustin' guy . . . an' it's either that or the chalkpits."

He don't speak for a minute. Then he says:

"Well . . . what's the break?"

"Look," I tell him. "Some time last night there was two people around in my apartment off Jermyn Street. Well, they sorta disappeared. Somebody hi-jacked these two. One of 'em was a guy who was workin' for me by the name of Nikolls an' the other was a baby by the name of Dodo Malendas—a cute little trick—who was just playin' around tryin' to get herself a stake. I suppose you wouldn't know where those two have got to?"

"No," he says, "I wouldn't know."

I give a sigh. Then I stick the barrel end of the Luger under his nose an' give it a nice little jab. He lets go a squeal an' flops back against the corner of the car. This boyo is no hero.

"Just think a little," I tell him. "Try an' get that big brain workin' otherwise I'm goin' to do somethin' to you that you won't find in the child's first primer."

He puts his hand up to his nose just to make sure that it is still there. He says: "I don't know where they are. Maybe they're at the dump on the Leatherhead road. Maybe they're there. But I don't know."

"Never mind, kid," I tell him. "You're gettin' warmer. So there's a dump on the Leatherhead road, is there? You tell me where."

He tells me. He tells me all about it.

"Fine," I say. "It looks like Rudy Zimman has got a whole lot of property around here. First of all there is The Waterfall—here at Capel, then there is Max Schribner out at Betchworth, an' now we got a dump at Leatherhead. We're doin' swell."

I smoke for a bit an' then I say: "I don't think you're tryin'. I think you could tell me a lot more if you wanted to. I think you got a whole lot of information that you're bein' clever about. I'm gonna start in on you, pal."

I smack him across the snout with the Luger. He starts whimperin'. "For chrissake . . ." he says. "I've given you the lot. I don't know any more. I told you I was only the guy on the door. What the hell . . .?"

I give him another smack on the snozzle. Then I lay off him. He is leanin' back against the back-seat, an' the tears are runnin' down his cheeks. He don't look at all happy to me. But I think he is tellin' the truth. I don't think this guy knows any more.

I light another cigarette. I take a look at my wrist-watch. It is just twelve o'clock. It is a bum night an' the rain is patterin' on the roof of the car. Maybe this is gonna be one of them nights.

"Listen, unconscious," I say, "you tell me somethin'. Are there any more cars parked over at The Waterfall?"

He says yes. He says there is a garage at the back an' that there are half a dozen cars parked there. He says they belong to the boys who are runnin' The Waterfall.

"O.K.," I tell him. "Well . . . we're gonna get one. We're gonna get a nice one. You got a key to that garage?"

He says it ain't locked.

"Swell," I tell him. "Well, here we go. You get outa this heap an' ease over to that garage. An' remember I'm goin' to be just behind you. Remember that I want just one crack outa you, one little noise or anythin' else to let any of these mugs know we're around, an' you're for it. Now scram."

We ease along the lane, across the roadway an' up the drive to The Waterfall. We go around the left-hand side of the house. The guy in front is movin' nice an' quiet an' I am just keepin' near enough to keep him in sight. After a bit we come to a low stone garage. He pushes open the door an' goes in. I go in after him, close the door an' switch on the torch.

There are five cars in the garage. Along at our end is a Lancia—a Sports model. I take a look at the dashboard an' see that the ignition key is there. I switch on an' check on the petrol tank. The indicator says it is nearly full.

"Get in," I tell him, "an' drive that bus out. I'll open the door for you. Wait for me when you get her through an' remember that I can blow the top of your head off just as easy through a car window as without. Get goin'."

He gets inta the car an' drives her out. Outside I shut the garage door, get in an' sit beside him. "Now ease her out onto the roadway," I tell him, "nice an' quiet."

We slide down the driveway in top gear at about five miles an hour. The heap is a honey an' runs as quiet as a lamb. When we get out into the roadway I tell him to drive down the road a bit an' then pull in to the side. He does this. "O.K., pal," I say. "Now you can get out an' come with me."

He gets out. He gives me an odd sorta look. The guy is still scared stiff. He still ain't certain about what I'm goin' to do with him. We go back to where I have left my car. I open the trap in the dashboard an' take out the flask of liquor I have got in there. I put it in my pocket.

"Listen, fella," I tell him. "Supposin' I was to tell you to get inta the drivin' seat an' scram. Suppose I told you I was gonna give you a break. What would you do?"

He licks his lips.

"I'd get outa here." he says. "I'd get outa here goddam quick. I'd make straight for London—I've got some pals there an' I'd get outa here an' get back to U.S. in such a goddam hurry that it'd be nobody's business."

I grin at him.

"That's O.K. by me," I say. "Scram. . . . Turtle. . . ."

I give him the ignition key.

He looks at me as if he didn't believe it. Then when he sees me put the Luger back in my pocket he relaxes. He gives a feeble sorta grin. The way his nose is fixed after bein' smacked around with a gun barrel makes the grin look sorta stupid.

"I'm on my way," he says. "Thanks. . . ."

He lets in the clutch an' the car moves off. He takes her down the lane an' onta the road nice an' easy. Then he treads on it. The rear light of that car goes dashin' down the road as if all the devils in hell was after it.

I stand in the roadway thinkin'. This mug is just another mobster with nerves. But Rudy Zimman ain't the sorta guy to employ boyos who scare easy. So I reckon that *somethin'* has happened that has scared this guy. Maybe things are gettin' a bit more serious than he thought. Or maybe Zimman got these heels workin' for him on one idea an' now they are beginnin' to find out that they're doin' somethin' that is not quite so easy. Maybe some of these other punks are scared as well.

I light a fresh cigarette. Then I ease down the road an' get into the Lancia. I look at my watch. It is ten past twelve. I reckon I got to get a ripple on. I got a coupla appointments to keep to-night an' I don't want to be late.

I let in the clutch an' slide off. Just when I am runnin' inta Holmwood I see a telephone booth. I pull up an' get out. I ease across the road an' go inta the booth. I dial operator an' when she comes on the line I ask for the Dorking police. After a bit a police guy comes on the line.

"This is Mr. L. H. Caution," I tell him. "I am an F.B.I. operative workin' over here with the American Embassy. Some guy has just pinched my car—about five minutes ago."

He says yes an' asks for some details.

"It's a U.S. Embassy car," I tell him. I give him the number an' the description. "I can give you an idea about the mug who pinched it," I go on. "I left the car away down the road while I called on a friend, about a hundred yards away from this box at Holmwood. When I got outa the car I noticed this guy standin' on the sidewalk. He is a guy who looks sorta foreign, slim an' of middle height, with a sallow skin. He has also got a funny sorta nose, it looks as it he'd been fightin' or somethin'. . . ."

He says that will be all right; that they will pick the car up. I say thanks a lot an' when they have got it, they might hold this guy an' return the car to the U.S. Embassy, London, pendin' further instructions.

He says all right an' hangs up. I go back to the car. I reckon they will pick up that mug before he's got halfway to London. I reckon he will be plenty surprised too.

Well . . . I said I'd give him a break an' what has he got to bellyache about? Life is just full of surprises. An' if he don't know that it'll be a nice change to find out.

I ease the car inta the side of the road, under a tree. I have stopped about a mile an' a half from Leatherhead.

The rain has stopped an' a bit of moon has come out. Overhead I hear a bunch of bombers comin' back from strafin' the Jerries on the other side of the Channel. I hope they gave it to 'em good.

Just on the right is a grass patch an' a hedge. I start up the car, drive it off the road, stick it alongside the hedge an' turn off the lights. I sit there, smokin' a cigarette, nice an' relaxed an' do a little considerin'.

This case is just another one of those things. It is just one of them cases where you never really get anythin' to work on. Where you go guessin' from one point to another.

Well . . . I got one point, an' that is that for some reason or other Herrick is stallin' me along. If he wasn't he woulda knocked off that guy Schribner on some faked charge when I asked him to. An' for some reason that he wasn't goin' to tell me he wouldn't do it. That is point one.

An' the second point is that I got onto Max Schribner in the first place *through* Herrick. When I started in on this job the U.S. Embassy gave me the address of the Schribner dump. They said Schribner was my first contact. They got that address from Charlie Milton an' Charlie Milton got it from Herrick.

So Herrick wants us to get on to Schribner, but when I want him knocked off he says no an' stalls . . . why? Maybe I am beginnin' to get an idea about that.

I sit there smokin' an' thinkin' about all the cases I been mixed up in where there was a lot of swell dames. Well, there are swell dames in this one all right. Dodo Malendas is an eyeful; Tamara Phelps is such a looker that she woulda made Rip Van Winkle talk in his sleep, an' I reckon that Mrs. Lorella Owen would also make you blink—that is when she ain't wearin' wigs an' generally messin' about with the original scheme of nature.

Some guys like handlin' guys an' some guys like workin' through dames. Me—I would rather kick around with this bunch of frails an' see what I can find than mess around with Rudy Zimman an' the other tough guys he has got. Women talk easier than men, an' they can make bigger mistakes when they get rattled. A dame is wise enough until somethin' knocks her off balance an' then she goes haywire. An' that's the way I'm gonna play this job.

I flick my cigarette end away, get out of the car an' start walkin' down the road lookin' for the turnin' over the bridge that leads to this dump the mug told me about. I take a look at my watch.

It is one o'clock an' the night is not so bad. I got a Luger under my arm an' a hip flask in my pocket.

Believe it or not I am almost happy.

I stand in the shadow of a hedge lookin' at this dump an' wonderin' what I am gonna find around here—that is if I find anythin'. The place is a long low sorta farmhouse an' you can see where they have joined on an old-time outbuilding by makin' a stone . passage like a corridor between the two buildings.

The moon is out full an' the wet grass is glistenin' an' lookin' one hundred per cent like the poets like it. I get around to rememberin' that I am a poetic cuss myself an' that one of these fine days when I am through with chasin' thugs around generally I am goin' to get myself a chicken farm down in Minnesota or some place like that an' get good an' poetic at any moment—that is if the dames are right.

Because poetry an' dames are sorta made to go with each other. When you see some guy sit down an' write a smash hit about love—one of them hot numbers that make you wriggle under the collarbone—you can bet your last nickel that he has had the right royal stand-off from some baby with a nice line in hips an' what goes with it. Any time a poet starts railin' at life the reason usually is that the frail he has been gettin' around with has found some other palooka who buys her hamburgers with that different flavour—if you get me.

I knew a dame who was so goddam poetic that she was practically a menace to anythin' in pants. I met this baby when I was on a counterfeitin' case up in Back Bay. She had eyes that looked like stars, a voice that sounded like your favourite crooner an' a wiggle when she walked that woulda made the guy who invented the law of gravity rush out an' buy himself a double rye with ice just to make sure he wasn't dreamin'. Believe it or not this frail was so goddam lovely that every time she looked in the glass she usta blush with confusion.

An' she usta write poetry. Everythin' was copy to her. She was workin' in with the neatest bunch of counterfeiters that ever pushed a snide bill across the bank counter where the teller was short-sighted an' boss-eyed. When I pinched her boy friend an' took him in for a ten to fifteen years' spell in the local pen she wrote a poem called "I must part from thee"; an' when I wiped her up two weeks later on a charge of bein' accessory to a Federal offence, she took four shots at me with a duck gun, kicked me in the stomach an' tried to put my eye out with a nickel-plated hatpin. After which she got down to it an' wrote a poem called "Trapped by the Law" that woulda made a Chinese dishwasher cry any time he was peelin' onions.

All of which will show you guys that there is not such a big gap between crooks an' poetry as you would think.

I ease along the hedge until I come to a gateway that leads around the side of the main farm building. I give it a shove an' hope it won't creak. It don't. Just then, standin' in the farm *patio* or courtyard or whatever they call it around here somethin' hits me in the brainbox like a well-aimed brick.

For some reason I don't know I find myself thinkin' of Mrs. Lorella Owen. O.K. Well, Mrs. Lorella Owen told me that she was contacted by Dodo Malendas who told her that Julia Wayles had been kidnapped by Rudy Zimman an' Tamara Phelps an' brought over here to England. Well, that is O.K. if you like to believe it but I got the idea in my head that I would rather believe what Dodo said.

You mugs will remember that she said she was hangin' around New York tryin' to get a stake somehow when she run into somebody who offered her a job that wasn't too honest. Remember when she said that? O.K. Well, supposin' that somebody was Mrs. Lorella Owen? Well . . . if it *was* Mrs. Lorella Owen who offered Dodo the job to come over here frontin' as Tamara Phelps, how the hell did Mrs. Lorella Owen know who had snatched Julia Wayles? How did she know that Rudy Zimman an' Tamara Phelps had engineered the job? You tell me that one.

I put this idea in the back of my head to think about some other time. I cross over the courtyard keepin' in the shadow until I come to the back wall of the farmhouse. I edge along this wall lookin' for a door because it looks to me that most of the back doors in England haven't got any locks on 'em—real ones I mean.

After a bit I find it. But it is a good sorta door an' for once it's locked an' locked hard. I try the other side of the house. About halfway along I come to a little window about eight feet off the ground. A sorta pantry window. It looks like I might just get through if I pull my belt in.

I go over to the other side of the hedge an' get some clay off a little bank that is there. I stick a pad of clay on the window, an' stick a bunch of grass on that. I hold on to the grass an' give the window a smart smack with my other hand. It cracks all right an' I pull a piece of the glass out.

In two minutes I have got the window open, an' in another two I am inside. I am in a sort of big cupboard place—I reckon this was an old-time farm pantry—but the door is open an' I come out into a stone kitchen. I go up a few stairs an' along a passage. I stand there in the dark, shadin' my torch with my fingers, listenin'. Away somewhere in the house I can hear some guy singin' in a quiet sing-song sorta voice.

I remember the last time I heard that number was in a club somewhere on Broadway an' I remember the cute little piece who was croonin' it. I take a quick grip on myself before I start gettin' poetic, an' get back to the business in hand.

I ease along the passage-way an' start walkin' up a flight of stone stairs. At the top is a door an' another passage. Right at the end of this passage there is a half-open door an' the singin' is comin' from inside.

I snap off the torch an' gumshoe along the passage. When I get to the end I take a peek through the crack of the door.

The room is a big square sorta room with no window. There is a sorta covered in skylight right up in one wall. I reckon the place was a barn or somethin' like that some time. But it is comfortably furnished an' there is a wall telephone. Right in the middle of the room is a table with some news-sheets on it, an' lyin' across the news-sheets is a sawn-off shotgun. Just a little bit of old Chicago stuck in the English countryside!

The guy who is doin' the singin' is a tough-lookin' *hombre* with a bust-in nose. This palooka looks like he has had a head-on collision with a tank. He is standin' openin' a tin of corned beef with one hand, an' any time he stops singin' it is to start cussin'. The guy has a nice selection of language. Just when he gets the tin open the telephone rings. He goes across to the wall an' takes off the receiver.

"Yeah . . ." he says. . . . "Yeh . . . it's me all right. I saw the guy a coupla minutes ago. . . . Yeh . . . he's still out an' he ain't likely to be anyhow else for a while. . . . O.K." He hangs up.

He goes back to the corned beef. He starts singin': "Everythin' is Jake." I push the door open an' go in. I step in pretty fast so as to get near the table before he lamps me.

"Hello, pal . . ." I tell him.

He spins around. He looks sorta surprised. He puts the tin of corned beef back on the table.

"What is this?" he says. He has got a voice that is like the rumble of a train goin' through a tunnel.

"Just nothin'," I tell him. "I'm just gettin' around makin' a few inquiries about a guy named Nikolls an' a dame who was knocked off with him—a dame named Dodo Malendas. You wouldn't know anythin' about these guys, I suppose?"

He says: "I don't know anythin'. An' if I did why do I have to talk to some bum louse like you?"

I grin at him. I walk around the table so that the shotgun is behind me.

"I got half a dozen reasons why you're gonna talk to me," I tell him. "But just one of 'em is enough to go on with. Here it is. I'm sore at rushin' around the countryside at this time of night tryin' to catch up with that cheap heel who's payin' you . . . a heel by the name of Rudy Zimman. I'm gettin' sort of bored with it. That's one reason. The second is I do not like guys who look like you. I do not like your face an' I got reasons to believe that you wasn't born in the ordinary way. Some special process musta been brought into play to bring a lousy flat-faced, evil smellin' bastard like you into the world. See?"

He gives a big grin.

"Sorta fresh," he says. "You wanna play, pal, hey?"

I look at his arms. He has got a pair of forearms on him like tree trunks.

"Any time I want to play with a muscle-bound scab like you I'll write you a letter," I tell him. "Where's Nikolls?"

He throws the corned beef can at me. I duck an' it goes over my head. Then he tries a rush.

I don't know whether I ever told you guys, but for a boyo who weighs two hundred pounds I am very sweet on my feet—only more so. I just do a nice little side step as the big boy comes level an' bring my knee up with a jerk. It catches him under the belly an' he lets go a gasp that you coulda heard out in Jamaica.

He jumps back a coupla steps an' reconsiders the situation. While he is doin' this I try an old one on him.

I take a jump forward at him an' then stop suddenly. He falls for it the whole way. He shoots out his foot an' tries a big kick at my guts. I take a step back, kick up an' kick his leg up in the air. He goes over on his back. I don't move. I just stand there lookin' at him.

The guy is very quick for a bozo of his size. He rolls over an' he is up on his feet before you can blink. He stands there considerin' the situation an' lookin' at me like I was the original snake in the Garden of Eden.

"Well, pal," I tell him. "For a guy your size you remind me of a cissy I usta know in Brooklyn. Only he was better than you. He could kick with both feet at once."

He says a very rude word.

"Ain't you the sweet bastard?" he says. "I'm gonna do somethin' to you."

"You don't say?" I tell him. "You an' who else? By the time I've finished pushin' you around you'll be able to use your pan for a pen wiper. Anyhow what are you waitin' for?"

He gives a snort an' comes in again. This time he is a bit more careful. He comes in nice an' easy an' don't try any rushin' tactics. I wait for him. He slings a punch at my face that woulda knocked my nose outa the back of my head if it had connected. But it don't. I block it. Just when I catch this punch of his I do somethin' else he don't expect. I take a little step forward an' stamp on his foot *hard*.

He lets go a gasp like a steam whistle. I take advantage of the pause in hostilities to punch him in the belly hard. He goes a bright shade of green so I hit him in the same place again with the other fist, just to show there is no ill-feelin'.

He goes back, backin' toward the wall. I go after him, pretend I am goin' to run in an' then side-step an' hit him under the kidney on his right side. He says: "Oh . . . Jeez!" an' drops his hands. I sling a smash hit inta his face that sounds like somebody droppin' a bomb on a flour factory, an' then bring my elbow up under his chin.

The big boob is an air balloon. His knees start slidin' down from under him. I catch him under the chin with my left hand and hold him up while I measure him with my right. Then I let him have it.

I hit that heel such a bust on the beezer with a full right arm punch, that Cruelty to Children woulda sounded like an old-time melody compared with the noise he made. He slides down an' lies on the floor tryin' to figure out whether the end of the world has come or if he is still in one piece. I stand lookin' at him. Then I light a cigarette an' ease over to the table. I pick up the shotgun an' take out the charge. I walk back to him.

"Little sweetheart," I tell him. "Before I go inta further action on you I would like to repeat a question while you can still talk. Where is that guy Nikolls?"

He don't say anythin' that you could repeat, so I drop the gun butt on his ugly schnozzle. When I pick it up again he is lookin' more beautiful than ever. His pan looks like a map of the world with the possessions of the British Empire marked in red. Any time you saw this bozo comin' towards you on a dark night you would give up drinkin' because you would think a guy could *not* look like that.

I put the shotgun back on the table. Then I go over an' take a long look at Little Lord Fauntleroy, but I don't haveta worry about him. I reckon it will be quite a while before he even begins to take an interest in life.

I go out into the passage an' snap on my torch. I start easin' this joint an' believe it or not the dump has got so many passages an' turnin's that it looks like the Coney Island Maze in the rush hours.

After a bit I get inta a long stone corridor. I reckon that this is the corridor I saw from outside—the one that connects up the two farm buildings. When I get to the end of this I find a little wood doorway on my right with a shutter over it. I open the shutter an' take a look. Then I do a big grin. It looks like I have found Nikolls.

On the other side of the doorway is a little flight of wooden steps; an' at the bottom is a stone floor with a lot of straw lyin' about. The walls are stone an' the place looks like an old-time stable.

Nikolls is lyin' propped up against the wall opposite the doorway. There is an oil lamp burnin' 'an' the light is on his face. He is right out. He has got a lump on his dome as big as a roc's egg an' he is breathin' good an' heavy.

I go down an' take a look at him. Then I get it. The guy has been shot full of dope an' is busily engaged in sleepin' it off. By the look of him he's goin' to be like that for a long time. I lift up his eyelid an' try the old touch on the eyeball. But it don't work. Nikolls is right out for hours.

I take a look around but I do not see anything that interests me except one thing. By the side of Nikolls the straw is pressed down as if somebody else had been lyin' there. I reckon that was Dodo Malendas. I wonder what these guys have done with that jane.

I go back into the corridor, close the door an' the shutter. I go back to the other room where I left the other sleepin' beauty. I take a look at him. He is still like I left him.

I go back into the passage an' take a look. Halfway down there is a little sort of cupboard cut in the wall. There are some packin' cases an' rope lyin' there. I grab off a length of rope, go back to the room an' start work on the big slob. I rope him up so good that by the time I have finished he looks like an advertisement for the Christmas Spring puzzle. Then I drag him along to the cupboard, push him inside with his head in one of the packin' cases an' shut the door.

If I get back in time the guy will be O.K. If I don't maybe he's gonna die of suffocation. Anyhow I reckon that will be a new experience for the mug, an' life is made up of new sensations—or so they tell me.

I go back to the room an' take the telephone receiver off the hook, so's if anybody rings through they'll think the line ain't workin', after which I ease outside an' walk back to the car.

Maybe I oughta have stopped an' looked after Nikolls, an' maybe not. Anyhow I feel that I ain't worryin'. An' I got another date to keep.

Besides which I am beginnin' to think that the Callaghan-Nikolls set-up have tried to pull a fast one on me.

When I get back to the heap I take a look at my watch. It is half-past two. I reckon I will go an' see a dame. Because if you wanta see a dame there is no time like the present . . . if she is that sort of dame.

I let in the clutch an' roll off towards London. Somehow I caught the tune that sourpuss—the guy I have left in the cupboard—was singin'—"Everything is Jake."

An' why not?

CHAPTER NINE
DUCK, TAMARA!

I GO rollin' along the London road croonin' to myself an' tryin' to add up how many beans make five. Maybe this bit of arithmetic is gonna come out right sooner than you expect.

Maybe you guys will think I am nutty to be doin' what I'm doin' right now; but if you will think around things for a coupla minutes you will probably come to the conclusion that I am not so crazy as you thought I was.

I figure it this way. When that swell baby Tamara Phelps gave me her address an' told me she would like to see me sometime she'd got some sorta reason in her head. Maybe you think that she was stallin' me along at the time because I'd told her I was Willy Careras. Well . . . you'd be wrong, because both you an' me know now that at the time she knew goddam well that I was Lemmy Caution. An' I reckon she wanted me to have that address at the back of my mind.

Maybe you guys are goin' to say that knowin' I was me an' knowin' that I was anyhow partly wise to what she an' her boy friend Rudy Zimman was playin' at, she must be nuts to expect me to go along an' pay a call on her. But you would be wrong again.

This Tamara is a crook. An' crooks do funny things. No matter how brave they may think they are they are always carryin' a little load of scare along with 'em. They are always wonderin' when they are goin' to slip up an' somebody is goin' to put the linger on 'em.

The guy who talked about "honour amongst thieves" was just one jump ahead of the nuthouse. This bozo musta been so goddam crazy that any time he really got an idea, sparks musta shot outa his eyelids. There ain't such a thing as honour amongst crooks of any sort. Directly things start lookin' a bit funny the boys an' girls start lookin' for an "out." They start wonderin' how they can save their own skins.

Maybe, says you, but in this case it's different. You're gonna tell me that I'm wrong in thinkin' that Tamara Phelps would sell out the mob she was workin' with just because she was scared, an' your reason is goin' to be that she is stuck on Rudy Zimman an' that a dame would not sell out a guy she was crazy about.

Well . . . wouldn't she! I have known dames to be so nutty about a guy that they would practically cut their throats for him at any given moment—so long as the mug is playin' it the way they want it played. But directly he does somethin' they don't like—some little thing—these janes have gone shoutin' copper so quick that you would think there was a fire alarm.

I knew some swell, stream-lined baby up in Hathkin County away in the Ozark country who was workin' in with a hold-up guy. This hold-up bozo was a nice one at his job. He had medals for stickin' up cars in lonely parts of the country an' persuadin' the people inside 'em that it would be good for 'em to keep their trap shut about it. He worked this racket for years an' he had a honeybelle of a side-kicker who usta work it with him by the name of Wandy Long. This

Wandy was a sweet piece with a nice way an 'a tremulous mouth. She looked like an angel.

She usta stand on the side of the road an' look pathetic an' pretend she was thumbin' a ride some place. Smart slickers drivin' along the road on their own an' feelin' a little bored with life would take one look at Wandy's streamlined figure an' put their foot on the brake. They would think that this baby was nice cargo.

Once she was in the car it was all up with 'em. That baby could put your left eye out with an old penknife an' look sorry while she was doin' it. She was so sorta apologetic an' sweet an' her mouth was so tremulous an' invitin' that havin' your throat cut by this dame was practically an honour.

The hold-up guy she was stuck on was a bird named Freemer. Wandy had stuck around with this bozo for years. She thought a hell of a lot of that one. When he got knocked off an' sent up for five years she was waitin' at the gate when he came out. He usta knock her about an' kick her around plenty . . . but that was O.K.—she could take that all right.

One evenin' Freemer stuck up a car that was bein' driven by some dame from the big city. Freemer was workin' on his own an' stuck her up on the country road near Fells Place. He gets inta the car an' tells her to drive it off the road. She does this an' Freemer then proceeds to grab off this dame's wallet an' rings an' bracelets.

When he has done this he takes a look at the dame an' thinks that she ain't so bad, so he puts his arm around her an' gives her a kiss. What he don't know is that Wandy is away up on the hillside lookin' at this neckin' through an old spyglass that her grandpap used at the Battle of Gettysburg. O.K. Next mornin' a coupla State cops drive around to Freemer's place an' pull him in before he's even got the sleep out of his eyes, little Wandy havin' shot her mouth over the telephone to Police headquarters the night before.

All of which will show you guys that when it comes to love you never knew which way a dame is gonna jump. But maybe you know that. Maybe you're had to duck yourself some time.

I pull in at Mount Street just after three o'clock in the mornin'. It is not so warm an' I wish I had got an overcoat . . . but maybe somethin' is going to happen that will warm me up a little bit or maybe I'd rather stay cold.

I park the car in a side turnin' an' start walkin' around tryin' to find the Grange Apartments. After a bit I connect. The Grange Apartment is a swell sorta dump formin' two sides of a square on the street an' a side street. The place is good an' dark an' when I find the main entrance it is all locked up. I ease around lookin' for some place I can get in an' away down the side street I find the Fire Guard entrance. There is a glass door with a black-out curtain behind it an' it is not locked.

I go inside. There is a corridor in front of me with a coupla elevator wells in it. The corridor is a long one an' there are blued-out lights in the ceilin' makin' it look very goofy an' mysterious.

I start gum-shoein' along the corridor towards one of the lift wells, an' I am lookin' around for an indicator to show me if Tamara is livin' here, although it won't be so hot if she is registered here under some other name. Just when I get near the elevator gates I hear it comin' down. I get a big rush of instinct to the head. Just on my left is a little sub-corridor leadin' off the main one. I duck inta this an' stand up against the wall, because just for one moment I get the idea that Rudy Zimman might be in that lift.

I hear the gates open; then somebody gets out an' passes the end of the little passageway in which I am standin'. It ain't Rudy Zimman. No, sir! Believe it or not, it is Dodo Malendas! I give a big sigh. This is what the wise guys call another convolution in this case—an' that is this jane Dodo Malendas who is supposed to have been put in on this job by Mrs. Lorella Owen to find out where Julia Wayles is, an' who by every sort of reasonin' oughta be somebody that the Rudy Zimman-Tamara Phelps mob would wanta push outa the way good an' quick, payin' social visits here at Tamara Phelps' place at three o'clock in the mornin'.

Ain't life wonderful? What the hell has happened to this dame since somebody hi-jacked her an' Windemere Nikolls who is lyin' doped to the world at that dump near Leatherhead? What has happened that makes this dame come easin' along here? I get to thinkin' that this is one of them cases where every time you add up two an' two it makes about seven.

I wait a few minutes so as to give Dodo plenty of time to get out of the building; then I light a cigarette. I go back inta the main corridor an' walk back to the street entrance. I go out inta Mount Street an' start lookin' around for a telephone booth. After a bit I find one. I go in, look up the number of the Grange Apartments an' ring through. After four or five minutes some guy with a yawn in his voice says "hello."

"This is very urgent," I tell him. "I just gotta speak to Miss Tamara Phelps. Can you put me through?"

He asks me to wait a minute while he looks at the list. Then he says: "Oh yes, Miss Phelps is on the second floor. Just a minute, sir."

There is a pause. I hang on, blow in' smoke rings, wonderin' what sorta reception I am goin' to get when I tell Tamara who I am, an' whether she is goin' to hang up the receiver an' take a run-out powder as quick as if the devil was after her. Maybe she's goin' to be plenty scared when she knows who's talkin' to her.

She comes on the line. She says in that low cool voice of hers: "Hello! Who's speakin'?"

I grin inta the mouthpiece.

"Hello, Tamara," I tell her. "How're you goin'? This is Lemmy Caution. Ain't you surprised to hear from me?"

She gives a little low gurgle.

"Well, I'll be doggoned!" she says. "You know, Lemmy, they always told me you was a hard guy to get rid of, although I must admit I thought Rudy was goin' to get rid of you all right the last time I saw you."

"Yeah?" I say. "An' with your assistance too, sweetheart. Ain't you the nice baby?"

"Look, pal," she says, "ain't anybody ever told you that it is a bad thing to come to conclusions too quick? Where are you speakin' from?"

"I've just this minute blown inta London," I tell her. "I'm talkin' from some call box at the Piccadilly end of Regent Street."

"All right," she says. "Well, you come round here good an' quick. I wanta talk to you. An' when you hear what I got to say you'll be glad you came."

"Yeah?" I tell her. "What guarantee do I get that some punk is not stickin' around behind your front door with a sub-Thompson gun?"

"Have a heart, Lemmy," she says. "Didn't I tell you when you came out to that Waterfall Inn place, trying to kid the world you was Willy Careras come to see me, that I knew who you was. Maybe you'd be surprised if I told you I was on your side."

"I wouldn't be surprised—I'd be slain," I tell her. "Any time you're on my side, baby, I'm goin' to sign a partnership agreement with the devil. . . . But I'll get around as soon as I can."

"Do that thing," she says. "I'm on the second floor here—No. 43. So long, pal." She hangs up.

I get outa the phone box an' start walkin' around the houses takin' up the time it oughta take me to get from Piccadilly Circus, because you mugs will realise that I don't want this dame to know I was talkin' from practically next door, in case she got the idea in her head that I mighta seen Dodo Malendas.

I smoke a coupla cigarettes; then I turn round an' go back towards the Grange Apartments. Maybe I am a mug, but I'll try anythin' once an' if I like it maybe twice. . . .

When I ring the apartment door bell an' Tamara opens it I get a shock. That old palooka Confucius that I told you about before said "A beautiful woman who is wicked is still beautiful. Fools see her beauty and not her wickedness." Well, maybe the old geezer was right, because I'm tellin' you that when I look at this baby framed in the doorway, with a soft sorta rose-shaded light behind her, my heart gives a kick. She may be wicked but she looks very good to me. An' if this Confucius guy had been stickin' around he'd have probably thought the same thing himself. Maybe he'd have wished he was a bit younger.

She is wearin' a pair of oyster silk pyjamas with the neck cut high—Russian fashion—an' over 'em she's got a long sorta lacy beige house-coat. I don't know what the lace is but it is good. Her hair is nicely done an' tied back with a ribbon. An' her pretty lips are parted over a set of teeth that are so white that they are just nobody's business. She says—just as if I was an old pal:

"Hello, Lemmy. . . . Come in! An' look . . . when I say there ain't anybody but us in this flat I mean that."

"That's O.K., Tamara," I tell her, "because even if there was somebody here I wouldn't worry. I gotta gun under my arm an' you'd be surprised how quick I'm goin' to use that rod if I see anything that smells even a little bit."

She says: "Aw, Lemmy . . . why don't you be your age?"

She turns around an' leads the way across the hallway inta the room on the other side. I close the door behind me, hang up my hat an' go after her. She goes over to the sideboard an' starts mixin' some drinks. Suddenly she turns around facin' me. She puts her hands behind her on the edges of the sideboard. She throws me a sweet smile. She says: "Gee, Lemmy, it's good to have you here. Just for once I'm feeling happy."

"You don't say!" I tell her. "Me too . . . I never knew what happiness was till I met you, Tamara—an' then it was too late. But let's cut out the neat stuff. I wanta talk to you. You're in a spot, aren't you? What're you doin'—tryin' to duck?"

She goes on mixin' the drinks. She throws me a quick sidelong look over her shoulder. "So I'm in a spot, am I?" she says. "Why, what have I done, Lemmy?"

I grin. "What have you done?" I tell her. "What about you an' Rudy Zimman tryin' to bump me off at Schribner's place in Betchworth? I suppose that don't count?"

She looks surprised. She even looks a little bit hurt.

"Me try an' bump you off," she says. "I like that! Who do you think it was put her foot on the electric light globe in the standard lamp when you knocked it over, so that Rudy shouldn't get another shot at you? I practically saved your life."

"Like hell you did," I tell her.

She gives another of them delicious little gurgles. I'm tellin' you mugs that when that dame laughs that way it sends tremors runnin' up an' down my spine. She comes over to me with a drink in her hand.

"It ain't even poisoned," she says. "It's just good Scotch whisky. You drink that an' sit down an' listen to me."

I sit down. The whisky tastes very good.

"I'm listenin'," I tell her. "But I'm tellin' you one thing, Tamara. It had better be good. I'm beginnin' to lose my temper with you mugs."

She looks sorta serious. "You don't mean that, Lemmy," she says. "You only think you mean it."

"I see," I tell her. "Well, what do I mean?"

She looks at me an' her eyes are so big an' round that you would think this dame couldn't tell a lie even if she was paid for it. "What you mean is, Lemmy," she says, "that you're fed up with Rudy Zimman—not *me*."

"That's a nice one," I crack back at her. "I suppose you an' Rudy ain't workin' in harness? I suppose you haven't been his side-kicker for years? I suppose you ain't in love with that guy? Everybody knows you've been stringin' around with Rudy for four five years, Tamara. So you'd better think up a better one than that."

She looks at the ceilin'. She looks like the dame in charge of the Sunday School class at Three Elks, Pa., tryin' to think up the text, for the next session. She says:

"Look, Lemmy, you get around plenty. You haveta know things. Don't you know that some dames have to do things that they don't want to do?"

I take a gulp of whisky.

"You're goin' to start makin' me cry in a minute, Tamara," I say. "You'll be tellin' me next that you come up from the chicken farm in Minnesota to try your luck in the big city; that you bumped inta Rudy Zimman by mistake an' never had a chance since. I've heard that story so many times that it's got mistletoe growin' on it."

"Yes?" she says. "Well, this time it's true."

She leans forward an' puts her hands on the arms of the chair. There are tears in her eyes. Sittin' there like that, she looks sweet an' sorta aristocratic. That's what I think for a minute. Then it hits me like a well-aimed brick that if this dame has got aristocratic blood in her veins it musta been by transfusion.

"Some of you guys are so cynical," she says, "that you don't believe anything. Maybe that stuff about the chicken farm is truer than you know."

She leans back an' puts her hands behind her head. She goes on: "It's funny you talkin' about a chicken farm because that's where I was raised, an' I wish I'd never left it. But I suppose I was like every other sorta girl. The only place I ever thought would be good was the big city. I used to stand down on the railway line where it cut across the fields behind the farm, an' watch the trains go by. I sorta envied them because they was goin' some place I couldn't get to."

"Well," I tell her, "what are you grumblin' about? You got there."

"Sure I got there," she says. "I asked for trouble an' I've got it—plenty trouble." She gives a sigh. "I got a job in a department store in Chicago," she goes on. "I was doin' well and I was happy . . . an' then I haveta meet Rudy."

Her eyes flash. Just at that moment she looks as if Rudy wouldn't have much of a chance if she got her hooks on him.

"I was a kid," she says. "Not only that—I was a mug." She smiles at me. "Rudy's got a nice line when he wantsta," she says. "An' he used it on me plenty. Maybe you're not goin' to believe this either," she says. "But I thought Rudy was goin' to marry me. I wasn't the sorta girl who goes kickin' around with a guy on the loose, but it was a year before I found out what he was an' when I tried to make a get-out of it, he told me what he'd do to me if I scrammed. The trouble was," she goes on, "I knew too much for Rudy by then."

I grin at her. "Well, I'm not believin' or disbelievin' you, baby," I tell her. "But why this sudden anti to Rudy? He's been pretty good to you, hasn't he—in the way that a mobster is good to a jane like you?"

"Has he?" she says. "Rudy's not so hot. He's a louse an' he's mean. That punk is so generous that he throws diamonds around like a guy with no arms."

She gets up an' comes over to me. She takes away my empty glass an' fills it. I notice when she pours herself a drink it is just ginger ale.

"So you're not drinkin?" I tell her.

"No," she says. "I'm on a diet." She smiles at me. "I have to watch my figure," she says.

"You're tellin' me!" I say. "I'm not on a diet, but I have to watch it too. Has nobody ever told you you've got somethin', Tamara?"

She comes back with a drink. She stands in front of me with a whisky in her hand, lookin' down at me.

"If I've got plenty, where's it got me?" she says. "You tell me that. Bein' pushed around the place by Rudy, bein' roped in on every lousy scheme he's got; an' I don't like some of his ideas."

I don't say anythin'. I think maybe this dame is goin' to get down to business.

"The reason why I wanted to see you, Lemmy," she says, "is just this: Believe it or not I don't know what Rudy is playin', an' even if I did I wouldn't like it. That's the way I feel."

I nod my head. "You think the time has come to duck, Tamara, hey?" I say.

She shrugs her shoulders.

"How do I duck?" she asks. "What am I goin' to do? Where am I goin' to go? I'm in this goddam country an' I can't even get out of it—not the way I'm fixed."

I think I'll try a line with this dame. I say:

"You could get outa this country if you wanted to easy enough. I could get you out."

She nods. She looks at me sorta serious.

"That's why I'm talkin' to you," she says. "You're a 'G' man—you can make things right for me here. You can fix me up with a passport. Maybe you can get me back to the States—some place where Rudy couldn't get his hooks on me."

"Why worry about Rudy?" I ask her. "He ain't goin' to get his hooks on anybody by the time I'm through with him."

"That's what *I* thought," she says. "But he's still got pals."

"Look, honey," I tell her, "you do somethin' for me. You go an' park yourself in that chair over there an' tell me a few things."

"O.K.," she says.

She goes an' sits down. She crosses her legs sorta prettily. I told you mugs that this baby has a nice line in legs, and believe it or not she knows how to use them. In point of fact I think there is goddam little that this dame don't know.

"You tell me about this Julia Wayles business," I tell her.

She makes a face.

"I wish I could," she says. "I know about as much as anybody else does in this game. Zimman is no mug. He believes that what you don't Know you can't shoot your mouth about. He's got a lot of people workin' for him over here, but if you was to ask any one of 'em what they are doin' they probably wouldn't know."

"Maybe not," I tell her, "but you gotta know somethin', haven't you?"

"That's right," she says. "What I know is this. Whatever this idea was about Julia Wayles, it originated with a guy called Jakie Larue, who's serving a prison sentence in Leavenworth."

I cock my ears. This sounds like business.

"The idea was," she goes on, "that Rudy should fix it that Larue was sprung. But they couldn't do it. They tried two or three times to get him out but there was nothin' doin'. The next idea was apparently that Rudy should handle the business. Well, if this thing was a snatch—an' I think it was—it wasn't carried out in the ordinary way. It was a classy sorta job, see? I don't know how it was done but somehow they got this Wayles dame over here. She was got over here first an' that mug Schribner was planted as a sorta reception committee to wait for her."

"Just a minute," I tell her. "What is this Schribner like?"

"A punk with brains," she says, "an' nasty brains at that. I don't like that guy. That's all I know about him."

I nod my head. "Go on," I tell her.

"Well, when this Wayles dame was over here, we came over. Some other guys came over too, but on different boats, and the job was very nicely fixed. All these mugs were issued with passports that were good enough to get 'em through the Customs at New York an' into this country." She gives a wry sorta grin. "I don't know whether they'll be good enough to get 'em out again, but havin' regard to the fact that you're around, I doubt it," she says.

"You tell me somethin', Tamara," I say. "What was the idea in snatchin' this Wayles baby?"

"Search me," she says. "I've never seen her an' I don't know that she amounts to anything very much. She certainly ain't an heiress an' I've never heard anybody talk about a ransom yet."

"I see," I say. "So it looks as if the job wasn't done for dough?"

"Not so far as I know," she says. "It might be, but I don't know."

"Where is this Julia Wayles?" I ask her.

She shakes her head.

"I don't know," she says, "an' I don't believe anybody knows except Rudy Zimman. But . . ." she throws me a smile. She looks sideways at me along her long eyelashes—"I'm goin' to know," she says. "In a minute somebody's got to know where little Julia is an' I'm goin' to find out. An' that's where I do a deal with you."

"Go on," I tell her. "What's the deal?"

"Ain't it obvious?" she says. "I'm goin' to find out where this dame Julia Wayles is. Then, when I've found out, I'm goin' to take a chance. I'm going to let you know. I'm goin' to fix it so that you can get her . . ." she sighs. "I'd like her to be the one dame that Rudy didn't make anything out of."

"An' then?" I say.

"Well," she says, "you'll knock Rudy off, won't you? When I tell you where Wayles is, you won't have any difficulty in findin' where he is. You get him Once you've got him, he'll talk all right, when he knows there's no out. Rudy is only a tough guy when he's got all his pals around him."

I don't say anythin'. But this little bit of information don't match up with what I've heard about Rudy Zimman.

"Well," she goes on, "when you've got this Wayles dame an' Zimman, you get me out of here. I'm goin' back to start over, again with a clean slate. An' this is the way I'm tryin' to clean it."

She sits there lookin' at me like a baby. I reckon butter wouldn't melt in this dame's mouth.

"That sounds O.K. to me," I tell her, "but I'd like to ask you a few more questions. Do you know anythin' about a dame called Dodo Malendas?"

She nods her head. "Yeah," she says, "I do. I heard about this dame. Somebody put her in pretendin' to be me. They tried to get her next to Schribner so's she could find out where Julia was. Well . . ." She gives a little smile—"it looks as if she's all washed up, don't it?"

"Would you know where this Malendas piece is?" I ask her.

She shakes her head. "How should I know?" she says. "I've never seen the dame."

I get up. "And you don't know anythin' else?" I tell her.

"I've told you the book, Lemmy," she says. "You know as much as I do. Well, are you goin' to play with me?"

I nod my head.

"O.K., Tamara," I tell her. "I'll play ball. You fix up to let me know where Julia is. You fix it so that I can get my hands on Rudy Zimman and the other boys who are workin' with him, an' I'm goin' to look after you. I'll see they don't get at you. I'll see you get a passport back to the States. I'll see you get a clean bill with the cops when you get there." I look at her sorta goofy. "How does that suit, kid?" I say.

She gets up. She comes over to me. She says:

"That suits me fine. You know, Lemmy," she says, "the first time I saw you—an' that was a long time ago—somebody pointed you out to me in the street in New York—I thought you was a hell of a guy. I haven't changed my opinion."

She puts her arms around my neck an' she gives me a kiss. Believe it or not this dame could run a correspondence course in kissin'. When she takes her mouth away from mine it's like takin' the porous plaster off grandpa's chest. You know—one of those sorta kisses. Then she stands away from me. She says:

"That's all right. You tell me where I can get at you."

I tell her. I give her the number of my apartment on Jermyn Street an' the telephone number. I tell her if I ain't there she can leave a message with the janitor. She says O.K. She walks across with me to the door. Then she hands me my hat. She says:

"Look, Lemmy. Maybe it ain't gonna be too good for me to come around an' see you at your apartment . . . that is if I *want* to see you. Maybe we better meet somewhere else . . . somewhere that's easier."

"Such as where?" I ask her.

"Schribner's cottage at Betchworth is the place," she says. "There's nobody there, but I got the keys. I can let you have 'em. That would be a good spot for us to contact if we haveta get together."

"That's O.K. by me," I tell her. "But what about Schribner? What's he doin'? Ain't he there?"

She shakes her head.

"Don't you worry about Max Schribner," she says. "He's all washed up. That guy has made a mess of this business. He's so dumb that he thinks circular letters have to be posted through a round hole. He's a punk. The guy is clever sometimes . . . but maybe he's a bit *too* clever."

"I see . . ." I light myself a fresh cigarette. "So Schribner is all washed up," I say. "Well . . . what's happened to him? Has Rudy given him the heat?"

She smiles—sorta mysterious. It looks to me like Schribner has got himself in bad with Rudy.

"I wouldn't know," she says. "But you can leave him right out. Max Schribner is through an' you don't haveta worry about him."

"O.K.," I tell her. "Well . . . his dump at Betchworth would be a good place." I give her a big grin. "Anyhow it's right in the heart of the Rudy Zimman country," I tell her. "So let's have the keys, baby."

She goes over to the sideboard an' opens a drawer. She takes out a coupla keys an' hands 'em to me.

"There you are, Lemmy," she says. She throws me a wicked little smile. "The idea of havin' a secret meetin' place with you goes well with me," she says. She sighs. "You do something to me, Lemmy. You sorta fascinate me."

I don't say anythin'. I am thinkin' just what I would like to do to this baby if I had my way. I reckon it would be somethin' with boilin' oil in it.

"So long, pal," she says. "An' remember one thing—I'm workin' for you now. I'm on your side."

"That's O.K. by me," I tell her. "So long, Tamara."

I close the door behind me, an' when I tell you mugs that I don't even laugh till I get out on the street I'm tellin' you the truth.

I light myself a cigarette an' ease around to where I have left the heap. I get inside, start her up an' roll off on my way back to the Leatherhead dump. I get a hustle on because I have got plenty to do to-night before I get through an' I am so goddam tired right now that I could go to sleep for a few years without even turnin' over.

An' I have got plenty to think about. This stuff that Tamara has been puttin' over on me sounds like dynamite. Maybe some of you guys will be thinkin' that there is a chance that this dame is on the up an' up. Well . . . if you are, all I can say is the sooner you get yourself measured up for a strait jacket the better.

I reckon there is just enough truth in what that cute baby has put across to be dangerous. Tamara is no mug.

The thing that is stickin' out as bein' the most important bit of business is the stuff about Schribner. You remember that she said that "Schribner was all washed up an' right outa the job." Well . . . why? If Schribner was important enough to be in this business from the start why do they have to throw this mug overboard? Maybe I got the answer to that one an' maybe to-morrow—*if* I'm still kickin' around—I'm gonna find out.

Then there is the Dodo Malendas business. Dodo Malendas, who is supposed to be workin' for Mrs. Lorella Owen, tryin' to find out where Julia Wayles is, is playin' some game on her own an' rushin' around an' havin' secret sessions with Tamara. It looks as if this baby is doin' a little double-crossin'. Well . . . maybe we can find out about that too.

Then there is this guy Nikolls. I reckon *he* has been doin' a little funny business on the side. But I think I got that worked out all right.

I got a lot of ideas. Some of 'em may be wrong, but they're all pointin' somewhere an' I'm goin' to try 'em all out. Anyhow it's gonna be funny—even if I *am* wrong.

I throw my cigarette stub outa the window an' light a fresh one. I start wonderin' what this Julia Wayles is gonna be like when we eventually get a look at her. Right from the start of this business this baby has been the queen-pin of the whole works an' I don't even know what she looks like. By this time I am through Fulham an' on the Wimbledon road. When I get on the bye-pass I put my foot down an' let her go.

Maybe, before we get through with it this is gonna be a good night.

CHAPTER TEN
CHINESE STUFF

IT IS just after five when I get back to the Leatherhead dump. I park the car where I left it before an' I go over the little bridge towards the back of the house. There is a mist all over the countryside, an' it feels good an' damp. I feel I could do with a whole lot of whisky. I stick around the back of the house for a bit an' listen, but I can't hear a thing. So I get in the same way as I went in before.

I go upstairs an' gumshoe along the corridor until I come to the cupboard where I left Sourpuss. I open it up an' flash the torch on him. The guy has come to all right. He is lyin' there trussed up like I left him, with his head doubled over, lookin' at me out of the corner of his eye. An' he looks as if he don't like me a lot.

"Well, Sourpuss," I tell him. "How's it goin'? Maybe I'll come an' untruss you in a few minutes, an' when I do you're goin' to talk."

"Yeah?" he says. "Who's goin' to make me?"

"I am," I tell him. "An' don't get any ideas about me bein' soft in the process either. Between now an' when I see you again I'll think somethin' up for you."

I close the door quietly an' go gum-shoein' along the passage till I come to the door with the shutter in it where I looked through an' saw Nikolls. I take a look. Nikolls is still lyin' there, but he's not breathin' so heavily. I reckon this guy has slept off the dope they gave him an' is now just asleep. Then I give a big grin, because lyin' beside him, with some cords stuck around her wrists an' ankles as if she was tied up, is Dodo Malendas!

She is lyin' on her back lookin' at the ceilin'. She looks sorta innocent. I get it. When they hi-jacked Nikolls an' her at my apartment on Jermyn Street, they brought 'em both here. They doped Nikolls so's he wouldn't know what was goin' on: then after he'd gone out they made a deal with this baby. Probably she talked an' talked plenty. She told 'em all sorts of things an' I reckon mainly she told 'em about Mrs. Lorella Owen. Well, whoever it was she was talkin' to—an' maybe it was Rudy Zimman himself—thinks it is important enough to let this dame go an' tell Tamara. I reckon they throw a big scare inta Dodo—big enough for them to think she wouldn't rat on 'em—alter which somebody runs her up to town, an' she has a session with Tamara. What they don't know is that I see her comin' out of the apartment.

Then I phone Tamara an' we have our meetin'. She pulls a story on me that is the result of what she's heard from Dodo.

In the meantime they have brought Dodo back here. They stick her in the straw beside Nikolls so that when that mug comes to he'll think she's been there all the time. The last thing he will remember is that both he an' Dodo were put inta this dump.

The guys who brought her back musta missed Sourpuss. They musta wondered where he was but they probably never thought of lookin' in the cupboard. Maybe they thought this mug had gone for a walk an' would be back. Anyway, I'm goin' to chance that. I stick my head through the shutter an' I say nice an' quiet:

"Hello, Dodo! How's it goin'?"

She looks up an' sees me.

"Gee," she says. "Caution! What a surprise."

"That's nothin'," I tell her. "You're goin' to get so many surprises, baby, you're goin' to wonder what's hit you. An' don't pretend you can't move because you're tied up. I bet you can get outa those ropes any time you want to. I know all about it, kid. I know you haven't been back here long from seein' Tamara Phelps. I saw you comin' out of her apartment."

"Oh well," she says. "Life is full of surprises, ain't it?"

She starts wrigglin' outa the cords that are around her wrists. I go down the stairs an' I stand lookin' down at her. Nikolls is still sleepin' like a log.

"Look, baby," I tell her, "maybe I'm gettin' wise to you. You tell me somethin'. When those guys who knocked you an' Nikolls off at my apartment in Jermyn Street brought you here, they made some sorta deal with you, didn't they?"

She sits up. She looks good an' scared.

"Something like that," she says.

"O.K.," I tell her "Well, my advice to you is to talk. If you don't you'll find yourself stuck in a English jail for about fifteen years, an' how would you like that? Now come on, baby, spill it, an' don't raise your voice too much. I don't want that mug to wake up. I want him to think what they wanted him to think—that you've been here all the time."

She says: "What the hell is a girl to do? All the time I'm tryin' to give a square deal to the people who've employed me, an' I find I'm always gettin' myself in a jam."

138 | PETER CHEYNEY

"Hooey," I tell her. "Any time you try an' give anybody a square deal you'll probably get paralysed through shock. . . . But go on . . . what happened?"

"Oh well," she says, "a coupla guys stuck up Nikolls an' me at your dump. They brought us back here. When they got here Nikolls tried some funny business so they hit him over the head; then they gave him a shot of morphia or something in the arm. Well . . . they told me I'd gotta talk or it wouldn't be so good for me. They told me what they was goin' to do to me if I didn't talk." She makes a little face. "It didn't sound very nice so I talked."

"What did you tell 'em?" I ask her.

"I told 'em about Mrs. Owen," she says. "I told 'em I was workin' for her. I told 'em that she'd got an 'in' with Scotland Yard here. . . ."

"I see," I say. "So Mrs. Owen has got an 'in' with Herrick at Scotland Yard, has she? This is interestin'." I sit down on my heels beside her. "Look, pal," I tell her, "you tell me somethin', an' if you don't give me the works what those Zimman boys said they'd do to you is goin' to be nothin' to what I'm goin' to do with you. Just who is Mrs. Lorella Owen? Why is she wearin' grey wigs an' puttin' lumps in her face to make her look different?"

She thinks for a minute. She looks straight in front of her. After a bit she says:

"Well, I suppose you've got to know. She's Karen Wayles—Julia Wayles' sister."

I nod my head. "So that's the way it goes," I say. "So she's Karen, an' I suppose she come over here tryin' to find where her sister Julia was. Is that right?"

She nods her head. "That's it," she says.

"An' I suppose she gave you the job of comin' over here an' helpin' her. Because you'd worked around with the mobs in New York she thought that you'd have a better chance of gettin' next to these mugs over here than she had on her own. Is that it?"

"That's right," she says.

I light another cigarette. I sit there on my heels lookin' at her, but while I am lookin' at her I am doin' some quiet thinkin', because although this story sounds very plausible it creaks in one or two places. Why should Karen Wayles have this "in" with Scotland

Yard, an' why the hell is Herrick doin' all sorts of things behind my back just because Karen Wayles wants him to do it? Who the hell is Karen Wayles anyway?

I start thinkin' about my conversation with Mrs. Lorella Owen, when she told me she was an old friend of the family. Well, what did she say about Karen Wayles? She said Karen was workin' for the W.P.A. in New York some place, an' she sorta suggested that Karen was a stupid sorta dame. So she was talkin' about herself. Well . . . well . . . well . . .! It just shows you how goddam clever some of these dames can be. "O.K., baby," I tell her. "Well, what happened when you went to see Tamara?"

"I told her just that," she says. "I told her that Mrs. Owen was Karen. I told her what she was tryin' to do."

"An' how did Tamara like that?" I ask her.

"She wasn't worryin'," says Dodo. "She knew goddam well that neither Herrick nor Karen, nor you for that matter, knew where Julia was. Tamara thinks she's still sittin' pretty. She's got the ace card in the pack. She's got Julia."

"I get it," I tell her. "It looks like this Julia is a pretty valuable sorta cuss, don't it?"

I blow a coupla smoke rings. I reckon Tamara musta been pretty pleased when I phone her so soon after she'd seen Dodo Malendas. She was all ready for me. She'd got a sweet line for me. I get to thinkin' that this is one of the sweetest set-ups I have ever been in in my life.

"O.K.," I tell her. "Now look, baby, you get upstairs an' get some water. It's time we brought this mug back to life."

"All right," she says.

She gets up. We go up the stairs an' along the corridor. In the corner of the big room where I met Sourpuss, is a water tap. She finds a glass an' fills it. I ease out to where I left the car an' bring the flask back. When I get back she is givin' Nikolls a drink. The big mug is sittin' up with his back against the wall lookin' surprised.

"Well, how's it goin', pal?" I ask him. "So they took you for a ride."

He puts his hand on his head. I believe I told you mugs he has got a lump on his dome as big as a roc's egg.

"You're tellin' me," he says. "Well, it ain't the first time I've been stuck up. But why they have to slip a lotta sleep juice inta me I don't know."

"That's nothin'," I tell him. "They probably wanted to keep you quiet. How're you feelin'?"

I give him a shot of the whisky. He takes a gulp that nearly drains the flask. "I'm feelin' good," he says. "All I'd like to do is to get my hooks on those bastards."

"Maybe you will, Nikolls," I tell him. "But we've gotta do somethin' first."

"Such as?" he says.

I nod my head towards the Malendas.

"The first thing we've gotta do is to take care of this baby," I tell him. "I think we'll tie her up good an' proper so's she can't move. I think she might be dangerous."

"Listen here," says Dodo.

I put up my hand.

"Look, kid," I tell her. "Take a tip from me. The trouble with you is you don't know which side you're playin' on an' there is nothin' worse in life than being undecided. So I'm makin' up your mind for you. You're goin' to play on our side. An' any time you get any other ideas it is not goin' to be so good for you. So keep your trap shut, an' take what's comin' to you. Get busy, Nikolls."

Nikolls gets up an' stretches himself. I give him a cigarette, after which he gets to work on Dodo. By the time he's finished with this baby she's tied up so tight that she looks like a silkworm.

"O.K.," he says. "What's the next move?"

I pick up the oil lamp.

"The next thing is that you an' me are goin' to have a little session," I tell him. "We'll leave this baby here, an' I hope she's not afraid of the dark. So long, Dodo."

It is nearly six o'clock in the mornin' when we get around to a discussion as to what we should do with Sourpuss. Nikolls has found some tea an' stuff an' we are sittin' in the big room with the fire made up havin a meal.

"Well, what are we goin to do from now on?" says Nikolls.

I don't tell him. First of all I'm not tellin' this guy anythin' for reasons which you will see pretty soon, an' secondly I gotta find out just what is goin' to happen around this dump. I tell Nikolls about Sourpuss.

"This guy is tied up in a cupboard along the corridor," I tell him. "He's a very tough guy. He says he ain't goin' to talk. Well, he's gotta talk. I think maybe we'll have a lotta trouble with that guy makin' him open up."

Nikolls fumbles around in his pocket for a packet of Lucky Strikes. He hands one to me. Then he strikes the match on the seat of his pants. He says:

"Did I ever tell you about that blonde I met up with near the Saratoga race course one year?"

I tell him no. I am wonderin what the hell this has gotta do with makin' Sourpuss open up. Nikolls says:

"She was a sweet dame—sorta passionate if you get me. She fell for me in a big way." He looks sorta coy. "I just did somethin' to that dame," he says. "She couldn't visualise life without me. You get what I mean? I have that effect on some dames."

I nod my head. I reckon this mug hates himself.

"I get it," I say. "So she was crazy about you. So what! What has this gotta do with Sourpuss?"

"I'm comin' to that in a minute," he says. "Well, I was stuck on some other baby, an' I'm a guy who never believes in crossin' his wires. So I gave this blonde the stand-off. Well, she didn't like it. She has a session with herself an' she comes to the conclusion that she's goin' to make me play ball. An' does she do it!"

"You don't say," I tell him. "What did she do, Windy?"

"I'll tell you," he says "She hires a coupla thugs to pick me up one evenin' when I'm goin' round to meet the other girl friend. They take me round to her flat an' they tie me in an Oxford chair in the kitchen. She tells me that if I don't give up this other dame an' stick around with her she's goin' to make things plenty tough for me. I give her the big ha-ha. I ask her who the hell she thinks she is that she can talk to me like that. Well . . . she went to work on me."

I grin.

"What do you mean?" I tell him. "You ain't tellin' me she went to work on you with a piece of rubber pipin' or somethin'. You're not goin' to tell me that a dame who was stuck on you like this one was supposed to be was goin' to slug you around."

"Oh no," he says sorta casual. "She didn't do anything like that. She'd got somethin' better than that."

"What was it?" I ask him.

"Chinese stuff," he says. "She used the Chinese water torture on me. An' boy, is it good! By the time that dame was through with me I'd have just done anythin'." He thinks for a minute. "An' believe me I did," he says. He smiles sorta reminiscently.

"The suggestion bein'," I tell him, "that we use this Chinese stuff on this Sourpuss mug?"

"That's the way it goes," he says. "That stuff would make anybody talk. An' it don't even hurt 'em. It just drives 'em nuts." He yawns. "I reckon it's the cutest torture I know," he says, "an' I know plenty."

I light a cigarette. "O.K.," I say. "Get busy."

Nikolls gets up an' stretches himself. It looks to me like this big boy is enjoyin' the idea of havin' a crack back at some of these mugs around here. He goes out an' in a coupla minutes he comes back, draggin' Sourpuss along the floor behind him. He ain't bein' gentle either. He leaves the big mug lyin' in front of me an' he goes over to the water tap. I can hear him tinkerin' about behind me.

"Look," I say to Sourpuss, "I want a little information from you. Not very much because maybe you don't know much. But just one or two things. First of all when do you expect Rudy's boys to come around here again? You're in charge of this dump, ain't you? When they slung this Nikolls guy an' the dame who was with him in here, how long were they goin' to leave 'em here for, an' when are they comin' back? You know that, don't you?"

"I know it," he says. "But I'm not tellin' you."

"O.K.," I tell him. "That's all right." I lean back in the chair. "Get to work on him, Windy," I say.

I stick around an' smoke. I watch Nikolls while he starts this business. I've seen a lotta things in my time, but I have never seen this Chinese water torture before, an' I reckon you can always learn. Nikolls sticks a chair in front of the sink. Then he takes an empty bean tin an' punches a hole in the bottom. He gets a piece of string an' hangs this tin from one of the rafters directly above the chair. Then he sits in the chair an' yanks it about until he's got it right underneath the hole in the tin. Then he sticks Sourpuss in the chair an' ties his head an' shoulders against the back of it so's he can't move. Then he fills up the bean tin with water from a jug an' moves it just a little bit so's it starts swingin'. Then he comes back an' gets another chair an' puts it by the side of mine. He sits down with his hands folded across his belly, watchin' Sourpuss.

The water outa the can starts to drip on Sourpuss's head, but the can is movin' a little bit so the drop don't always fall in the same place. Sometimes it even misses him. Sourpuss yawns. I reckon he's sorta bored with this business.

He says: "Is this stuff supposed to make me talk? What do you guys think I am—a cissy?"

"That's O.K., pal," says Nikolls. "You wait a minute." He says to me, "This is goin' to take about an hour."

"All right," I tell him. "If it works you wake me up. If it don't we'll try something else."

I put my head against the back of the chair an' I go to sleep. I think I told you guys I was plenty tired.

Nikolls gives me a jab in the ribs. I wake up. He's grinnin' at me.

"O.K.," he says. "The big boy has decided to talk." Nikolls looks at his wrist-watch. He seems sorta pleased. "It took an hour an' ten minutes," he says. "The guy was tough."

I open my eyes an' take a look at the mug who's tied up in the chair by the sink. He's cryin' like a baby. I reckon this Chinese stuff is good. I go over to him. He starts whimperin' for somebody to turn off the water. Nikolls takes the can down.

"Well, pal," I tell him, "so you're gonna talk. Well, say your piece an' if you don't tell us the truth we'll fix a whole bathful of water above that dome of yours an' leave you there till you go nutty."

"O.K.," he says. "There ain't anybody comin' back here. I'm supposed to stick around here for two or three days an' look after these mugs an' not let 'em get out of the place. There's plenty of food an' stuff here. They also told me I'm not to go outside myself.

They reckon in two or three days' time they're goin' to pick me up an' these other two mugs, an' take us off some place. That's all I know an' that's the truth."

I reckon this guy is tellin' the truth. I reckon he's too scared to do anythin' else. It's wonderful what a little water can do in the right place.

"How long have you been over here?" I ask him.

"About seven weeks," he says.

"Did you come over with Rudy Zimman?" I say. "How did you get over here an' how many thugs are there with you?"

"I came over with four of them," he says. "Rudy got our passports for us. They was O.K. We're supposed to be some business firm that's goin' in the munitions business over here. That's all I know."

"What did you think you was goin' to do over here?" I ask him.

"I wouldn't know," he says. "I was hangin' around with a mob in Chicago. They asked me if I'd like a sweet job. Well, this was it. It's been O.K. They said I'd get a coupla hundred dollars a week an' no risks."

"O.K.," I tell him. I reckon this bum is tellin' the truth. I reckon he's just a stooge like a lot of other guys, bein' used by the big brain who is Rudy.

"All right," I tell him. "But I tell you what we're goin' to do with you. We're goin' to leave you here. We're goin' to fix it so's you can't get out. We're also goin' to fix it so's you can get a little food when you want it, an' if you take a tip from me you're goin' to play ball. Any time you or your girl friend tries any funny business you're goin' to be for it. Have you got that?"

He says he's got it. I smoke another cigarette. Then Nikolls an' I get to work on this guy. We take him down to the room where we got Dodo. We rope him up good an' hard. We fix 'em both so's they can't move except to get at some milk an' stuff that we put in between 'em. I reckon they got enough to live an for a coupla days, an' if we don't get back by then it's just goin' to be too bad.

"So long, you babies," I tell 'em. "Just stick around an' behave yourselves an' you'll be all right. Maybe if I've got time to remember you I'll come back some time. So long!"

We go out. We go back to the place where I've left the car an' get it on the road towards London.

"Look, Windy," I tell him. "When we get back, you go back to the office. You tell Callaghan I'm layin' you off. I'll be around an' tell him why some time in the day."

"Say, what the hell is this?" he says. "I thought we was doin' swell on this case."

"Maybe you did," I tell him. "But there're just one or two little points I want cleared up. Maybe I'll have 'em cleared up by some time to-morrow afternoon. Then I'll be seein' you. You got that?"

He says he's got it. He don't say anythin' else. I reckon he knows what I mean.

CHAPTER ELEVEN
THE CALLAGHAN DEAL

I WAKE up at twelve o'clock an' grab off a cigarette. I lay there in bed, nice an' comfortable, lookin' at the ceilin' an' wonderin' what the day is goin' to bring forth. I got an idea that as days go this ain't gonna be such a bad one.

I grab off a cigarette an' reach for the telephone. I order some breakfast an' tell the service guy to try an' get Chief Detective-Inspector Herrick on the telephone.

After a coupla minutes Herrick comes on the line.

"Hello, pal," I tell him. "I wanta see you. Will you be around?"

He says yes, he'll be around all the time. He asks how I am getting along with the Wayles case.

I give a big grin. I say: "Look . . . it's in the bag. I got everything where I want-it."

He starts to ask somethin', but I cut in.

"I ain't talkin' to you about it now," I tell him. "I'm gonna get some breakfast an' then I'll come along an' see you. I got a coupla complaints to make."

"Not really," he says. "I hope nothin's gone wrong, Lemmy. . . ."

"Not so you'd notice it," I say. "But that ain't the fault of several people concerned. I'll be seein' you, Herrick." I hang up. I reckon I will give him a little time to think that one out.

I have my breakfast an' a bath an' just one little shot of rye just in case I get rheumatism some time, after which I look out a very cute suit for myself an' doll up a little, because I am one of those guys who likes to feel well-dressed any time he thinks somethin' is gonna happen.

Then I go downstairs an' grab a cab in the street. On the way down to Scotland Yard I work out in my mind just how I am gonna play this thing. I reckon I wanta say just enough an' let it go at that.

I am feelin' pretty good. Because I am an old hand at the poker game an' when guys try an' pull one on me I am liable to pull a bluff myself. I reckon I'm gonna tell Herrick just enough of the truth an' just enough lies to make that guy feel that he has just gotta put this job where I want it.

An' if he does . . . Boy . . . will I go to town or will I?

Herrick is sittin' at his desk, smokin' a little pipe an' lookin' as if butter wouldn't melt in his mouth.

"How are you, Lemmy?" he says. "I'm glad things are going all right with you. What can I do for you?"

"Not much," I tell him. "Because even if I wanted you to do somethin' for me I don't know that I'd ask for it. You tried a double cross on me once an' you ain't goin' to do it again. See, pal?"

He opens his eyes. He is puttin' on a big surprised act. He says: "I don't know what you mean, Lemmy. What's been getting at you?"

"Nothin'," I tell him. I light a cigarette an' throw my hat on the corner of his desk. I stand there lookin' down at him.

"Look," I tell him, "you been tryin' to make a stooge outa me. You been givin' me the big run-around. You an' your friend Mrs. Lorella Owen—the dame with the grey wig an' the false bumps in her pan. The only thing is you guys will have to get up a lot earlier if you aim to catch me out."

He starts to say somethin', but I hold up my hand.

"Save it," I tell him. "I reckon I am next to the big business you tried to pull. But you ain't done yourself any good. I got this job where I want it. Tamara Phelps has got good an' scared an' spluttered so much you'd be surprised. Well . . . you know what that means. I'm on top of the job. I know where Rudy Zimman is; I know where Tamara is; I know where Julia Wayles is an' I know where Karen Wayles is. In fact," I go on, "I could have the whole goddam lot of 'em here inside five minutes if I wanted to an' how d'you like that?"

He looks serious. He says:

"Why don't you stop talking in riddles, Lemmy? If you've got something up against me why don't you say what it is? I'm all out to help."

"You better had be," I tell him. "An' I'm tellin' you, Herrick, I don't like this idea of sorta usin' me so's you can pull a lotta stuff behind my back. Any time you want me to help you just say so. I'll be glad to oblige. But don't try any funny business. See?"

"What funny business?" he says. I reckon he is stallin' to try an' find out how much I know.

"First of all," I say, "there is this business about Max Schribner. I call through on the telephone an' ask you to pinch this guy an' what do you do? You put up a lot of *alibis*. You say you can't do it, that you got no proper charge against him. You tell me a lot of hooey to stall me off an' then what do you do?"

"Well . . . what do I do?" he says. He is beginnin' to grin a little bit.

"You go right out an' pinch Max Schribner," I tell him. "You think you've pulled a fast one on me. You think you've got one of the guys in this job who is gonna talk. So you pinch him an' you think I don't know. Well, what you didn't know was that you did the very best thing you could for me!"

His eyebrows go up. He looks plenty interested. I start to turn on the little story I have rehearsed comin' down in the cab.

"Look," I tell him. "When you knocked off Schribner, Tamara Phelps got to know about it good an' quick. How an' when an' why I don't know. But she got the news an' it scared her plenty. So what does she do? She gets in touch with me an' she makes a deal. She says if I will promise her a safe conduct outa this country an' see that the Zimman boys don't get at her she will blow the whole goddam works. So I tell her I will deal. So she tells me the whole book an' how do you like that . . . you an' your pal Mrs. Lorella Owen?"

He starts drawin' on the blottin' paper. He looks serious.

"From now on," I tell him, "I'm gonna play this my own way without any help from you. I'm gonna get these mugs an' if there's any shootin', I'm gonna do it, an' *you* can do the explainin' afterwards. . . ."

"Listen, Lemmy . . ." he says. But I bust in again.

"Listen nothin'," I tell him. "You been pullin' fast ones on me—or tryin' to ever since I started in on this job. When I ask you to put me next to some guys who will work with me you put me on to some firm called Callaghan Investigations. I suppose you're gonna tell me that you didn't instruct that guy Callaghan to wise you up to every move in the game I made; I suppose you're gonna tell me that that side-kicker of his, Windemere Nikolls, wasn't wisin' Callaghan up all the while, an' Callaghan wasn't comin' through to you an' tippin' you off. Well . . .?"

He gives a big sigh.

"It's not much use tryin' to pull any wool over your eyes, Lemmy," he says. "I never liked this business from the start. But how did you know about Callaghan?"

"That was easy," I tell him. "I sent Nikolls an' Dodo Malendas back to my apartment on Jermyn Street from some dump at Betchworth. I never told Nikolls to try an' get anythin' out of that dame; but directly he gets there he gets through to Callaghan an' gets a dictaphone sent around. If the Malendas cutie had said her piece it woulda been recorded on that dictaphone, an' Nikolls woulda grabbed off the record an' sent it around to Callaghan, who woulda wised you up. Then you'da had somethin' else to work on.

"So Nikolls starts tryin' to get the story outa that baby, but he was unlucky. Before she can get goin' a coupla Zimman's thugs come in an' knock the pair of 'em off. They took 'em to some dump in the country."

Herrick starts puffin' on his pipe. He don't say anythin' for a minute or two. Then he says:

"Lemmy, you and I have got to have a straight talk. We've got to get this thing cleared up from the start."

"You don't say, big boy," I tell him. "So now when you find you're in a jam you wanta start talkin' straight. O.K. I'm listenin'."

He says: "I can understand you feeling fed up, Lemmy. But it's not my fault. I'll prove that to you. just wait a minute."

He goes outa the room. He's away for about ten minutes; then he comes back. He's got a letter in his hand. He says:

"I've just seen the Assistant Commissioner. I've explained the circumstances. He's given me permission to put *all* the facts of this case in your hands." He sits down at his desk. "You'll want to know why I've done what I *have* done, Lemmy," he says. "Well . . . I'm a policeman. I've got to obey orders. Here's the explanation. . . ."

He hands the letter to me. I read it. It is dated ten days before. It is from the U.S. Embassy. It says:

Dear Mr. Herrick,

I am writing to you confirming a conversation I have had with the assistant Commissioner of Police in reference to the Wayles case. We have been trying to get in touch with one of our Federal Bureau officers—Chief Agent L. H. Caution—who is in this country on leave of absence, but we cannot contact him. However, I have no doubt he will report within a day or two, and in the meantime we are temporarily appointing another F.B.I. operative—Special Agent Charles Milton—to this case.

Please see Mr. Milton who will contact the man Schribner at Betchworth and endeavour to get some information about the whereabouts of Miss Wayles.

Immediately Chief Agent Caution returns he will take the case over from Milton.

Now I must ask your assistance over a matter which I consider delicate. Chief Agent Caution will merely investigate the disappearance of Julia Wayles. He will endeavour to find her. Nothing should be said to him about the main point of this case, i.e. the Fifth Column Group who have been operating both from the United States and from England. This part of the investigation should be kept entirely separate, and in this connection I shall be most grateful if you will render every possible assistance to a special officer of the United States Secret Service who is in charge of the Fifth Column part of the case—Mrs. Lorella Owen.

It may well be that Caution, who will doubtless carry out his investigation into the whereabouts of Miss Wayles in his usual forthright manner, will provide you with pointers which may be of the greatest assistance to Mrs. Owen in her part of the business, and it would perhaps therefore be advisable if any people detailed by you to assist Special Agent Caution were to report to you from time to time without his knowledge, so as to enable you to pass any pertinent information to Mrs. Owen.

I am, Sincerely yours,

Charles C. S. Senley,

Counsellor, United States Embassy.

I give a big grin an' hand the letter back to Herrick.

"Just like I thought," I tell him. "So I was to be the stooge—the big mug. I'm to go rushin' around doin' the donkey work, gettin' myself pushed around by a lot of cheap thugs, just so's Mrs. Lorella Owen can stick on grey wigs an' pad that pan of hers out an' think she's bein' a secret service operative. Well . . . well . . . well . . .! Now what are you goin' to do about it?"

Herrick looks me straight in the eye.

"You've got to realise, Lemmy," he says, "that once or twice before, when you've been working on cases in this country, your methods have been a little bit peculiar. I expect the U.S. Embassy realise that. Perhaps they thought that Mrs. Owen—and after all she seems to be an experienced person—would prefer to handle her part of the case more delicately."

"Maybe," I tell him. "It looks to me as if this Mrs. Owen is over here on some fifth column business, and I suppose Rudy Zimman is behind it. An' I suppose this Wayles snatch is somehow tied up in it. Well, I told you I was on top of the job an' I am. I'll handle it my own way or I'm just goin' to sit back an' smoke cigarettes an' watch you guys make mugs of yourselves, an' you can tell Mrs. Owen that—that goes for her too."

He puts his pipe down. He says:

"Lemmy, I'm goin' to believe everything you say. I'm going to take it as being the truth when you tell me you can pull in Zimman and Phelps; that you know where Nikolls and Malendas are. In other words that you've more or less got this case tied up. Is that the truth?"

I don't bat an eyelid. You guys know how much this case is tied up. This case is about as finished as I am. We ain't even started on it yet. But I ain't goin' to tell him that. I look him straight in the eye with an expression of sincerity that woulda made the senior Sunday School mistress burst inta tears at any given moment. I say:

"Yes, pal. That is the truth, an' that is the way it is."

"All right," he says. "Well, that bein' so I'm goin' to suggest that from now on you go right ahead with the whole business. All we want is Zimman, Phelps and the people who are running this business. Once we've got them the rest is easy. How do you propose to handle it?"

"You go fry an egg," I tell him. "I'm handlin' this my own way, an' I want a little assistance too. Are you goin' to tell this Callaghan guy to lay off this funny business an' get behind me on this job, or am I goin' to throw him overboard too?"

He says: "Don't do that. Callaghan's pretty good. He's got brains. He'll be useful. I'll put that matter right now."

He takes off the telephone. He asks the switchboard to give him Callaghan Investigations. Two minutes afterwards he's talkin' to Callaghan. He says:

"Is that you, Slim? Listen. The instructions that I gave you about reporting direct to me on what Caution was doing are cancelled. He knows all about it. He's just been telling me we'd have to get up very early in the morning to catch him." He grins. "I'm inclined to agree with him," he says. "Will you take your orders direct from him? . . . All right." He hangs up.

"I'm sending a note round to Callaghan confirming the conversation I have just had with him," he says. "His organisation is at your disposal, Lemmy. From what you say I take it you'll have this case finished in a matter of hours."

"Maybe not as soon as that," I tell him. "Maybe a coupla days, but it won't be long."

"All right," he says. "Directly I can I'll get in touch with Mrs. Owen and tell her what the new situation is."

"Oh no, you won't," I tell him. "That dame makes me tired. Another thing," I go on, "she's a darned sight too good-lookin' to be a secret service operative. What's a woman with a figure like that doin' in the secret service? We could use a dame like that in the Federal Bureau of Investigation."

He grins. "I reckon you could use a woman with a figure like Mrs. Owen's wherever she was, Lemmy," he says, "if, I know anything about you. But if I'm not going to tell her, you'll have to give me your word that you'll explain the circumstances to her."

"You bet," I tell him. "I'll go round an' see her. I'll tell her the whole works."

He lights his pipe again. He looks happier. I think to myself like hell will I tell Mrs. Owen the whole works. By the time I've finished with that good-lookin' baby she won't try an' pull another fast one on little Lemmy. No, sir! Maybe you mugs will remember that old Confucius said: "The way of the lying man is hard, but the woman who lies and knows not truth is like a snake in the grass." Well, if this Owen cutie is a snake in the grass, I gotta swell way with snakes. Anyhow you can always tickle a snake before you catch it.

I say so long to Herrick an' promise to let him know just what happens—sometime. I pick up my hat an' I scram. Outside I take a cab. I tell the guy to drive me round to Berkeley Square.

Callaghan an' Nikolls are sittin' up on high stools in front of the bar at the Zouave Lounge in Albemarle Street. Each of 'em has got a double rye in front of him. Callaghan grins when he sees me.

"Hello, Caution," he says, "I suppose they told you where we were. Have a drink?"

"That's right," I tell him. "An' I'd like to put it on record that it ain't right for a private dick like you to have a secretary who is as good-lookin' as Effie Thompson is. Maybe somebody told you that before."

"Many times," he says.

He orders another double rye. I get myself a high stool. He says: "You were with Herrick when he phoned through to me, so you know what the position is. You realise that we were simply carrying out instructions. Callaghan Investigations always carries out its client's instructions—when it feels like it."

He looks at Nikolls. Nikolls grins.

"O.K.," I tell him. "Well, if you guys are goin' to work in with me, you've gotta play ball Maybe this case isn't started yet."

"No?" says Callaghan. "When is it going to start?"

"It's goin' to start right now," I tell him. "Look, here is the set-up. Some of it maybe you've guessed at, but here's the whole job as I see it. Rudy Zimman an' his mob, for some reasons best known to themselves, snatch a dame called Julia Wayles an' bring her over here. O.K. Her friends an' family, an' the guy she was engaged to, *if* she was engaged to a guy, get all steamed up about this, an' eventually the Federal Bureau of Investigation is put on the job of tryin' to find her.

"In the meantime I reckon the U.S. Secret Service have discovered that this Zimman mob are on some other racket over here—some fifth column business. They wanta pull in Zimman on that, so they put one of their operators—a swell lookin' baby called Mrs. Lorella Owen on to the job. It looks like her business is to work on this fifth column end. Then I reckon they find out that the Federal Bureau have got me over here lookin' for Julia Wayles, so Mrs. Lorella Owen comes over here an' the U.S. Embassy give instructions to Scotland Yard that I'm to go on with the Wayles investigation, but I'm not to know anythin' else about the other business. You guys, who are put on to help me, have gotta report to Herrick, an' Herrick in turn reports to that smart baby Mrs. Owen." I take up my drink an' sink it. It tastes pretty good to me. I order three more.

"All that is very nice an' straight," I tell 'em. "But here's where the issue's got clogged a bit. Last night I come up to town an' see this Tamara Phelps baby. When I get there Dodo Malendas—the dame who was knocked off with Nikolls here—was just leavin' her apartment."

Nikolls' eyes pop. "For cryin' out loud . . .!" he says.

"O.K., pal," I tell him. "That's why they shot that dope inta you, so that you should be right out while they was makin' a deal with Dodo. Well, I reckon Dodo's plenty scared. They probably told her they was goin' to give her the heat. Those guys threatened to do all sorts of things to that baby. She got good an' frightened. So she tells me something. What do you think she tells me?"

Callaghan says: "I wouldn't know, but I bet it's goin' to be good."

"You're tellin' me," I say. "Well, here it is: She told me that Mrs. Lorella Owen was Karen Wayles—Julia Wayles' sister—who come over here lookin' for Julia."

I stop talkin'.

Callaghan looks at Nikolls. Nikolls looks back at Callaghan. Callaghan whistles a little, very quietly.

"What do you know about that one?" I tell 'em.

Callaghan says: "I'm beginning to see daylight. I think I've got it."

"Me too . . ." I say.

Nikolls says: "I reckon I have too. Did I ever tell you the story of that dame with the strawberry coloured hair that I met up with in Minnesota? Well, this baby . . ."

Callaghan says: "Shut up, Windy. I've heard that one before. Anyhow it's redundant."

"O.K. . . . O.K. . . ." says Nikolls. "Whenever I'm goin' to tell a story that has a direct bearin' on anythin' it is always redundant." He finishes his rye.

Callaghan says: "You've got an idea in your head?"

I nod.

"I got a big idea," I tell him. "An' this is the way it goes. You guys have gotta help an' you've gotta keep your traps shut. There mustn't be any slip-ups on this business."

Callaghan says: "I think this is goin' to be a very interestin' case."

"Me too," I say.

He orders three more double ryes, an' we get down to a little quiet business.

Chapter Twelve
THE SNATCH

I GET back to my apartment at three o'clock an' relax. I get inta a huddle with myself an' go over all this business in my mind, tryin' to find some place where I mighta slipped up in my calculations.

But I don't reckon I have. With a bit of luck everything is gonna pan out all right.

Because you guys will realise that it is stickin' out like Coney Island Pier that Rudy an' Tamara are goin' to pull somethin' drastic good an' quick. They have *got* to. They're in bad an' they gotta find some way out. They just can't afford to wait any longer an' I reckon they're gonna try an' play it the way I worked out.

I stick around an' smoke cigarettes an' think of all the cases I been mixed up in where there was good-lookin' dames. I reckon that any time you get skulduggery you get cute janes with it. Then I start wonderin' which of these three babies—Tamara Phelps, Dodo Malendas or Mrs. Lorella Owen—is the one I would really go for if I hadta be wrecked on a desert island with one of 'em. I rule out Dodo Malendas because the dame is two-faced an' when it comes to considerin' Tamara I reckon I would rather elope with a shark than stick around with that one. Well ... that leaves the Lorella cutie an' I don't really know enough about her temperament to get excited.

I reckon I will have to get to know this dame better.

At five o'clock Nikolls blows in like we arranged. He says everything is O.K. He says that Callaghan's got a coupla guys planted near Lorella's flat in an empty basement an' that he has got another three guys parked on the first floor in the house opposite the apartment block. He reckons that these five bozos—who are all pretty tough palookas—can take care of anythin' that blows up. I ask him whether he knows what Lorella is plannin' to do.

"She's stayin' right where she is," he says. "We put a guy in frontin' as a man workin' for the Gas Company goin' around an' inspectin' meters. This guy shoots a line on the maid in the Owen flat an' she tells him that Mrs. Owen will be in all day. She's arranged to have her dinner served there an' everything."

"O.K.," I tell him. "Well, you stick around an' don't leave that office dump of yours, because directly I call through to you you gotta get action—quick."

He says O.K. an' scrams. After which I have one little shot of rye just to keep the germs away an' go to bed, because I reckon that anyhow I owe myself a little sleep an' I also got the idea in my head that maybe I am not goin' to get any for quite a while.

I lie there for a bit thinkin' things out an' hopin' that this job is goin' to come off like I want it to. I also do a little thinkin' about Mrs. Lorella Owen.

I reckon that dame has got somethin' good. Besides her figure I mean. Maybe she has a little brains as well. I feel sorta interested in her. I would like to get a good look at her when she ain't wearin' that wig an' doin' things to her face. An' I would also like to hear what her voice—her real voice—is like.

Because, as I have already told you guys before, I am a poetic sorta cuss. An' I am also very curious by nature an' inclined to experiment—especially where dames are concerned.

Well . . . I have met plenty of babies in my time. But I ain't ever come up against a dame workin' for the U.S. Secret Service Department who looks like Lorella, an' with a little encouragement I feel that I could easily get sorta interested.

I close down on this great thought an' go to sleep, which, believe it or not, is a good thing to go to if there ain't anything better breakin'.

It is eight o'clock when I wake up. I take a warm shower an' call through to Service to send me up some dinner. When I have finished eatin' I sit around, drinkin' coffee an' a little rye an' wonderin' whether anything's goin' to pop an' if so which way.

An' the more I think about it the more it seems that I mighta made a mistake in my ideas, in which case I am goin' to look a goddam fool an' Mrs. Lorella Owen an' Herrick an' all the rest of these mugs are goin' to give me the big ha-ha.

Maybe you've been on the dead-line yourself. Maybe you guys have planned somethin' out an' got it all set an' then, just when you think that the time has come for the job to break, you start gettin' scared in case it don't. Well . . . if you been like that you know how I am feelin'.

I give myself another four fingers of old Kentucky just for the nerves an' I have still got the glass in my hand when the telephone rings. It is the desk downstairs. They say that there is a lady on the line an' she will not give her name. Do I want to take the call?

Do I? I tell 'em to put her through quick. While I am waitin' for 'em to switch her on I can see my fingers twitchin'. Me . . . I am gettin' jittery in my old age . . . maybe!

But I don't haveta worry. It is Tamara all right. She comes through in that soft cooin' voice of hers that sounds just like spreadin' treacle on a satin bed-spread.

"Well . . . Tamara . . ." I tell her. "So you decided to go through with it. You decided to sell out the rest of that lousy mob you been workin' with *an'* Rudy, an' play ball. I think you're a wise dame."

She gives a little gurgle. That dame has a way of laughin' that would make a cripple get up an' do a *rumba*.

She says: "Look, pal, I am one of those dames who know which side their bread is buttered on. You get me? I reckon this job is too hot for me . . . an' I reckon before you get through with it, it is gonna be too hot for anybody. I'm duckin', see? An' I'm keepin' my bargain with you. An' you gotta look after me."

I think I will tell one now. I say:

"Look . . . I got everything fixed for you, Tamara. I got you a special passport from the Embassy an' you can get a boat to-morrow. An' you don't haveta worry about Rudy gettin' at you. I'm gonna look after you, baby."

"Thanks, Lemmy," she says in a nice thankful sorta voice. "An' I would like you to remember this. I would like you to remember that you will always stay in my mind as a big guy who was good to Tamara. One of these days maybe I can do something for you, pal . . . ."

"Maybe, sweet," I tell her. But I am thinkin' that the only thing this baby would ever want to do for me would be to cut my throat with a blunt penknife while somebody was holdin' me down. "Maybe you can," I go on, "an' if that time ever arrives you will find me there with bells on. In the meantime what is the set-up? Have you fixed things like you said?"

"Better," she coos. "I done better than I said I was going to, Lemmy, but I can't talk to you on the telephone. Maybe I'm goin' to be interrupted, see? I've gotta see you an' I've gotta see you some time an' place where I can get away so that Rudy don't suspect anythin'."

"O.K.," I tell her. "You tell me when an' where an' I'll be there."

"We better meet at Schribner's cottage," she says. "There's nobody there. I've got a key an' you've got one. Can you be there to-night between eleven an' twelve?"

"I'll be there," I tell her.

"Everything's O.K.," she goes on. "I've got it all fixed about a certain person—you know who—an' you can pick her up to-night. I'll tell you where when I see you."

"Right, Tamara," I say. "I'll be there. Schribner's cottage between eleven an' twelve, an' get there as early as you can because if we got any time to spare I would like to show you a new system of neckin' I've invented since I saw you last time."

"Oh, Lemmy," she says, sorta plaintive. "I wish you wouldn't talk like that. You don't mean it an' it hurts me a lot. I mean to say bein' stuck on you like I am, I don't like you tryin' to make a goat outa me."

"Nobody is goin' to make a goat outa you while I'm around," I tell her. "An' I wasn't even kiddin', Tamara. I go for you so much that any time I think of you I get the staggers. But don't worry, I'll tell you about it when I see you. So long, kid."

"So long, Lemmy," she says. "An' remember I've done what I said I'd do. . . ."

She hangs up.

I give myself another drink for luck. This looks like business! Then I call through to Callaghan's office. When Nikolls comes on the line I give him the works.

"Look, Nikolls," I tell him. "This job is now gonna start. Tamara has been through an' done her stuff. The baby has made a date to meet me down at Schribner's place at Betchworth between eleven an' twelve o'clock. That. means that they're gonna try an' pull something about that time—when I am outa the way. So you get around an' stand by your guys an' see that there ain't any slip-ups."

"O.K.," he says. "I been through once or twice but nothin's happened up to date."

"It won't," I tell him. "They'll wait till it's dark before they try an' pull this one. You stick around an' directly you got that business fixed you let me know. I'll keep in touch with you on the telephone. If anythin' turns up that stops me gettin' you, you know what to do."

"I got it," he says. "But there is only one thing that is worryin' me. Supposin' this dame makes a hell of a noise?"

"She won't," I tell him. "That dame is too clever to make a noise for nothin'. She ain't that sorta dame."

"You can be wrong about a dame," he says. "Anybody can. Me . . . I have always found it wrong to judge dames by appearances."

"You don't say?" I tell him. It sounds like this Nikolls mug is a philosopher.

"Yeah," he says. "You'd be surprised. There was a dame I knew up in Mayola County one time. Believe it or not this baby usta give me the spasms. I was takin' a holiday on a farm next to the one she lived on an' I usta look at her outa the window of my room most of the day while she was workin' around the place.

"Well, believe it or not, the top half of that kid was marvellous. I never saw what her legs was like because there was a little wall between my window an' the farm an' I could only see the top half of her. But what I could see was one hundred per cent. She had swell hair, an' a skin like cream, an' a figure that woulda knocked you for a row of pins. You got me?"

I tell him yes, I have got him.

"O.K.," he goes on. "Well, I was dyin' with curiosity to see the other half of this honey-belle. I wanted to see if her ankles was as good as the rest of her. So I got up early one mornin' an' snick around leanin' over the wall waitin' for her to come out an' start milkin' the cows. Well, she come out, an' boy . . . I'm tellin' you that *everything* about that dame was perfect. Well, what do you think happened?"

"I wouldn't know," I tell him. "But I can make a coupla guesses."

"Well, you'd be wrong," he says sorta miserable. "Because it was this way. I reckoned I'd gotta do somethin' about that blonde. I thought it was just too bad for a beautiful dame to be workin' around a farm in the sticks like that with nobody to make a pass at her. So I snapped inta action an' did I get a surprise!"

"Go on," I tell him. "Tell me . . . the suspense is killin' me."

"Well," he says, "this dame had got a coupla cork legs. She usta let me stick pins in 'em for fun." He gives a big sigh. "It just shows you can't always judge dames by appearances," he says.

"Maybe," I tell him. "But in this case it don't matter. If you think *this* dame is gonna bawl her head off yon better stick a bag over her head. Anyway that would be a good idea."

"O.K.," he says. "I'll do that. Well . . . I'll be hearin' from you an' I hope it goes all right your end."

"Good luck, Nikolls," I tell him. I hang up. I give a big grin when I think of Nikolls workin' the bag act on that baby.

That will be one in the bag anyhow!

It is just after eleven o'clock when I roll the car around the roundabout at the Reigate end of Dorking an' spin along by the golf course. I pull up an' leave the car in the little lane where I left it before. I stick the rye flask in my hip, an' ease up my shoulder holster under my arm. Maybe we shall get a little shootin' before the evenin' is out.

I turn off the car lights an' then I grab the dictaphone that I brought away from my apartment, stick it under my arm, lock up the car an' move off towards the avenue of lime trees.

It is damp an' dark; there is a little bit of moon comin' out from behind the clouds an' there is a sorta mist hangin' over the golf course an' makin' the whole place look so goddam mysterious that you get around to thinkin' that somethin' might really happen around here sometime.

Me . . . I am a poetic cuss. Walkin' across the fairway an' up the hill I start wonderin' whether I shall ever get away from this thug-chasin' game an get myself that little chicken farm down Minnesota way. The only thing about a chicken farm is that you gotta have a dame an' the idea hits me like a well-aimed brick that you might get sorta tired of one dame on a chicken farm. This leads me to a bigger an' better idea which is that a wise guy would have a lot of chicken farms an' a lot of dames, after which he would be a goddam sight more tired than when he started.

Maybe there is some philosophy in this idea because it looks to me like every guy spends his time thinkin' just what a helluva time he could have if he only got the one dame he really wants, an' when he has got this dame he spends the rest of his time thinkin' what a helluva time he could have with a lot of other dames if he hadn't got this one. You get me?

By now I have got to the top of the rise an' start walkin' into the avenue of limes. The moon has come up a bit an' there are shadows lyin' around the place, an' away on the other side of the avenue I can see the green of the golf Course, on the high ground, stickin' out of the low-lyin' mist like green islands.

I pull up behind a tree an' light a cigarette. I am just takin' the first puff when somebody says: "Hey . . . Lemmy. . . ."

I look around an' Nikolls comes out from behind some tree. "Look . . ." I tell him. "What the hell is this! What's happened?"

He gives me a big grin. "It's O.K.," he says, "but they pulled it a bit earlier than you thought."

"Yeah?" I tell him. I sit down on a tree stump. I take a look at my wrist-watch an' see it is just a quarter past eleven. I reckon Tamara can wait a bit.

"What happened?" I ask him.

He takes a cigarette outa his pocket. I wait to see whether he is gonna strike the match on the seat of his pants. He does. When he has got the cigarette alight he says:

"It was a honey. Just before ten o'clock some guys come into the Mayfield Apartments. Four of 'em. Well-dressed guys, but tough." He gives another grin. "I was workin' the lift," he says. "I slipped a coupla pounds to the liftman an' told him to take the evenin' off. When these guys come along an' ask for Mrs. Owen's apartment I told 'em to stick around for a minute. I eased down the passage an' signalled to the guy I got outside. I then get these four mugs in the lift an' take 'em up to the third floor, get outa the lift an' say I'll be back in a minute. They don't look so pleased but they don't say anything. After a minute I come back an' take the lift down to the first floor.

"When they get out of the lift my boyos are waitin' for 'em. Not one of those mugs had time to even get his hand around to his hip pocket for a gun. On the second floor we had an empty apartment fixed an' we shot the four of 'em in there, roped 'em up an' got to work on 'em. Three of 'em was plenty tough but the other guy was easy. He talked."

"An' what did he say?" I ask him.

"What you expected," says Nikolls. "These guys was to snatch Lorella. They got a car outside—a big Mercedes—an' the idea was they was to run her down here to some place on the Brockham Road—a place called The Marsh. But they wasn't to get her down there before half-past one. They was to run down here an' pull the car up this side of Brockham Green somewhere where it wouldn't be seen, wait till one-thirty o'clock an' then take Lorella along to this dump they call The Marsh."

"I got it," I tell him. "An' what happened then?"

"We snatched Lorella ourselves," he says. "We went along an' did a big Rudy Zimman act with guns an' everything. We got her out the back way an' in the car before she knew which way she was pointin'. Everything went like clockwork an' she didn't even yell."

"Where is she now?" I ask him.

"Where you said," he says. "We got two cars parked about a quarter of a mile down the road from Schribner's cottage—but well off the road. Lorella's in one of 'em. We tied her up an' blindfolded her an' I don't think she's too happy. I got two guys in the car with her, an' a couple more boys in another car with 'em."

"Nice work." I tell him. "Well, here is the way we're gonna play this. You go back to where you left the cars an' get one of 'em. Then drive towards Schribner's cottage but don't come in sight of it. I'm goin' there now. Tamara is either there waitin' for me or else she'll be along pretty soon. O.K. When you've got the car pretty near to the cottage come along on foot but keep outa sight. Come up the back way an' take a look at the kitchen door. If it's open that's gonna mean that Tamara has arrived. She'll have a car an' she'll leave it outside. You go an' bring your own car up so's when she leaves me you can tail her. Don't let her get an idea that there's anybody tailin' her an' keep that dame in sight. Because when she leaves me she'll be goin' back to Rudy Zimman an' I wanta collect that bastard before the mornin'. You got that?"

He says he's got it.

"When Tamara goes an' you go after her, I'll go back to where you've left the other car an' Lorella an' take her along to the cottage. I wanta talk to her. Your boys can go straight on to this Marsh dump an' hang around there just in case they're wanted later. There might be a spot of trouble along there. Tell 'em that."

"That's OK.," he says. "But supposin' Tamara goes off a helluva way to some place. Do I still keep after her?"

"Be your age," I tell him. "If those thugs who was goin' to snatch Lorella was supposed to deliver her to this Marsh dump at one-thirty you can bet your life Tamara an' Rudy Zimman are goin' to be around there at that time. But the place she's goin' to when she leaves me is the place that Rudy is usin' as a headquarters. I wanta know where that is."

"I got it," he says. "Well . . . I'll be gettin' along. It's been a nice evenin' up to date." He scrams.

I light myself another cigarette an' go on my way. Pretty soon I get in sight of Schribner's cottage. There is no car outside so I reckon that Tamara has not arrived. I go through the gate an' open the front door with the key she gave me. I get inside an' pull the Luger outa its holster just in case anybody is tryin' to start somethin'. Then I go over the place. All the rooms are like they was before except the front sittin'-room has got the windows boarded over an' blacked out where I bust 'em when I did a dive through last time I was here.

I go downstairs an' take a look at the cellar, but everything is O.K. there. I go back to the sittin'-room, switch on the light an' make myself at home. There is still some whisky on the sideboard an' glasses an' a siphon, so I mix myself a little one.

Then I sit down an' light a cigarette.

About at ten minutes before twelve I hear a car pull up outside. Then the door opens an' Tamara comes in. Maybe I told you mugs before that this baby knows how to sling her clothes on, but I'm tellin' you that the way she looks an' the way she is dressed would hit you for a row of pins.

She has got on a short fur coat that is open. Underneath she is wearin' a grey flannel frock that was slung together by a guy who knew his tangerines. There is a little amethyst blue collar on the frock an' it is simple an' sorta sweet—if you get what I mean. It makes this dame look like one of them innocent an' wide-eyed babies that don't even know the secrets of life an' who blush any time somebody talks about oomph.

I get up an' stand lookin' at her. She throws me a sweet little smile an' comes over an' drapes her arms around my neck. Then she gives me a kiss that makes my back hair stand up. After which she stands away from me an' just looks at me with big pleadin' eyes like somebody had just sentenced her to death by mistake an' she was glad of it.

"Well, Lemmy," she says. "Here I am an' now you gotta admit that I been on the up-an'-up with you." She puts a curl back in place. "Maybe I've done some pretty screwy things in my time," she goes on. "Maybe I've been a bad baby now an' again, but here is where I put the book right."

"Nice work, Tamara," I tell her. "An' I have done the same thing by you. I've got everything fixed for you. An' you're gonna be O.K. from now on. So just sit down an' relax while I take a look around this dump an' see that there is not anybody lurkin' in the undergrowth."

"There ain't anybody here," she says. "I can tell you that; but if you wanta make sure you go ahead."

She takes out a cigarette case an' lights a cigarette. She goes over to the sideboard an' opens it an' finds another bottle of rye an' glasses. I leave her pourin' the drinks.

I take a look around the place just to make it look right, then I ease along the passageway to the back an' open the kitchen door so's Nikolls can see it. Then I go back.

She has poured the drinks. She gives me one.

"Here's to Julia Wayles," she says, "an' Lemmy Caution an little Tamara."

She sinks the drink like an old hand at the game.

"Take the weight off your feet, honey," I tell her. "An' start talkin'. I don't wanta waste any time."

"Nor me," she says. "Well . . . here's the way it is. This Julia Wayles baby is at some dump called The Marsh. It ain't far from here. Right now there's only one guy lookin' after her an' he's so goddam dumb that he don't matter. All you got to do is to ease over there. Ring the bell, give this guy a bust in the puss an' grab that dame. I reckon she'll be plenty glad to be grabbed too. She ain't had too good a time what with bein' roped up an' havin' her trap stuck up with adhesive tape for about the last ninety-nine years. I reckon she'll be glad to see if she can still talk."

"Swell," I tell her. "I'll go right over when I leave here." I take a pull on my cigarette an' blow a smoke ring. "You tell me somethin', kid," I tell her. "What is all this business about? Who is this Julia Wayles baby an' what the hell is all this song an' dance about?"

She answers up right away. She don't even hesitate. I reckon this dame is feelin' so good an' so goddam certain that everything is goin' all right for her that she is goin' to tell me as much of the truth as she dares to.

She says: "Rudy got himself mixed up in a swell racket. You know as well as I do that things wasn't too good fox the mobs after this goddam war started, so Rudy is lookin' around for some dough. He finds it. The German Bund in the U.S. had a swell job for anybody like Rudy. . . ."

"So that's it?" I say. "I mighta guessed.".

"Rudy starts a phoney war production business," she says. "He has two or three legitimate guys—palookas with no police records—frontin' for him. Schribner was one of 'em. O.K. The idea is that Rudy runs a sorta depot between here an' France—Fifth Column an' espionage. Guys workin' between U.S., Germany an' France get passed through here. An' believe me it *was* organised. They got Willie Karenza an' a coupla swell counterfeiters fakin' passports an' a regular set-up. They been gettin' away with it too an' Rudy has been cleanin' up plenty."

"I got it," I tell her. "An' just how does this Julia Wayles come into the set-up?"

She waits for a minute. Then she says:

"She comes in it through a dame called Mrs. Lorella Owen. This Owen dame is a U.S. Secret Service operative an' she puts Julia in to find out this an' that. She puts Julia in because Julia looks a bit of a mug even if she ain't one. Well . . . Julia does her stuff. She finds out plenty. She finds out what Rudy is doin' an' she also gets to know who the guys are who are workin' this racket with him. See?"

I nod my head. "I see," I tell her. "But Rudy gets wise, hey? Before Julia has time to shoot the works Rudy gets wise to what she's doin' an' snatches her?"

"Right," says Tamara. "He grabs her off an' he reckons he's got somethin' to do a deal with. He gets a big idea an' has her sent over this side an' kept under cover so that if things get too hot he reckons he's got somethin' on his side. The next thing is that some guy that this Julia baby was engaged to starts tryin' to find her. I reckon that's how you come inta this game."

I nod some more.

"Well . . ." she goes on, "the U.S. Secret Service bunch get a line on this business an' they send Lorella Owen over this side. Lorella picks up some baby called Dodo Malendas an' gets her workin' on the job. She puts this baby in callin' herself me, an' as Schribner ain't ever seen me at this time, Dodo gets away with it . . . but not for long. You got all that?"

"Yeah," I tell her. . . . "It's as plain as daylight. Go on, Tamara."

"There ain't much after that," she says. "Rudy gets wise to Dodo eventually an' scares hell outa her. So she spills the works about Lorella Owen an' there you are."

"Well . . . all that looks pretty good for Rudy," I tell her. "So why did you have to sell out?"

"I'm scared," she says. "This business is too big an' too hot for me. I don't like it. Me, I like mob stuff. I don't like this international Fifth Column business an' what goes with it. It's outa my line. Another thing," she says with a little smile. "I'm scared of you. I reckon you'd get this job cleaned up as soon as maybe an' I reckoned it was time I got out."

"O.K.," I tell her. "So I get along to this Marsh dump an' grab off Julia. All right . . . an' then where an' when do I get my hooks on Rudy?"

"There's a house on the coast," she says. "A marvellous set-up." She opens her handbag an' takes out an envelope. "I got it all written down here," she says. "Where the house is an' the names of the guys an' everything. All you got to do is to get your hooks on Julia to-night an' take Rudy an' the rest of the mob to-morrow—or when you want to. They won't know anythin' about Julia bein' snatched off 'em until it's too late. They won't be around here. . . . See?"

I nod my head.

"I see," I tell her. I take the envelope an' put it in my pocket. "Now," I go on, "just where is this Marsh dump?"

She tells me. Then she gets up an' stands lookin' at me.

"I'm in your hands now, Lemmy," she says. "What d'ya want me to do now?"

"You scram outa here," I tell her. "Get back to London an' put yourself up some place for to-night. To-morrow about three in the afternoon come around an' see me at my dump on Jermyn Street. Then I'll look after you. Got that?"

"O.K.," she says. She puts out her hand. "So long, big boy," she says. "Am I goddam glad I'm on your side . . .?"

She throws me one of them long lingerin' looks of hers an' gets out sorta quick as if it was all too much for her. A minute later I hear her car start up outside. I switch off the light an' pull up the corner of the black-out. I can see her tail light goin' down the road towards the Dorkin'-Reigate road. A coupla seconds later I see Nikolls' car go past. He is takin' it nice an' easy.

I give a big sigh. I reckon that is *that*.

I take one quick shot of rye just to keep things nice an' square, after which I grab my hat an' scram. I start walkin' towards the Brockham road, keepin' in the shadow of the bushes.

After about ten minutes I find the car. It is stuck away down a little side-turnin' an' you'd never see it if you wasn't lookin' for it. I go over. There are a coupla tough lookin' babies hangin' around smokin'.

"My name's Caution," I tell 'em. "An' how's Mrs. Owen?" One of 'em grins an' looks towards the car.

"She's all right," he says. "Just a little bit bad-tempered but otherwise fine."

I look in the car. Lorella is sittin' in the back seat, relaxed against the corner of the car. She has got a handkerchief tied over her eyes an' her hands are tied. When I stick my head through the window of the car to look at her I get just a suggestion of the perfume she is wearin', an' I'm tellin' you mugs that that scent of hers is good an' easy on the nostrils.

I don't say anything. I turn away an' speak to the guy standin' by the bonnet.

"Look," I tell him, "here's what you gotta do. . . . In ten minutes' time just drive the car down the road until you come to the cottage I just left. There's nobody inside. Just off the kitchen you'll find a flight of stone steps leading down to a cellar. Take the girl friend down there. Fix her up with an armchair from the sittin'-room an' give her a drink an' a cigarette if she wants 'em. But you ain't to take that handkerchief off her eyes an' you ain't to untie her hands. You got that?"

He nods his head.

"When you done that you two can go back to the sittin'-room an' give yourself a whisky an' soda. Stick around until I get back an' then I'll tell you what else I want."

I ease off an' go back to the cottage. I grab the dictaphone that I brought down with me an' take it down inta the cellar. There is a spare electric plug in the wall, an' I plug in the dictaphone an' leave it up against the wall, so's I can start it off by kickin' the lever with my foot any time I want.

Then I scram. I go outa the cottage an' cut across the fairways to where I left the car. It looks to me that I have never done so much walkin' across a golf course in my life. Maybe—one of these days—I'm gonna learn this game.

When I get to the car I slip inside an' relax. I light myself a cigarette an' wonder if the rest of the evenin' is gonna be as good as the start. After a bit I let in the clutch an' drive down to the Dorking roundabout. I go inta the telephone booth an' ring Scotland Yard. I ask for Herrick.

After a coupla minutes he comes on the line.

"Listen, pal," I tell him, "I think everything is very nice an' that we are goin' to have a nice night. I told you I had everything in the bag. Well, that's the way it looks to me."

He says he's damn glad to hear it an' what do I want.

"You gotta get a move on," I tell him. "It is now half-past twelve so you got an hour. What you gotta do is this. You gotta get a strongarm squad an' be at a dump called The Marsh on the other side of Brockham village about twenty to two. You gotta stick around there until I come along. After which you can clean up the whole lot of these bozos. They got a big date there."

He says that is fine. Then he says have I got any ideas about where Julia Wayles is. He asks me if I was kiddin' when I said I knew where she was.

"I was kiddin' *then* but I ain't *now*" I tell him. "I'm just goin' to see the dame. I'll be seein' you at twenty to two. So long, Herrick."

I hang up. I think the joke is on him.

CHAPTER THIRTEEN
MEET JULIA

I GO rollin' along the road towards Brockham. I am whistlin' to myself because between you an' me an' the gatepost, I am not what the politicians call displeased with the situation, an' any more trouble that's comin' is gonna be Herrick's headache. It is nearly ten to one when I find this place. It is a big sorta house set back behind a lotta trees well away from the road. There is a high wall round it an' it smells of damp vegetables. I don't like the look of this place.

I take a look around an' start walkin' along by the side of the wall, but when I get tired of lookin' for a gate I decide to get over the top. I find a tree standin' along by the wall, scram up an' make it.

When I drop down on the other side I'm standin' in some bushes on the edge of a big lawn that stretches between me an' the front of the house. There is a drive leadin' up to it, so I reckon the gate is on the other side. I light myself a cigarette an' take a look at the Luger just in case anybody is goin' to start any funny business. Then I walk across the lawn, go up the steps an' ring the doorbell.

It is one of them bells. When you ring it it sounds like somebody has started the Fire of London again. It goes ringin' right through that house, an' from where I am the noise sounds sorta ghostly. This is one of them houses that feel empty even if there are a million guys livin' in it.

I wait two or three minutes an' nothin' happens. Then after a bit I hear a noise on the other side of the door. Somebody starts undoin' a chain; then the door opens a bit—just a little way. I stick my foot in quick. Some guy on the other side says: "Say, what is this?"

"This is Mr. Caution," I tell him. "Just open up, will you, pal? I wanta talk to you."

He opens the door an' I step in. In front of me is a big hallway with a wide flight of stairs leadin' out of it. There are animals' heads an' swords an' things stuck all around the walls. This I reckon is one of them old-fashioned English country houses, but the guy who is standin' in front of me is not English or old-fashioned. He is nobody else but Lanny Flayne—an Irish Italian who used to work in a numbers racket on the East Side. Well . . . well . . . well . . .

"Lanny," I tell him. "Ain't it nice meetin' up with you again? What are you doin' over here? Was you afraid you'd get caught in the Draught or what . . .?"

He says: "Look, did you come here to ask me that? Whatever you want we ain't got it. So take it an' scram."

"No, Lanny," I tell him. "You can't talk to me like that." I look over his shoulder. "Say, look, who've we got here?" I say. I'm lookin' sorta surprised.

He takes a look behind him, an' I let him have it. I hit him a sweet one on the jaw-bone—one of them staccato raps that sounds like breakin' wood.

He subsides. He goes over on his back an' stays there. I take a look at him. I reckon I'm not goin' to be worried with this guy for a bit. I frisk him an' take a gun outa his hip pocket an' a bunch of keys. Then I start takin' a look around.

The place is big and empty. Down in the basement and on the ground floor I don't find a thing. The furniture is covered with dust. I try the upper regions. When I get to the corridor on the first floor, away along at the end I can see a crack of light comin' under a door. I grin to myself. You might almost think that these mugs were tellin' me where to look.

I go along an' try the door. It is locked, but one of the keys I got opens it. I go inside. When I step over the threshold I close the door behind me. I stand there grinnin'.

There she is!

Lyin' on the couch on the other side of the room is a dame. She is blindfolded an' her mouth is taped with adhesive tape. Her hands an' her feet are tied, but even with all this it is good an' easy for me to see that this dame is a looker. I get to thinkin' that I ain't had a case for a long time with so many swell dames in it. She moans a little when she hears me walkin' across the room. I say:

"Look, baby, your troubles are over. My name's Caution—Lemuel H. Caution—Chief Agent Federal Bureau of Investigation—an' when I cut that plaster off your mouth you can tell me how that sounds."

I get to work on her. I cut the rope round her wrists an' ankles, take the cloth off her eyes. She looks at me with big blue eyes an' believe me she don't look sorry either. Then I start in on the adhesive tape.

I don't know whether you mugs have ever had to take adhesive tape off a dame's mouth, but, believe me, it ain't much of a job. It hurts. The only thing to do is to get the corner up an' pull quick. It takes her about five minutes to get over this. Then she says:

"What a relief. Are you really a 'G' man?"

"That's right," I tell her. "An' you're Karen Wayles, aren't you. The funny thing is every guy in this business has been tryin' to kid me that you was Julia. But I knew you was Karen. Anyhow, I will tell you about that later."

She nods her head.

"Look," she says, "will you tell me why this has to happen to me? I've been kicking around with my head in a bag an' my mouth taped up any time I could let go a yell, for weeks. What's goin' on around here?"

I grin at her. "It's a helluva story," I tell her. "But you'll get to know it soon enough."

"I hope so," she says. "I don't like this sort of business."

I look at her. I remember that Mrs. Lorella Owen told me that Karen was stupid. Well, maybe she is a bit dumb.

"Look, baby," I tell her, "you an' I are goin' to get outa here quick. I don't think this place is goin' to be particularly healthy in about half an hour's time. Do you mind if we scram? There'll be lots of time to talk later."

"That suits me," she says. "Say, listen, do you mind tellin' me where I am?"

I laugh.

"Of course you wouldn't know," I tell her. "Look, this is 1941 an' there's a war on, an' you're at a dump called Betchworth, Surrey, England, an' how do you like that?"

"Oh, my God!" she says. I catch her as she falls.

"It's funny how a dame will faint just because she finds she is in some other country but the one she thought she was in. This dame don't even know she's out of the States."

I pull up outside Schribner's cottage. I get Karen outa the car an' take her inside. In the sittin'-room are the guys I told to stick around there, an' Nikolls. Nikolls is smokin' a cigarette an' drinkin' whisky, which I reckon is his idea of life. He gets up.

"So we've got company?" he says.

"Yeah," I tell him. "Meet Miss Karen Wayles, an' you might give her a drink. I think she's been havin' a tough time." I say to one of the other guys: "Is Lorella downstairs?"

"Yes," he says. "She's in the cellar. She's quite happy."

Nikolls says: "What is this? This is a sorta blind-man's-buff or musical chairs, ain't it?"

"You keep your trap shut," I tell him, "an' amuse the lady. Maybe you can tell her some of those tales about the blondes you've known in different places. I'll be seein' you, Karen. Maybe I'll have a nice surprise for you sometime."

I go outa the sittin'-room along the passageway inta the kitchen, down the stairs to the cellar. I go in an' shut the door behind me.

She is lyin' back in one of the armchairs from the sittin'-room that they brought down for her, an' does she look good or does she? I take a good look at this dame. She has still got the handkerchief over her eyes. She has got on the green velvet house-coat that she was wearin' when Nikolls' bunch snatched her. She has got auburn hair an' a skin that's one hundred per cent, Of all the babies I have met up with in this case this one is tops.

I light a cigarette; then I put on a helluva tough voice, speakin' through my nose to such an extent that it almost hurts:

"Well, Julia," I tell her, "so we got you at last, even if we did snatch your sister by mistake first time. Not that that matters. Me—I am a guy who believes that if you don't succeed the first time you have to try again."

She moans a little bit. She says in a very quiet icy sorta voice: "That would be Rudy Zimman, I suppose?"

"That's right, baby," I tell her. "Now, you better make the best of your time. Maybe you'd like a cigarette."

She says: "I don't want anything from you."

"Aw, shucks, kid!" I tell her. "Have a cigarette. Maybe you won't have the chance of smokin' many more."

I go over to her, put a cigarette between her lips an' light it for her. Then I ease over to the wall where I planted the dictaphone. I kick the lever over an' hear it start.

"So we caught up with you," I tell her. "Ain't you the mug? If you'd played this the right way, maybe you'd have been all right."

"How very interestin'," she says. "When I want any tips from you, Mr. Zimman, I'll ask for them. And another thing, maybe you have got me, but where's it going to get you? Someone's going to catch up with you pretty soon, and sooner than you think maybe."

I laugh. "Yeah?" I tell her. "An' who?"

"Caution," she says. "Did they tell you Caution was in on this job? He'll get you."

"Hooey!" I say. "If Caution hadda been in on this job from the start maybe I'd have got scared. They got him over here kickin' around tryin' to find Julia Wayles. It looks like they didn't tell the mug what the real job was. I suppose *you* thought you was goin' to handle that." I give a laugh. "It looks like you Government guys ain't been straight with each other," I say.

She says, sorta bitter: "You think you know everything, don't you, Zimman?" So I reckon I have touched a sore spot.

"Well," I say, "I think I know plenty. In fact I'm sure of it. Ain't this the way it went? I reckon the Secret Service got wise about the little set-up I got over here. Well . . . things can't go on for ever. So they put you on the job—Julia Wayles, the big Secret Service operator."

I give another laugh.

"Look, kid," I tell her, "I knew all about you before I started on the job. I fixed up to get you outa the way. I thought it would be a swell idea to knock off Julia Wayles, bring her over here so that if things got a bit tough I'd have something to bargain with. Well, I made a mistake. I put a coupla punks on the job an' what do they do? They grab off the wrong baby. They grab off her sister, Karen. But we don't know that.

"I have Karen sent over here an' think she's Julia. When you find that out, you don't like it, do you? You don't like havin' your little sister in the hands of a guy like me. So you come over here. But you get a big idea. You don't wanta show in this business. You wanta keep in the background, so's you can do your snoopin' nice an' quiet. You know that whoever it is tries to find the missin' Wayles dame is goin' to get in some tough spots an' maybe will make a few mistakes. So you get the mug that Karen was engaged to to go to the F.B.I. an' get a 'G' man put on the job of findin' out where Julia Wayles is. But he's not to be told anythin' else. So they put Caution on to it."

I give another laugh.

"Now that guy has got brains," I tell her. "If he'd been handlin' this job from the first, you wouldn't find yourself in the jam you're in, baby, because now I got the two Wayles dames—Julia an' Karen. An' I got 'em just at the right time, see?"

She says: "Maybe you're getting the breaks, Zimman, but they won't last. You're right about one thing though. I've been a fool. I ought to have played straight with Caution. If I'd done that from the first, I wouldn't be where I am now."

"Sure you wouldn't," I tell her. "Look, you heard about Caution? That guy is a big guy. He's tough an' he's got brains. Why, goddam it," I go on, "every mobster in America is afraid of Caution—even me. *I* get a bit scared sometimes, an' look who I am . . . Rudy Zimman—one of the best mobsters in the game; been runnin' it for years an' never pulled in. Even I get a little bit scared of Caution sometimes. Why, they tell me that guy is positively brilliant.

"Anyhow," I go on, "he's been brilliant enough to get wise to what I'm doin'."

She perks up at this. "Do you mean that?" she says.

"Do I?" I tell her. "Caution has made things so hot for us that I reckon the only thing I can do is to scram an' take the boys with me. An' that's what I'm doin'. We're gettin' outa here to-night. Everything is all set."

She makes a little hissin' noise.

"That's what I was afraid of," she says. "So Caution's scored again, hey? What a fool I've been. Why didn't I trust that guy?"

"Sure," I tell her. "Why didn't you? Anyhow," I go on, "I'm goin' to make up my mind what I'm goin' to do with you an' your sister. Maybe it won't be so nice."

She says: "I can take my medicine. I haven't played this the right way. I've tried to be too clever."

"That's always the way with you dames," I say. "You muscle inta a man's job an' think you can handle it. Well, here's one time you slipped up. You know, I thought you didn't treat this Caution guy right."

She says: "Why are you so interested in Caution?"

"I'll tell you, kid," I say.

I go over to her an' untie the handkerchief that she's got round her eyes. She blinks for a bit; then she takes a look at me.

"My God!" she says. "So it's *you.*"

"You're tellin' me, Julia," I say. "Were you scared sick or were you? Look, what would you an' your sister do if I wasn't rushin' around lookin' after you . . . you big Secret Service operative?"

She don't say anything. I get to work untying her hands.

"Come on, baby," I tell her. "Come upstairs. Karen's up there. We picked her up this evenin'. Everything is O.K."

It is near two o'clock when I stop the heap outside the main gateway that leads to The Marsh. Away down the carriage drive I can see torches flashin' an' guys beefin' about the place. I reckon Herrick is dealin' with the Zimman proposition.

I get outa the car an' go up the driveway. On the steps of the house I find Herrick. He is smokin' his pipe an' lookin' pleased with himself.

"Well, Lemmy," he says. "So you've done it again. You must have a system. You ought to tell me about it some time."

"The only system I have got is follow my nose," I tell him. "Have you collected all these thugs?"

He nods.

"We've got Zimman and Tamara Phelps and a dozen of the main people we want," he says. "Some of the smaller fry have got away but that doesn't matter. They're quite helpless without Zimman and the organisation."

He takes out his pipe an' starts fillin' it.

"What about the Wayles girls?" he says.

I grin at him. "I've got 'em," I tell him. "Both of 'em. They're near here. I ain't quite finished with Julia yet—your pal 'Mrs. Lorella Owen'!"

He shrugs his shoulders.

"It's no good your havin' it in for me, Lemmy," he says. "I have to obey orders. Julia Wayles wanted it played that way an', in this case, she was the boss—on this job anyway." He gives me a sly look. "I don't know who's doing the bossing now," he says.

"Julia is O.K.," I tell him. "She had a good idea but she didn't know how to work it. It woulda been all right if it hadn't been for me buttin' in. As a matter of fact," I go on, "it was only because of her playin' it the way she did that I got next to these mugs."

"That's as maybe," he says. "But I don't see that it did much good our keeping you in the dark."

"Listen, Herrick," I tell him. "This Julia Wayles, besides bein' a damn good looker, has also got some brains. If this job had been played the way she meant it to be she woulda come out tops an' so would you."

"How d'you make that out?" he asks me.

"It's stickin' out a mile," I tell him. "You work it out for yourself. Rudy Zimman gets word that a Secret Service dame by the name of Julia Wayles is after him in U.S. Somebody tips him off that this baby is wise to him an' some of the guys he's got workin' for him. So he gets a bright idea. He reckons he's gonna snatch her. This way he's gonna find out what she knows an' either bump her or keep her on ice so as to have somethin' to deal with if he gets in a spot. See?"

He nods his head.

"O.K.," I go on. "Well, Zimman's thugs snatch the wrong dame. They snatch Karen instead of Julia. An' believe me they wouldn't find out much from that baby. First of all she don't know a thing about Julia bein' in the Secret Service, an' secondly she is so dumb that it almost hurts. All she has is looks an' any time she opens her mouth you even forget she's easy on the eyes. That dame is practically sponge cake above the ears.

"But Rudy don't know that he's got the wrong dame. He has sent her over here to Max Schribner an' reckons to come over here himself later an' fix things. Meanwhile Julia has got the good news that Karen has been snatched. She knows she has been brought over here, so she gets a big idea. She comes over an' brings with her a mobster's pet who is lookin' for a job—a cutie named Dodo Malendas. Julia knows that Schribner, who is supposed to look after the supposed Julia dame, has never seen Tamara Phelps, so she puts in Dodo as Tamara Phelps an' Schribner falls for that line.

"O.K. Julia then pulls the second part of her scheme, an' that is to have a 'G' man put on to investigate the disappearance of Julia Wayles. I'm away on leave so Charlie Milton is put on the job. He comes to you an' on Julia's instructions you tell him that his first contact is Schribner. Right?"

"Right," he says. "But I still don't see why."

"You will," I tell him. "Because here is the clever idea. Julia thinks that directly Schribner is approached by a 'G' man he's gonna get scared. He's gonna start worryin', an' the first person he's gonna talk to about it is Tamara Phelps. This way Julia expects to find out where they was holdin' Karen, an' once she's found that out she reckons she will be on to the main job."

"I see," says Herrick. "That idea wasn't so bad. But it didn't come off."

I grin at him.

"That was *my* fault," I tell him. "Because it was me that told Schribner that the phoney Tamara Phelps was nobody else but Dodo Malendas, as a result of which Rudy Zimman snatches *her* an' forces the truth outa her. She tells him that they got the wrong dame, that the dame they've got is Karen an' that she, Dodo, is workin' for Julia Wayles who is over here after 'em."

Herrick nods. He is beginning to see daylight.

"I got at Dodo again," I go on. "I found out where she was an' that she'd been seein' Tamara. Then I knew that they'd put the screw on this dame. I told her to open up an' she *had* to tell me somethin'. An' the best thing she could think of on the spur of the moment was that Miss Lorella Owen was Karen Wayles. Directly she said that I was on to it. I knew Mrs. Owen was nobody else but Julia.

"Then I had a bit of luck. I went to see Tamara. She is waitin' for me with a swell story. Her story is that she is fed up with Rudy Zimman an' tryin' to duck out of it while the goin' is good. She tells me a lotta stuff that she's arranged with Rudy an' it's a goddam good story too. She tells me that to prove she is on the up an' up she's gonna tell me where Julia Wayles is. In other words she is goin' to hand over *Karen* Wayles to me.

"Well . . . what they wanted was as plain as a pikestaff. Dodo has told 'em they got the wrong dame an' they're now plannin' to get the right one. Tamara says she will hand over Karen to me. This makes me believe that she is O.K., an' it also, she thinks, ends the job so far as I'm concerned. Then they planned to pull a very fast one. While I am down here takin' delivery of Karen from Tamara, some more of Rudy's thugs are snatchin' Mrs. Lorella Owen, otherwise Julia Wayles, from the Mayfield dump in London. So they're gonna be better off than ever. You got that?"

He whistles. "That wasn't a bad idea," he says.

"It was a goddam good idea," I tell him. "But I was wise to it. I fixed with Callaghan to have some of his boys around there an' when the Zimman mob arrived he knocked 'em an' you'll find 'em any time you want 'em in an empty apartment on the second floor there. Nice work, hey?"

He grins at me.

"You're just the same old Lemmy," he says. "Except you get a bit better and take more chances each time."

"Nothin' venture nothin' have," I crack at him. "Well, to cut a long story short, Nikolls an' his boys snatched Julia. She thought it was the Zimman mob! They brought her down here an' in the meantime I have taken delivery of Karen. So everything is hunky dory . . . hey, pal?"

"Look!" he says. "There are your friends Tamara and Rudy. . . ."

Down at the bottom of the steps the cops are loadin' a bunch of mugs inta a police wagon. I can see Tamara, lookin' like the Queen of Sheba in a snowstorm, handcuffed to a tall guy—Rudy Zimman.

I ease down the steps an' go over.

"Hey, Tamara," I tell her. "How's it comin'? I'm sorry to see you got yourself in another mess. What you been doin'—stealin' a baby's gold teeth or stayin' out after curfew. You be careful or I'll tell Hitler about you an' he'll get tough."

"You bastard," she says. "You low, lyin' double-crossin' son of a green-eyed snake. You heel . . . you cheap four-flushin' beat-poundin' copper. You hellion. . . . You . . ." She calls me some very rude names includin' a couple that even I never heard before.

"Look, Virginia," I tell her. "You got what was comin' to you an' . . ."

"My name ain't Virginia," she says. "You . . ."

"I know," I tell her. "But Virginia was my grandmother's name an' you remind me of her—except that she was younger lookin' than you are. Anyhow, take it easy, sweet, because you're goin' to be on ice for quite a while."

Zimman says: "You're clever, ain't you, Caution? You're on top of the job, but one of these fine days I'm gonna get you. An' when I do it ain't gonna be very nice for you. Bein' shot quick would be good compared with what I'm gonna do to you."

"Sarsaparilla, you big ape," I tell him. "You ain't got a chance. You're so unconscious that you practically don't exist. You're gonna get about fifteen years here an' when they're through with you I'm goin' to have you extradited an' sent to Alcatraz for a coupla million years. Before I get through with you it woulda been cheaper for you not to have been born at all. So long, little playmates."

The wagon drives off. I stand there lookin' at the tail light, wonderin' what Rudy will look like in broad arrows.

Herrick says: "Well . . . I'll expect you to-morrow. We've got a lot to talk about."

"Sure," I tell him. "But make it late in the afternoon. I haven't done yet. I've got some more investigatin' to do. So long, pal. . . ."

I start walkin' down the driveway to the car. Halfway down a guy comes out of the shadows. He is a tall, well-dressed guy an' he has got a dame with him who looks like a million. I stare at him. Then I get it. It is Callaghan.

"I thought I'd like to be in at the kill, Caution," he says. "It looks as if you've pulled it off. Congratulations."

"Thanks a lot," I tell him. "An' thanks for what your boys did. You gotta nice crowd around you . . . an' that guy Nikolls is a pip. . . ."

"Windy's all right," he says. "Except he talks too much. Drop in at Berkeley Square before you go back to the States. I've got some straight Kentucky there. You'll like it."

"I'll be seein' you," I tell him.

They go off towards the house. I take a quick look at the dame who is with Callaghan, an' I'm tellin' you that guy has got a taste in ankles that is pretty near as good as my own.

One of these fine days I'm gonna have a long talk with that guy.

It is a half after three when I get back to Schribner's cottage. The moon is good an' the mist has cleared away. The place looks like a sorta fairyland with the fairways an' the rollin' greens. Me . . . I reckon I am feelin' very poetic to-night.

I stop the car an' get out. I go over to the cottage. Nikolls an' Karen Wayles—who is wearin' his raincoat—are leanin' on the fence talkin'. I reckon Nikolls is tellin' her what some blonde did to him in Maryland some time. Anyhow, she looks like she likes it.

I whistle him over to me.

"Look, Nikolls," I tell him. "You've done a swell job an' now you can top it off. You take that dame Karen an' run her back to Julia's apartment in your car. When you get there wait for me. I'll be along."

I go inta the cottage.

Me—I have never thought that a main bye-pass road could look so swell in the moonlight. The car is hummin' along nice an' easy. I just drag on my cigarette an' say nothin'.

Julia says: "Anyhow, this is a Secret Service assignment. It's got to be handled the way I want it. Your job was merely the kidnap part of it. You understand?"

"Sure," I tell her. "That's O.K. by me. That suits me fine. I suppose you wanta stand around an' grab off all the credit. Well . . . why not?" I give a big sigh. "The trouble with you U.S. Secret Service people is," I tell her, "that you don't know a thing. An' when you get inta a jam you have to ask the F.B.I. to get you outa it."

I turn off towards Leatherhead. She says:

"Where are we goin'?"

"I got a little business," I tell her. "I got a friend of yours tied up in some dump near here. She's been there for a helluva time. Maybe she'll wanta stretch."

She takes a quick look at me. "My God!" she says. "Dodo Malendas. I'd forgotten about her!"

"Sure you had," I tell her. "You'd be in fine shape if it wasn't for me. I'm practically your nurse. The trouble with you, Julia, is that you don't know you're alive. When a little thing like bein' snatched turns up, you go all funny."

"You hate yourself, don't you?" she says. "They tell me you're very clever, Mr. Caution. It must have been very annoying for you to have to work for a woman."

"I like workin' for women," I tell her. "*Some* women. An' you get anythin' you want off your chest. Because *I've* got the big laugh in this job."

"Meaning what?" she says. I can feel her lookin' at me sideways.

"When you was in the cellar at Schribner's cottage," I tell her. "When you was blindfolded an' you thought I was Rudy Zimman an' you was sayin' all that stuff about you wished you'd left things to Caution, an' what a swell guy he was, I had a dictaphone workin'. I've got the record in the car boot. When I get back to U.S. the 'G' boys are gonna be plenty tickled to hear that record. I reckon I'll play it every mornin' just to make me feel good."

She makes a little hissin' noise. She don't say anything for a bit. Then: "What does a girl have to do to get that record?" she says. I grin at her. "Well," I tell her, "she hasta be nice an' polite, an' make me sorta feel that she is really *tryin'*—if you know what I mean."

She looks at me sideways. I can see her smilin'. I believe I told you that this dame had everything—an' then some. She says:

"I suppose I've got to emulate Tamara. I've got to try and do a deal with you."

"Correct, sweetheart," I tell her. "You will notice that I always leave myself *one* ace in the pack."

"*And* one up your sleeve," she says. "Well . . . what is the deal?"

"The first thing is to get me in the right frame of mind," I tell her. "An' for that I need a lot of atmosphere. I can see a big tree just down the road with the branches hangin' over an' that looks like the right sorta scene."

I stop the car under the tree.

She says: "Just a minute, Lemmy. Do you mean to tell me that just because you've got that dictaphone record you think you can kiss me just when and where you like?"

I give her a big grin.

"That's right, honey," I tell her. "That's the way it goes."

She sighs. "I thought that was how it was going to be," she says. "I must have second sight."

I ease in the clutch an' we start rollin' towards the Leatherhead road. Julia lights a coupla cigarettes an' gives me one. There is a suggestion of perfume hangin' around that cigarette which goes one hundred per cent with me.

I get around to thinkin' about that chicken farm in Minnesota. Maybe the idea would be all right when I am about ninety years older than I am . . . but not now.

Right now I got an idea in my head that this thug-chasin' business has got its compensations. I got another idea that one of the compensations is in the passenger seat alongside.

Listen . . . *you* mugs can have the chicken farm.

THE END

Lightning Source UK Ltd.
Milton Keynes UK
UKHW012001030322
399530UK00001B/147

9 781914 150999